"What Did You Say?"

stammered Brooke.

"I said I want to have dinner with you tomorrow."

"I already have plans." She was grasping at straws, trying to put things back on an even keel. He was playing with her because she represented a challenge, and she resented it.

"Tell him you're not interested."

"Please . . . the answer's still no. Now if you don't mind, I'd better be going."

"I want to take you out," Ashley said quietly. "And I usually get what I want. Maybe this will convince you that I mean to have my way."

Before she had time to avert her mouth, his lips covered hers with a searing, branding kiss.

MARY LYNN BAXTER
owns and manages the D & B Book Store in Lufkin, Texas. Romances have been her favorite books for years, and she sells more romances in her store than any other kind of book.

Dear Reader,

Silhouette Special Editions are an exciting new line of contemporary romances from Silhouette Books. Special Editions are written specifically for our readers who want a story with heightened romantic tension.

Special Editions have all the elements you've enjoyed in Silhouette Romances and *more*. These stories concentrate on romance in a longer, more realistic and sophisticated way, and they feature greater sensual detail.

I hope you enjoy this book and all the wonderful romances from Silhouette. We welcome any suggestions or comments and invite you to write to us at the address below.

Karen Solem
Editor-in-Chief
Silhouette Books
P.O. Box 769
New York, N. Y. 10019

Twila Chiesi

MARY LYNN BAXTER
All Our Tomorrows

Silhouette Special Edition
Published by Silhouette Books New York
America's Publisher of Contemporary Romance

SILHOUETTE BOOKS, a Simon & Schuster Division of
GULF & WESTERN CORPORATION
1230 Avenue of the Americas, New York, N.Y. 10020

ISBN: 0-671-53509-9

First Silhouette Books printing March, 1982

10 9 8 7 6 5 4 3 2 1

America's Publisher of Contemporary Romance

Printed in the U.S.A.

This Book Is
Dedicated to
Linda Shaw and Parris Afton Bonds

All Our Tomorrows

Chapter One

Brooke Lawson was no longer the same carefree young woman she had been. She would never bounce off a tennis court again, the doctors had told her. Her career and plans to have a family had come to an abrupt halt with the accident.

Yet, as the Boeing 747 lifted off the runway of Houston's Intercontinental Airport, she felt a keen sense of excitement. For the first time since her car had skidded, barreling into a concrete embankment, she was hopeful. She was actually on her way to Hawaii.

"You don't need to play professional tennis to be happy," her friends said.

"A woman doesn't have to bear children to be fulfilled," her ex-fiancé, Cody, tried to convince her.

An extended vacation was the excuse she had given her friends and Cody when she left for Hawaii. She absolutely couldn't endure any more sympathy from them. All she wanted was to be left alone with the

9

sunshine and sand. Time was what she needed to experiment with the new vigor returning to her limbs, to reevaluate her life.

Were the doctors wrong? she wondered. Could she be the tennis champion she had once been? Would she risk permanent injury if she threw herself back into the grueling profession?

Upon returning to her apartment from weeks in the hospital, a letter was waiting for her from her brother insisting she come and let him and his wife take care of her. Her roommate had written, he said, and told him about the wreck. Cindy had assured him that in time Brooke would be all right, but would never be able to play tennis again. There was severe damage done to her muscles, as well as internal injuries.

Jonathan had wanted to fly to Houston and see about her, but Brooke insisted that there was nothing he could do. So they kept in touch through phone calls and letters.

After fighting for weeks with Cody, she had finally convinced him that she must have time alone to decide what she wanted to do with her future. Cody badgered her to marry him immediately. Even though he kept saying over and over that the possibility of her not being able to have children made no difference to him, she knew it really did. They had talked too many times about the children they hoped to have one day.

Brooke remained firm and told him she was going to Hawaii regardless of what he thought. She knew, deep down, he was really relieved. As far as she was concerned, the engagement was over and Cody was no longer a part of her life. Cindy kept telling her they would both change their minds. Brooke knew, however, that it was too late for Cody and her. In fact, she realized for the first time that they probably had never really loved each other. She had met him in college where he taught a computer science course. He was likable and friendly and they had drifted into a comfortable relationship—nothing more.

Now, she planned to put the accident and Cody behind her for a while and enjoy her brother's company and the healing sun of Hawaii. She hoped against hope that she would be able to play tennis again one day—in spite of what the doctors said.

So intent was she on her thoughts that she was startled when the flight attendant interrupted her by saying, "Miss Lawson, are you all right? Can I get you anything?"

It was then that she realized tears were running down her face. Quickly she brushed them away and smiled rather uncertainly at the young woman before replying, "I'm fine, thank you. If you don't mind though, I would like a cup of coffee."

"Are you sure you don't need anything else?" Concern, as well as curiosity, was present in her voice.

Completely in charge of her emotions once again, she assured her that she was really all right and required no further attention. It was rather embarrassing to be caught in one of her emotional moments. Most of the time she was able to keep better control of her thoughts.

The rest of the flight was rather uneventful, passing much more quickly than she had anticipated. The next thing she knew the attendant was gently shaking her and helping her fasten her seat belt for landing.

The pilot's voice was coming over the speaker loud and clear announcing that they were approaching Honolulu's airport. He asked all the passengers to turn and look at beautiful Oahu, the third largest of the Hawaiian Islands. He then went on to give the island's population. About 725,000 people lived there, which made up about eighty percent of Hawaii's population.

"Waikiki and Diamond Head are favorite attractions among visitors to beautiful Hawaii," he mentioned.

"Peace and quiet," she thought, "are my favorite attractions. And a new Brooke Lawson."

By the time she departed from the plane, most of the crowd had dispersed. However, there were several Hawaiian girls still putting lais of flowers around the passengers' necks. She was not exempt from this custom and was delighted with the string of orchids they dropped around her neck. Standing alone to one side was her brother, Jonathan. They spotted each other at the same time and each hugged the other with unrestrained enthusiasm.

"Brooke, my girl, it's great to see you." Pushing her away from him, he looked closely. "You look much better than I expected you to, considering what you've been through. A little on the thin side, perhaps, but as beautiful as ever. Those dark shadows under your eyes add to your beauty, if that's possible."

"Oh, Jonathan, it's so good to see you. You haven't changed a bit—always did know how to make a girl feel good!"

"All joking aside, Sis," said Jonathan with concern in his voice. "Are you really all right? I should have flown over to see you myself. But I knew you really didn't want me to, and I certainly didn't want to upset you any further. Is there anything you're not telling me that I ought to know, other than the fact that the doctor has forbidden you to pick up another tennis racket?"

"I'm fine, Jonathan, really I am. I just need time to rest and get my strength back. I want to look forward to doing absolutely nothing. I'm so grateful to you and

Anne for inviting me to stay with you. By the way, where is Anne?"

"She's at the doctor's office. I'm hoping she's going to have some great news for me when I get home."

"Do you mean what I think you mean?" exclaimed Brooke.

"Yes, there's a good possibility that she's pregnant. We've been wanting to have a baby for a long time, but it just wasn't meant to be until now. That's one reason why I'm so glad you're here. You'll be good company for Anne."

"You know I'll do anything I can to help. Don't let my looks deceive you. Although I still tire rather easily, I'm in pretty good shape due to all the physical therapy I've had."

Brooke could tell he wanted to argue the point, but all he said was, "Thanks, Sis, I knew I could count on you. Let's get your bags right now and head for the house. We have a lot to talk about, but I'm sure you want to settle down a bit first."

"I am rather exhausted," replied Brooke. "But I'm so glad to see you that I can almost forget about being tired."

As they walked to the parking lot, Jonathan told her about his work. He worked for a sugar manufacturing company and had managed to work himself up to an executive position in the family-owned company.

Ashley Graham, the company's president, had taken a special interest in a project Jonathan had been working on and, because of this, he had earned a rather comfortable position with the firm. However, he went on to tell her, his eye was on the newly created position of vice-president, Ashley Graham's right-hand man.

"Sis, it's the one opportunity for me to really secure

my future for Anne and our baby. I want this position so badly I get a sick feeling in my stomach just thinking I might not get it. Do you know what I mean? Or have you ever wanted anything that badly?"

"Oh, yes," said Brooke with bitterness in her voice, "or at least I thought I did. But that's all in the past now."

"I'm sorry, Sis. What an unfeeling swine you must think I am. I know you've been through hell these past months, but dammit, I can't help you if you won't let me."

"Please, Jonathan," begged Brooke, "don't worry about me. Everything's fine, really it is, especially now that I'm here with you. Come on, now, get that frown off your face and finish telling me about your chances of getting this job. We'll talk about me later, okay?"

"Okay," grinned Jonathan, "but I'm going to hold you to that."

"Seriously," questioned Brooke, steering the conversation away from her, "do you think the job will be yours?"

"I think I have the best chance at it. Although with Ashley you never really know what he's thinking, or which way he may turn. He's a self-confident devil, he doesn't have to answer to anyone except his old grandfather, and that's only on rare and really important decisions. However, I'm determined not to let anyone else beat me out of it. I've just *got* to have it!"

Brooke noticed the tone of desperation creeping into his voice, and he seemed to be talking more to himself than to her. She certainly hoped all was well. Maybe she was just imagining any problems.

"I'm sure they know what an asset you would be to their company as vice-president. Just hang in there," laughed Brooke.

He was all the family she had, and although they did not get a chance to see each other often, she knew she could depend on him for anything. Since the death of both their parents in a boating accident when she was in high school, Jonathan had always made sure she had not been without his support and love. He had been in Honolulu several years now and had married a young girl who had been a secretary in his company. She had only been around Anne on two occasions, but they had gotten along well together. She was looking forward to getting to know her better.

Brooke was delighted to be part of a family again—especially since she learned about Anne's baby. It would help to make up for those lonely weeks and months in the hospital. Cody had been super up to a certain point, but she knew she could never marry him now. She could not go through life at cross purposes, because he refused to accept how important tennis was in her life. He always referred to "it" as her hobby. However, she knew she was better off without him. When she allowed herself to think about Cody, their separation left a painful void.

Pushing these painful thoughts aside, she turned her attention back to her brother who was now unlocking the door to his car.

"My, but you have come up in this old world if this car is any indication of your importance," Brooke teased with a twinkle in her eyes.

"Well, Sis, you know how it is—I have to keep up my image," laughed Jonathan. "However, I'm glad you approve. It's a new Mercedes. I had it shipped over from the mainland a few weeks back. Actually, it's more or less a company car. I'll let you drive it while you're here."

"Oh, no, I couldn't do that," Brooke exclaimed

quickly. "I haven't driven at all since the accident. Now, Jonathan, don't lecture me, please. I know what you're thinking, but don't say it. I'll drive again one of these days, but just not right now."

"All right, Brooke. We won't push it for now."

Changing the subject, Brooke said with excitement in her voice, "I love this climate! Everything smells so good and clean. I can't wait to see everything I can while I'm here. I don't want to miss seeing one of the islands!" I can't wait to take the time to learn what my arms and legs can do again, she added to herself.

"Whoa! Slow down," laughed Jonathan. "You are supposed to be here to rest and relax and get your health back. I promise you'll not miss seeing a thing, but all in good time. I want those dark shadows gone from under those beautiful brown eyes and some weight back on those bones."

"Yes, sir," answered Brooke with mock severity in her voice.

"As I said before, though, even with the shadows and weight loss, you're still a beautiful woman. I'll consider the man extremely lucky who gets you. By the way, what about you and Cody? Is that relationship still intact?"

Trying to hide the pain from his inquisitive eyes, she turned her head to stare at the passing scenery. But she knew he would demand an answer so she said, "Right now our marriage plans are in cold storage." She didn't mean for her statement to sound so bitter and flat, but she just couldn't help it.

"Brooke, look at me," demanded Jonathan. "I get the feeling in my gut that you're hiding something from me that I should know. I just want to help, you know."

"I know you do," replied Brooke, "and I love you the more for being concerned about me. But I have to work some things out by myself. One of these days we'll have a long serious talk, but not right now, please. At this moment I want nothing more than to enjoy the drive down Kalakaua Avenue and see the famed Waikiki Beach. You see, I've been doing my homework."

"For now we'll play it your way. No more personal questions from big brother, I promise," laughed Jonathan.

"Is it out of your way to drive along the beach? I don't want to keep Anne waiting, or you either for that matter. I know you're more than anxious to get back home."

"Kalakaua Avenue is on our way home. In fact, we live close to Waikiki. About a year ago I bought a town house and wanted it close to the beach. Although there are many other beaches that are more beautiful and serene than Waikiki, I love all the excitement and glitter that surrounds this particular area. Also, my office is in walking distance of our house."

They were rapidly coming into the heavy traffic from the beach population. Since it was July and the height of the tourist season, the beaches were jammed with brightly colored bathing suits and people of all types, shapes and colors. Brooke could feel the excitement in the air and was happy for the first time in months. She couldn't wait to join the gay-hearted vacationers and natives on the beach.

Sensing her excitement and anticipation, her brother laughed out loud at her obvious pleasure. "You would at this moment make an ideal ad to attract tourists to this island," declared her brother. "I'm really glad you're looking forward to your stay here."

"By the way," he continued, a little too casually, "Anne and I are giving a small dinner party tomorrow evening to introduce you to our friends and my boss, *if* he's not away on business. He's an awfully busy man, but I'm hoping he'll be able to come. I'd like very much for you to meet him. Even though some consider him a playboy, he's still my ideal of what it means to be a complete success in life."

"Sounds like a swell fellow," said Brooke sarcastically.

Raising his eyebrows in mock alarm, Jonathan laughed and said, "As a matter of fact, I was going to ask you to do me a favor, and be nice to Ashley. You would take to each other like ducks to water. What do you say, think you're up to handling that?"

"What do you mean, be nice? How nice?"

Jonathan shrugged. "Oh, you know—just act interested."

"Why?"

"Because I'm asking you to, that's why!" exclaimed Jonathan.

"I'm sorry, but I just can't. I don't need any more complications."

"Oh come on, Sis! I'm not asking you to do anything other than be nice to him, that's all! Who knows, maybe you'll even like him. Your being nice to Ashley certainly won't hurt you, and it sure might help me. So, will you do it?"

"Oh, Jonathan, please not tomorrow night," wailed Brooke. "I'm not ready to be the main attraction at a party, or make goo-goo eyes at some over-sexed man—even if he is your boss. I just want to enjoy your and Anne's company for a few days first."

"I'm sorry you feel that way, Brooke. Everything's all set now, and it's too late to change it. Anyway, I thought you would be eager to meet people. You're going to be here for a while, and you need to meet other young people so you can join in the island activities. Just forget about Ashley Graham for right now. We'll see what happens after you meet him."

Brooke could tell from his tone of voice that she had hurt his feelings, but she just wasn't up to coping with any man. Jonathan had no right even to ask her! But without causing a big scene, she would have to go along with them and at least pretend to enjoy herself.

From what he said about his boss, she already knew she was not going to like him. She definitely was not interested in having anything to do with a known womanizer. For now, she was totally uninterested in forming any type of relationship, lasting or otherwise.

"I'm sorry, Jonathan," she hurriedly replied, "I don't mean to sound ungrateful. Of course, I'll look forward to the party and will probably have a good time once it gets started. Don't pay any attention to my moods."

The rest of the trip home passed with Jonathan pointing out various points of interest along the way. At last they reached the town house. She was beginning to feel the effects of the long trip. All the excitement of seeing her brother, and their slight disagreement, had made her more tired than she cared to admit even to herself. If she looked as bad as she felt, Anne would think she was still ill.

As they drove into the drive, the front door flew open and Anne came hurrying out laughing and shouting, "Hey, you two, where have you been? I've been waiting on pins and needles for you to come home."

"We've been taking our time, visiting and looking. I didn't think you would be back home so soon," said Jonathan as he soundly kissed his wife.

"It didn't take me long at the doctor's office. For once I didn't have to wait!" replied Anne.

By now Brooke had gotten out of the car and was caught in a bearlike hug from her sister-in-law. "I'm glad to see you! It's about time you've come to stay with us." Although she was talking to Brooke, her eyes sought Jonathan's.

"Well? Are you or aren't you?" he questioned huskily, before Anne said anything further to Brooke.

Anne grinned from ear to ear and nodded her head.

Jonathan's eyes lit up like a candle. He then grabbed her and began twirling her around and around, both of them laughing out loud. With misty eyes, Brooke turned and hurriedly made her way back to the car with the pretence of retrieving her overnight bag. She did not want to intrude on this happy and private time. It belonged only to the two of them.

The moment quickly passed, however, when they realized Brooke had disappeared.

Untangling herself from Jonathan's arms, Anne called, "Hey, sister-in-law, don't I rate a hug from you?"

"Of course you do, silly!" said Brooke as she brushed the tears from her cheeks. "You can't imagine how happy this news makes me." She then proceeded to give Anne a bear hug and a kiss on the cheek.

"I'll tell you one thing right now," chimed in Jonathan. "*I'm* going to name this kid. I've already got the name picked out."

"Not if you're going to name him after your Uncle Henry," retorted Anne as she winked at Brooke. "I'll not have a son of mine stuck with *that* name," she went on to say with mock severity in her voice.

"And just exactly what is wrong with the name Henry?" questioned Jonathan, indignantly. "I happen to like it!"

"Oh, you!" groaned Anne laughing. "There is no way I'm going to . . ."

"Whoa, you two," cut in Brooke. "How do you know it's going to be a boy?" Turning toward her, they both grinned sheepishly. "Actually, I'd prefer a blue-eyed little girl," said Brooke, "I rather fancy myself watching a little girl wrap you, brother dear, around her little finger. Girls have a tendency to do that, you know."

"Well, that's true," admitted Jonathan. "To tell you the truth, I don't care what it is as long as it's healthy."

"Amen!" responded Anne and Brooke simultaneously.

Stepping back, Brooke peered at her sister-in-law closely. "By the way, what did the doctor say about your health? Does everything appear to be normal?" she questioned.

Shifting her gaze, Anne stammered, "Well, I—er—"

"Quit stalling, honey," cut in Jonathan. "Let's have it."

Sighing, Anne said, "He's afraid that I might have trouble with my blood pressure. He wants me to keep a close check on it. Other than that, everything else seems to be okay, except, of course, the constant nausea."

"Don't worry, Jonathan," exclaimed Brooke, "I'm going to be an ever-present watchdog. She won't be able to make many moves without my knowledge."

"Now listen, you two," began Anne putting her hands on her hips. "I—"

"No," cut in Brooke, "you're the one who's going to be listening. You will do exactly as you're told." She turned toward her brother. "Right, Jonathan?"

"You bet! I'm going to be depending on you, Sis, to

keep this woman in line while I'm at work. When I get home, I'll take over the watch."

Anne looked exasperated. "Would you please quit talking about me as if I wasn't standing here? I can see right now, I don't have the chance of a snowball in hell as far as doing what I want to." She wanted them to think she was mad, but Brooke knew that Anne was actually touched by their concern and would be glad of their help.

Grinning, Jonathan finally said, "Ladies, how about us continuing this discussion in the comfort of the house." He stepped aside with a sweeping gesture for them to precede him.

With arms around each other, they entered the cool house.

Brooke was delighted to be here, even more so now that there was going to be a baby. She meant what she said to Jonathan about taking care of Anne. It would keep her mind off her problems and at the same time, she would be accomplishing something really worthwhile.

Yes, coming here was definitely the best thing she could have done. She was welcome, and this added a glow to her scarred heart.

"You'll never know how much it means for me to be here. You two are my anchor in this time of need," Brooke forced a laugh. Now was not the time to think of the children she would never have.

It had been a long time since Brooke had seen her sister-in-law, but she hadn't changed one bit. Anne was still the same sweet person she always had been. Although she wasn't pretty in the sense of possessing real beauty, she nevertheless had a way about her that drew people like a magnet. Her small dark features were always smiling and eager to please. Her brother was lucky to have found someone like her. With his blond good looks, they made a striking couple. Pregnancy definitely agreed with her, adding a glow that went deeper than mere beauty.

Brooke noticed that Anne refrained from commenting on her haggard appearance. But she did notice the concerned look that passed between her sister-in-law and her brother before she was quickly whisked into the house and upstairs to the guest bedroom. In all the excitement about the baby and Anne's problems, she hoped her appearance would go unnoticed.

"I hope you'll be comfortable here, Brooke," smiled Anne.

"Oh, I shall," she replied. "It is lovely. I can't wait for you to show me the rest of the house. From the glimpse I got of it, it's really something!"

"There's all kinds of time for that later. You must get some much needed rest before dinner. I'll wake you later to dress. If there's anything else you need, just call."

After Anne left, Brooke turned and her eyes caught her reflection in the mirror on the door. She was astounded at how terrible she looked. The first thing she noticed was her huge brown eyes in a pale and thin face staring back at her. In fact, she was all eyes. Her delicate features were completely devoid of color, and the circles under her eyes were almost black. How Jonathan could possibly have thought she was still beautiful was beyond her.

What she was not aware of was that the weeks in the hospital caused her to look more fragile and appealing than ever. She was a lovely young woman by anyone's standards, being of average height and slender as a reed, with firm, high breasts that were obvious, due to her slender figure. Her hair was honey-colored, and she wore it fairly long with the sides swept back away from her face. Her cheekbones were high and her lips were full and sensuous. She had always had her share of attention from men, but had never taken any of them seriously until Cody. *That* one time had been a mistake!

After finally getting together the energy to remove her clothes, she fell onto the bed with the intention of merely resting a moment. Anne's gentle shaking made her open her eyes.

"I almost didn't wake you up. You were sleeping so soundly that I hated to disturb you," confessed Anne, "but I know you also need to eat, and we very much want your company at dinner."

Quickly Brooke flung her legs to the side of the bed and smiled at Anne. "Please, don't apologize for waking me. I would have been upset if you hadn't. Anyway, my stomach's telling me it needs something to eat and soon, too. Do you have a minute to sit down and talk while I throw on some clothes?"

"I sure do," exclaimed Anne. "You can't imagine how glad I am to have you here to keep me company. We are going to have such fun. I have so much planned for us to do."

"Wait just one minute, my friend," laughed Brooke. "Remember what we discussed outside a little while ago. The name of the game is for *you* to take it easy. I can see right now I'm going to have my hands full with you."

"Oh, come on now," sighed Anne. "Please don't let my pregnancy take all the fun out of your visit." She grinned impishly. "You know I'll be good."

"I know, because I'm going to see that you are," stated Brooke firmly.

Changing the subject, Anne asked hesitantly, "Do

you really think Jonathan is happy about the baby? You know how men are."

"Of course he is, silly. Whatever made you think he wasn't?" questioned Brooke frowning.

Shrugging her shoulders, Anne said, "To be honest, I don't know. It's just that Jonathan seems to have so much on his mind of late. He's so overworked, I'm thinking a baby would be just another added burden."

Brooke's eyes widened in surprise. "Oh, for heaven's sake, Anne, can't you see that a baby is exactly what he needs? It will make all those other things much less important. You wait and see if I'm not right."

Anne shook her head. "I know. It's just . . ."

"Hey," interrupted Brooke. "I don't want to hear any more gloom and doom from you. Understand?"

"All right," smiled Anne. "You win."

"Now we can get back to your health?"

"Oh, please, no," cried Anne, rolling her eyes upward in agitation. "Not again."

"Okay," laughed Brooke. "But I do insist that you answer one question and then I'll shut up. Did he give you anything for nausea?"

"Yes, he did," stated Anne. "He gave me a little white pill that I'm supposed to take three times a day before each meal. I'm keeping my fingers crossed that it will do the trick."

"That makes two of us," responded Brooke. "To me, there's nothing worse than an upset stomach."

Looking at her watch, Anne jumped up and said, "I've got to go and see about dinner. We've been jabbering and you haven't even dressed yet. It's a wonder that Jonathan hasn't been up to check on us."

"Oh, I'm sure he knows we're talking ninety miles an hour."

She laughed. "I'm going anyway and let you get dressed."

"All right. See you shortly."

"Come to the den and we'll have a drink before dinner," said Anne as she left the room.

After taking a quick shower, Brooke chose a long gaily colored caftan to wear. To make it fit her as it should, she put a thin gold chain belt around her slender waist. Since she had lost so much weight, her clothes didn't fit. Next she put on a little makeup hoping to cover the circles still evident under her eyes. She brushed her hair vigorously until it shone. Quickly looking at the overall effect, she decided she didn't look half bad.

When she entered the den, Anne and Jonathan were already having a drink, and to her surprise, they were not alone.

Pausing just inside the door for a moment, Jonathan noticed her immediately.

"Hi, Sis," he said. "Come on in. There's someone I'd like you to meet. This is my sister, Ashley. Brooke, I'd like you to meet Ashley Graham, my boss. He dropped by for a moment to bring some papers for me to sign. I talked him into having a cocktail with us, but only after he refused to stay for dinner."

Brooke wished that she could have met this man later. She resented the intrusion and having to share Jonathan and Anne with anyone, especially the first evening of her arrival.

"Hello, Brooke!"

Dressed in a light gray suit, Ashley Graham was undeniably the most physically attractive man she had ever seen. He was tall with broad shoulders, deeply tanned, had jet black hair and his blue eyes were enhanced by long thick eyelashes. His voice was deep, and although he spoke quietly, it was with obvious self-assurance. There was no excess flesh on his big vibrant body. She surmised he must be around thirty-seven or so due to the sprinkle of gray hair at his temples. He radiated an animal magnetism!

Upon realizing that she had been staring, she turned slightly away in embarrassment before she was forced to return the greeting. Flushing, she finally said, "It's nice to meet you, Mr. Graham."

As she spoke, her voice had a tremor she couldn't quite conceal. Her reaction to him was so strong it made her almost physically sick. What in the world was the matter with her?

She could sense that Ashley Graham was aware of her discomfort and was thoroughly enjoying it. Although the conversation had swung around to include the others, Brooke could feel his blue eyes looking at her with deep intensity and a hint of mockery in them. His virility was completely stripping her of her confidence and making her feel like a fumbling teenager instead of the twenty-five year old woman she was.

Before she realized it, she found herself alone with him for a moment while Anne had gone to see about dinner. Her brother was quickly looking over the papers Ashley had brought for him to check.

"Jonathan tells me you're going to stay with them indefinitely," said Ashley, making conversation.

"Yes, that's correct," she replied rather tersely.

Relaxing against the bar, he questioned further. "What are your plans while you're here?"

Nervously brushing a loose strand of hair back into place, she answered him with cool politeness, "At the moment I have no plans."

Remembering his manners, he asked, "Would you care for a cigarette?" His deep voice held a hint of something she could not quite identify. Was it concern?

"Thank you, but no, I don't smoke."

He looked at her empty hands questioningly and asked, "What about a drink?"

"I don't think I care for one of those, either." She smiled politely, hoping he would get the message and go away.

"What's the matter, do my questions make you nervous?"

"No, of course not," she replied.

"Well, then, do *I* make you nervous?"

Flushing, she said, "Mr. Graham, I don't know you well enough for you to make me nervous."

He merely raised his eyebrows and smiled.

She looked distressed. "I don't really see that this conversation is accomplishing anything."

"Oh, I don't know," he smiled. "I'm rather enjoying it."

Her temper flared. "Would you please excuse me! I—"

As she moved, he astounded her by placing himself in her path and saying quietly, "What's your hurry, Miss Lawson?" He was looking at her now, his eyes narrow and gentle. "Brooke?" he repeated softly.

She willed herself to stay where she was.

Sensing that he had won this round at least, Ashley said, his voice serious, "Your brother said that your accident left you unable to resume your career as a professional tennis player. I'm sorry about that." Before she could reply, he continued, "Jonathan insinuated that you were nursing wounds from a broken engagement."

Unable to believe what she had heard, Brooke gasped! "You have no right to question me like this and my brother had no business telling you anything about me, much less something that was totally untrue."

"You still haven't answered my question," he insisted.

Brooke shook her head. "And I'm not going to, either," she stated, her eyes sparkling with anger.

Ignoring her anger, Ashley said, "Well, I hope you take your doctor's advice and stay away from the tennis court. From what I understand, you'll be jeopardizing your health for the remainder of your life if you don't."

Brooke turned her face away, averting her eyes. "Please, I don't want to discuss this any more. . . ."

"You'll get your wish for right now. Here comes your brother. We'll continue our discussion tomorrow night," whispered Ashley conspiringly.

"That's where you're mistaken!" she returned swiftly.

"We'll see," he said and grinned.

Before she could say anything else, Jonathan interrupted them, saying, "Ashley, can I get you another drink? Brooke, I'm sorry, I didn't offer you anything. I guess my head's not on straight."

Smiling sweetly to cover her agitation, Brooke said, "That's all right. I think I'll pass. It will soon be time to eat and I need the food much more than the drink."

"Are you sure you won't stay for dinner, Ashley?" asked Jonathan. "It would indeed be a pleasure to have you for dinner two nights in a row."

Ashley shook his head. "Thank you, but no. I won't intrude any longer on your reunion celebration with Brooke. But I felt you needed to have those papers immediately."

By now Anne had rejoined them and again tried to get Ashley to change his mind, but he was adamant in his refusal. Turning his charm full force on Anne, he assured her that he would look forward to dining with them tomorrow evening, and with a reminding nod in Brooke's direction, he took his leave.

That man! Brooke fumed to herself. He had no right to involve himself where he wasn't invited. She shouldn't have lost her temper; it only let him know he had gotten under her skin. How did a person cope with meeting him? Her brother could just forget any help from her. There was no chance of her having anything else to do with him. He was totally out of her league. Fooling with a man like Ashley Graham would be like playing with dynamite.

After Ashley Graham's departure, the rest of the evening was something of an anti-climax. Not that she didn't thoroughly enjoy her brother and sister-in-law's company, but *he* had upset her and dented the shell she had so diligently built around herself. It scared her.

Throughout the remainder of the evening, she felt Jonathan's eyes on her, a puzzled look on his face. But, fortunately, he knew better than to say anything to her.

Anne, completely ignorant of the undercurrents, sung Ashley's praises all evening and couldn't understand why Brooke's only response was to remain quiet with a somewhat determined expression on her face. By the time Brooke said good night, she had a headache and was dreading the dinner party the next evening even more.

However, she had already decided how she was going to handle the situation. She planned to completely ignore Ashley, pretend he didn't exist, or at least try to.

But for some reason, she couldn't quite squelch the

guilt feelings for refusing to help Jonathan. After all, he and Anne had taken her into their home. All Jonathan wanted was for her to be cordial to Ashley Graham. It wouldn't be hard. He was a handsome devil, as Jonathan had previously stated. With that thought in mind, she finally drifted off into an uneasy sleep.

Chapter Two

$\mathcal{B}$rooke awoke the next morning feeling anxious. Today she hoped to begin slowly and experiment with exercises that would enable her to recover the full use of her arms and legs. She was itching to pick up a tennis racket and put what strength she had gained to a test. She was determined to recover the full use of her limbs.

Brooke had not slept well, tossing and turning all night, and it was only in the wee hours of the morning that she fell into a troubled sleep. She didn't even want to think about the reason for her sleepless night. She couldn't admit the truth, that Ashley Graham was the cause.

Turning to look at the clock on the bedside table, she noticed it was after ten. Why in the world hadn't Anne awakened her? She did not want to waste a minute of her day. She might as well be up and about. It did her absolutely no good to lie in bed. However, she was going to have to make an all-out effort to quit letting things upset her and get the rest she needed to regain her strength. Otherwise Anne and Jonathan would worry. They might even call the doctor, and that was the last thing she wanted. She wouldn't think about Ashley Graham; he was nothing to her!

Pushing these thoughts aside, she got out of bed and, not bothering to put on her robe, made her way to the bath adjoining her bedroom. She took a quick shower, knowing that before the dinner party she would have time to take a relaxing bath. Sighing, she quickly turned her thoughts away once again from the evening ahead. She dreaded it, but refused to let it ruin her entire day. As she tucked the towel around her to make her way back into her room, there was a knock at the door. "Come in," she called. "I'm finally awake."

Smiling, Anne strode into the room. "Well, sleepyhead, you don't look as if going to bed did you any good!"

Laughing away her concern, Brooke changed the subject by asking the question, "What are we going to do today? You look like you're full of vim and vigor."

Brooke saw the hurt look that fleetingly crossed her sister-in-law's face, but she was tired of her appearance being the sole topic of every conversation. She wanted so badly to put her troubled thoughts behind her. Having to talk about herself and review past pains with everyone she came into contact with could hardly be called healing. She knew she wasn't being fair, because Anne and Jonathan weren't just everybody, they were her family, but still . . .

Sighing, Brooke turned her thoughts back to what Anne was saying. "I do feel good, you're right, and after you eat breakfast, I'll show you the house. I'm so very proud of it. Jonathan has always given me everything I've ever wanted, although mind you, he's certainly not perfect," she teased.

"You're telling me," laughed Brooke. "But like you, I wouldn't trade him, faults and all, for anyone else."

Brooke felt good about having such an easy friendship between Anne and herself. It was going to be good for her to be around her sister-in-law and brother. She couldn't even remember the last time she was able to tease or joke about anything. Thank goodness her luck was beginning to change in more ways than one.

After a leisurely breakfast of cereal, toast and coffee, which Anne insisted on preparing for her, they began touring the house. Anne was proud of it, and well she should have been, because it was lovely. It reeked of elegance, but at the same time it was cozy as a home should be. Brooke felt that she had truly come home the moment she had arrived.

Even though Anne showed Brooke every detail of the house, it didn't take long at all, because everything was so compact and there wasn't any wasted space. There was a large den with a bar in the corner. Along one wall was a complete stereo system. Across the back of the den there was nothing but glass from floor to ceiling, overlooking the patio and swimming pool with a breathtaking view of the beach in the distance. The kitchen was small but extremely efficient, with a breakfast room adjacent to it.

Anne had laughingly explained that she spent more time in the kitchen than any place else and she designed it explicitly to fit her taste. To complete the downstairs, there was a large formal living and dining room used mainly for entertainment, and a small study which both Anne and Jonathan used.

The upstairs consisted of three lovely bedrooms; the

large master bedroom, a guest room which Brooke was now occupying and a third one that was being redecorated for the nursery. There was a bath adjoining each room.

By the time they finished, Brooke was beginning to tire, but she was determined not to admit it, even to herself. Anne looked at her with concern and sympathy in her eyes.

Trying not to let her worry show, Anne said, "Why don't you go lie down for a while and then go for a swim later? I wish I could join you, but I have to run some last-minute errands for the party."

"No, no. I'm fine, really I am. Let me help you get ready for the party."

"Now that you've mentioned it," Anne continued, "are you sure you're up to this party tonight? Your brother has a way of putting the cart before the horse. Don't let him push you into doing anything you don't want to do."

"Don't worry about that. I know how to handle my brother. Or at least I used to," laughed Brooke as she climbed the stairs to her room.

Brooke sensed from these last quietly spoken words that her sister-in-law was talking about more than her health. Jonathan's insistence that she be "nice" to Ashley Graham would be a disadvantage with the persistent man. It made her behave like an idiot when she didn't mean to. She had to get control of herself before tonight or she would once again find herself in a position that she would not be able to handle. After all, Jonathan's request was not an ultimatum, merely a friendly suggestion. But had there been just a tinge of anxiety underlying his words? Or had she only imagined it?

Before reaching her room, she called down the stairs to Anne, "I have some letters that need to be written, so when you get back, call me."

After several attempts to write her roommate and a couple of her old friends in Houston, she threw the pen down in utter frustration. What in the world was wrong with her? She could not keep her mind on anything, and she felt far too restless to lie down. Her thoughts were torn between wanting to prove to herself that her hands and arms were indeed getting stronger, and behaving herself at the approaching dinner party. It would actually be a relief to see Ashley Graham once again so she could dispel the attraction she felt for this man and put him in his place without offending her brother.

Not wanting to remain in her room any longer with her thoughts, she whisked a pair of knit shorts and a shirt out of the drawer and went to the bathroom to change. It was too early to eat, but she felt she needed to do something to keep her mind occupied. There was nothing like volleying a few tennis balls off a wall to tire one out.

Just the thought of holding a racket in her hands once again made her feel lightheaded and giddy. She could never accept that she was doing something wrong. The doctors simply did not realize how determined she was to be an ace tennis player again.

Anne and Jonathan would have a fit if they knew she was planning to go back onto the courts and the words of Ashley Graham came to her mind in full force. "You'll be jeopardizing your health for the rest of your life if you don't stay away from the tennis courts."

Brushing those disturbing thoughts aside, she made her way out the door.

When Brooke came downstairs, she checked to make

sure she had the house all to herself. She certainly had no intention of getting caught with her racket in hand! Just as she was about to go back upstairs to retrieve her racket and shoes, out of nowhere came Anne's voice, "Hey friend! You're supposed to be in your room! What do you mean trying to sneak out of your 'nappy' time?"

Laughing, Brooke said, "Please don't fuss at me. I'm too restless to stay cooped up in my room. However, I hope my stay here will cure that problem." That was a close call, she thought, congratulating herself for handling it.

"You bet it will," replied Anne. "Remember too, my shoulder is always handy anytime you feel you want to use it."

"Thanks," said Brooke frowning, "but I have to work my problems out on my own. Besides, I'm much better, both mentally and physically. You're the one that needs taking care of now, not me."

"Oh, pooh," said Anne, "I'm fine. I've been looking forward to having you here and taking care of *you*. . . ."

Brooke interrupted. "Don't encourage me to become too dependent or you may not ever get rid of me."

"Oh, I seriously doubt that, Brooke, just because you've had a bad experience with one man doesn't mean there won't be someone that will come along and be Mr. Right for you. Then you won't even miss not being able to play tennis anymore." She paused. "Take Ashley Graham for instance, I'm sure you were aware that he was completely fascinated by your good looks. Why weren't you impressed with him? Women fall over their feet for that man."

Striving to keep her voice light, Brooke said, "I

honestly don't know why I reacted to him the way I did. Maybe it was his macho attitude that I didn't care for. Who knows? Maybe I'm just paranoid."

"I didn't mean to sound as if I was criticizing," began Anne hurriedly.

"Please don't apologize," interrupted Brooke. "All I know is that for some reason he frightened me, but at the same time I felt strangely drawn to him. I felt, too, as if he were a spider drawing me into a tight web from which there would be no escape. Sounds crazy doesn't it?"

"Not really," answered Anne.

"Well, it sounds crazy to me!" said Brooke. "But then I don't handle things too well right now. It seems as if I blow everything out of proportion."

"Brooke," said Anne, her tone suddenly becoming serious, "Jonathan told me last night that he had asked you to more or less make a play for Ashley, to maybe improve his chances of getting that job he so desperately wants. I'm really sorry he asked you to do something like that, especially after all you've been through." She frowned. "But I'm not sure I shamed him enough to stop him from pushing the point any further. I just hope there's not more to his wanting this job than meets the eye," continued Anne, her voiced laced with emotion.

"Oh, Anne, I feel like an utter heel for making a big deal out of such a small request. I owe you both so much for making a home for me when I need it. I hate to refuse Jonathan anything. But let's not worry about it right now. We can't have you getting upset, especially now."

"Ha!" laughed Anne, some of the tension leaving her face with the changing of the subject. "The doctor said as long as I took care of myself I could do anything

I wanted to, within reason, that is," she finished lamely.

"Within reason, remember!" exclaimed Brooke grinning. "That's the catch. Now admit it, you'll enjoy us coddling you a little now, won't you?"

"Oh, I'm sure I will. When the time comes, I'll be the world's biggest baby. Well," continued Anne, getting up from the lounge chair, "I'm enjoying this, but I've just got to run to the store and pick up a few last-minute items for tonight. I won't be gone too long, I hope."

"Are you sure there's nothing I can do to help?" asked Brooke.

"No really, there isn't. Just go ahead and rest or swim. When you get through help yourself to a salad plate in the fridge. I'm going to pass on lunch since I made such a pig of myself at breakfast."

After Anne left, Brooke quickly grabbed her racket and shoes and headed for the back of the house, where she was relatively hidden from view.

Before beginning her volley, she did several knee bends and toe touches to loosen up. When she had finished, she felt a little shaky, but was determined nevertheless to continue.

So, squelching an acute sense of frustration at her weakness, she began slowly and methodically bouncing the ball off the brick wall of the garage. The more she volleyed the stronger she became and the better she felt. To think she had regained her strength to this degree. She was almost afraid it was a mirage. Thank goodness for physical therapy and the many hours of secretly exercising against a backboard before she left Houston, and last, but not least, determination.

The next best thing would be to actually play on the

tennis court itself. Was that possible? This thought kept plaguing her throughout her work session. The more she thought about it, the better she liked the idea. Why not? She had virtually the whole afternoon ahead of her with no one the wiser as to what she did.

Brooke was positive that sooner or later she would play again as a professional. A comeback was inevitable. It just had to be.

By the time she devoured a lunch of tuna salad, crackers and fresh fruit, she was nervous. What if she got caught? No, she chided herself, as long as she went to one of the public courts, she would be safe.

As soon as she finished eating, she went directly to the phone and called a taxi. When she put the receiver down, she was trembling. Could she actually go through with it?

Before she lost her nerve, she dashed upstairs, grabbed her tote bag and stuffed a towel, hairbrush, lip gloss and money in it and hurried back downstairs to wait for the taxi.

She instructed the driver to drop her off at the nearest public tennis court. She was so excited she found it hard to contain herself. After paying the driver and thanking him with a brilliant smile, Brooke walked onto an uncrowded court. She was surprised that there were not more people playing at this time of day.

Without wasting a moment of her precious time, she began her warm-up volley. She was hard at the task when she felt, rather than saw, someone staring at her. Pausing, she turned and saw a young man leaning against the umpire's box watching every move she made.

"Hey, you're good," he said as he nonchalantly strolled over to her. A grin was plastered on his face. "I haven't seen form like that in a long time!" His eyes scrutinized her lithe body.

The way he looked at her, Brooke wasn't too sure exactly what form he was referring to. He seemed harmless enough, however, so she smiled in return and said, "Hello. Who are you?"

"My name is David Ritter. What's yours?"

"Brooke Lawson."

"Not *the* Brooke Lawson who's the tennis pro?"

She smiled. "The one and the same, I'm afraid." The fact that he recognized her name gave her deflated ego a tremendous boost. She had been off the circuit for a long while now.

"Gee, it's sure a pleasure to meet you," he said excitedly. He stuck his hand out and Brooke put her slender one in his to seal the greeting.

"By the way, I haven't seen your name in the papers lately. You are still playing, aren't you?" He looked uncertain.

Brooke licked her dry lips. "No. Actually, I'm not, right now. I had a car accident, and I've been recuperating these last few months. To be honest, this is my first time on a court since the accident."

"Well, from what I saw a minute ago, you certainly don't have anything to worry about. Your moves are almost perfect."

"Oh, thanks a million," cried Brooke. "Your words are music to my ears."

"As soon as you recover completely, do you plan to play professionally again?"

Brooke faltered. "Yes—I—I do. Just as soon as I can." There was no reason to go into the fact that she wasn't ever supposed to pick up a racket again. It did not really matter what the doctor said anyway, because she knew her own inner strength and that soon she would compete in and win professional matches.

David Ritter was watching her with admiration in his eyes. He made no apologies for staring at her. He merely grinned. He was good-looking in a boyish sort of way. Tall and lanky, with sandy hair and freckles, he was dressed in the usual tennis whites. His blue eyes were twinkling and mischievous. He couldn't be more than twenty years old.

He was a total opposite of Ashley Graham.

Now why on earth did that thought cross her mind? Surely she was not going to compare every man she met with *him?* Absolutely not! she told herself.

Breaking into her thoughts, David said, "I would consider it an honor if you would play a short practice game with me, just for fun. Is that possible? He hesitated a moment. "I realize that you said this was your first time on a tennis court, but . . ."

Interrupting him, Brooke said, "I'd love to play, but only for a few minutes. All I really want to do is test my stamina and strength."

"Great! Let's get started."

Brooke's mouth was so dry she could hardly swallow. Was she up to this? Was she actually capable of playing so soon? All of a sudden, she was having mixed emotions. Maybe she *was* pushing her body too fast. No, she argued to herself, it was now or never. She was positive she could meet the challenge.

As they began their warm-up, Brooke felt the adrenaline course through her veins. No matter what the circumstances, she always felt the same competitive tension as soon as she walked onto the court. For that reason alone, it was an exciting sport.

For the next few minutes, they actually did little more than volley the ball back and forth across the net.

Brooke practiced her serve and worked on getting the stiffness out of her limbs.

The pace was slow and David was quick to give her encouragement when he would accidentally lob her a difficult shot to return. The fact that she was able to hold and swing the racket firmly and move around the court totally free of pain was a feat in itself.

She was elated. Even though it had been no challenge to David, he seemed to enjoy playing a part in her comeback.

Feeling herself weakening, Brooke laughingly called a halt to their play. She definitely needed to get back home before Anne did; she also had a long evening ahead of her and she did not want to be dead on her feet.

As he came around to her side of the net, David said, "It won't be long before you'll have it all back together. I pity the poor soul who'll have to face you in a real game."

Brooke squinted her eyes. "Oh, David, you make me feel so good!"

He shrugged and grinned. "I'm just telling it like it is."

She expelled a sigh. "I really hated to quit, but I was afraid to push my luck. My legs are a wee bit wobbly as it is," she finished breathlessly.

"I can certainly understand that. You don't need to push yourself," he chided.

"I don't intend to." She stopped to glance at her watch. "Goodness, I need to call a taxi and get myself home."

"Taxi?" He looked puzzled. "You don't need to call a taxi. I'll take you home."

"Thanks," she said and flashed him a smile.

The drive did not take long. After being walked to

the door, at David's insistence, Brooke promised to play tennis with him again if at all possible. He seemed satisfied with her half promise and left smiling.

After closing the door, she leaned against it. She was too excited to move. She had actually played tennis today, and although she was tired, she had never felt better.

After a moment, she forced herself to climb the stairs to her room. Thank goodness she was alone! Her day's activity was still her secret.

After discarding her shirt and shorts, she donned a light terry cloth robe and fell onto the bed. When she next opened her eyes, it was to stare at the clock radio beside her bed. Ten minutes after six? The guests were due to arrive for the dinner party at seven-thirty! When she moved to get out of bed, she groaned. She hoped she wouldn't have to pay for the short moments of pleasure she had experienced earlier. A good hot bath was just what she needed.

Before running her bath water, she crossed to the door and made her way downstairs to let them know she was awake. As she reached the bottom of the stairs, Jonathan came around the corner of the den, drink in hand.

"Hey, Sis," he remarked, "I was just on my way to your room to tell you to rise and shine."

"I was wondering why nobody had awakened me," said Brooke. "I was shocked when I rolled over and looked at the clock and saw what time it was."

"Well, Anne said not to disturb you as there was absolutely nothing for you to do except get dressed. Anyway, it may be a rather late night, if our friends run true to form. By the way," he continued, "I'm sorry about being pushy about Ashley yesterday. Anne made me feel awful about it. I still don't think it was anything for you two to make such a big deal out of, but—I'm sorry," he shrugged petulantly.

At this moment, Brooke's brother reminded her of a small boy who was prone to pout when he did not get his way. Sighing, she did not like remembering this spoiled side of Jonathan, but she recalled it well from past experiences. She knew there was much more behind his request than he wanted her to believe or he would not keep bringing it up.

"Jonathan," she said hesitantly, "let's just wait and see what happens, shall we? Who knows? Your Mr. Graham might be as turned off by me as I was by him. As I said before, let's just see what happens! Now, if I don't go and take my bath, I certainly won't be ready when the first guest arrives." Smiling fleetingly at him, she turned and ran up the stairs.

After a hasty bath, she began putting on her lacy underwear. Her breath quickened at the thought of seeing Ashley Graham again. All day she had refused to let herself think about him. When his dark arrogant face would pop up in her mind, she quickly turned her thoughts to other things. Now that it was almost time to see him again, she dreaded it. For reasons she did not want to pursue, she would not ask herself why she wanted to look her best.

The dress she chose to wear was very simple. The material was soft white chiffon with sheer belled sleeves each with a slit from the shoulder to cuff. The V-neckline ended in an elasticized waistline and flared into a full pleated skirt. A belt with a matching clasp further enhanced the outfit.

Stepping into heeled sandals, she brushed her hair until it looked like spun gold. Cleverly using the curling iron on the tips and sides, she swirled it back away from her face. Her only jewelry were small diamond stud earrings that had been a gift from her parents the Christmas before they were killed, and a thin gold chain around her neck which she rarely took off. A quick spray of Chloé perfume and she was ready to go.

Swallowing, she tried to calm the butterflies in her stomach before leaving her room.

When Brooke finally came downstairs that evening, it looked as if most of the guests had already arrived. At least fifteen or twenty people were enjoying the hospitality of the Lawsons; they clustered in small groups, drinking cocktails and visiting.

The massive stereo system in one corner of the den filtered soft music throughout the room, but didn't interfere with the conversation. Rich perfume and tobacco blended with the sweet fragrance from the flowers and drifted through the open patio door.

All day she had dreaded this moment. Now, the prospect of joining the group did not seem so bad. When Anne noticed her standing inside the door rather uncertainly, she came to her rescue.

"Wow, but do you ever look great! From just one day of rest and a few hours in the sun, you have already begun to show signs of improvement," she declared.

"The company and the wonderful sunshine can take all the credit," laughed Brooke. "Plus the fact that I'm so happy to be here. It makes me feel one hundred percent better already. I hope you won't get tired of hearing me say that."

"No way!" exclaimed Anne. "We're more than glad to have you as you well know. Come on, I want you to meet our friends. They are a nice bunch of people— rather on the rowdy side, but harmless," she cautioned with twinkling eyes.

As Brooke was introduced, she noticed that half the

couples were American, the others Hawaiian. Most of them were from Jonathan's office, with the few others being their neighbors in the town house complex.

As soon as Anne felt secure in leaving her, she went to take care of her duties as hostess and left Brooke in the company of a rather homely, but affable young man. He had wandered up to the group around Anne and Brooke and received a lot of good-natured bantering from his friends about always trying to hustle all the good-looking girls.

Grinning, he turned to Brooke and said, "Please don't let these so-called friends of mine influence you against my insurmountable charms. By the way, the name's James Gregory. Jim to my friends."

"Oh, I definitely caught your name, Mr. Gregory."

"Please, please, don't offend me by calling me Mr. Gregory," he said with mock humility in his voice. "No one ever refers to me as that."

He was making fun of himself, but in such a way that people laughed with him and not at him. After being around him for only a few minutes, she could see why he was the life of the party. She enjoyed his good-natured bantering and his uninhibited attempt at openly flirting with her. There was not one thing that could label him as handsome, or even good-looking for that matter. He was extremely tall, rather on the rangy side, with dark auburn hair and freckles. His nose was too broad for his long thin face. But his eyes were a brilliant blue and full of merriment and his grin was infectious.

"Hey, I heard that you're a crackerjack tennis player," he said. Admiration seeped from his eyes.

"Shhh!" hushed Brooke. She glanced around to make sure no one heard his statement, before continuing in a whisper, "Who told you that?"

"Why, David Ritter, of course." He seemed surprised at her question. "I saw him this afternoon at the tennis club. He told me that he had played you a practice game earlier today."

She licked her suddenly dry lips. "That's not supposed to be public knowledge." She looked uncomfortable. "My brother and sister-in-law aren't aware that I've even picked up a tennis racket since my accident."

Jim looked confused. "Accident. What accident? Dave didn't mention anything to me about your having an accident."

Brooke looked surprised. "You mean David didn't tell you?" Open mouth, insert foot, she thought to herself. But she had no idea David would not repeat what she had told him. "I had a car wreck and as a result, I'm not supposed to be able to play tennis again. But as you can see, the doctors were wrong."

"Sure sounds like it after what Ritter told me today."

Brooke flushed. "I want you to promise that this will be our secret, and will you please do me a favor and tell David, when you see him, to please not tell anyone else about my playing tennis."

"He was so excited after having met you that he wanted to brag a little." He grinned. "But I'll make it a point to tell him."

Brooke flashed him a smile. "Thanks, I'd appreciate it."

His tone casual, he asked, "How about playing a game with me sometime. We can practice together. Are you game?"

Brooke didn't hesitate. "I'd like that."

He relaxed. "Good. I'll call you soon and we'll make a secret date." He winked at her.

She laughed aloud.

It was the tinkling sound of Brooke's laughter that drew the attention of Ashley Graham as he was ushered into the den by his host. These affairs were a dead bore to him; he usually avoided them like the plague. But since his meeting Jonathan's sister the evening before, the vision of her kept appearing before his eyes. She was so lovely, so standoffish, so challenging that his senses quickened at the thought of seeing her again.

At the same time, Brooke saw Ashley enter the room and she felt her stomach drop to her toes. She knew she should avert her eyes, but she simply could not. Ashley was openly staring at her and they were so engrossed in looking at each other that they might as well have been the only occupants of the crowded room.

With a jerk, Brooke finally came to her senses and turned her head to answer a question asked by Jim Gregory. She could tell by the rather confused look on his face that he must have repeated the question at least once before he finally claimed her attention.

"I'm sorry," apologized Brooke rather breathlessly. "My mind seems to be in the habit of wandering lately." She smiled at him as she lamely made the attempt to cover her rudeness. But she knew he did not believe her because she saw his mouth tighten when he looked in the direction of her stare and saw Ashley Graham.

"You're forgiven. It's certainly not in my best interest to get mad at the most beautiful and available female in the room, now, is it?" He was grinning broadly and went back to his good-natured bantering, but Brooke noticed that his laughter never really reached his eyes. She knew he wanted to ask her about Ashley but knew he would be stepping completely out of his bounds if he did.

Although Brooke made it a point not to be caught staring at Ashley again, she nevertheless felt his eyes boring into her on several occasions. In fact, she could almost sense his frustration at not being able to get her alone so that he could talk to her.

During the course of the evening, Jim Gregory remained with her like a second skin. She was grateful to him, because the very last thing she wanted was to have to talk to Ashley Graham alone. She danced several dances with Jim and another one with a young Hawaiian who worked in her brother's immediate office. While dancing, she also noticed that her brother's eyes followed her very anxiously around the room. She knew he expected her to make an effort to seek out Ashley and she actually felt sick to her stomach when she would catch Jonathan looking at her with an almost desperate look in his eyes.

If she was in doubt before, she suspected now that her brother was definitely in some kind of serious trouble and it involved Ashley Graham. Whether it was directly or indirectly, she did not know, but tonight after the party, she intended to find out.

As he took a breather from dancing, Jim went to the bar for a Tom Collins to quench her thirst. She stood on the patio waiting for him, her back to the den and the loud laughter and dancing from within. Although the air conditioning was going full blast, it was still hot and stuffy inside with so many people milling around. She needed some fresh air.

She was beginning to feel tired from the long evening and her intense worry about Jonathan. She could not mask the feeling of impending doom where he was concerned. She knew, beyond a doubt, that she would play a large part in the outcome one way or another.

Before he uttered one word, she sensed that Ashley was behind her. After what seemed like forever, but in reality was only a moment or two, he said in a subdued voice close to her ear, "I was beginning to think I would never find you alone. Have you by any chance bribed that vulture Gregory to keep you away from me?" His warm breath teased her ear, causing her senses to reel.

Trying to keep her feelings from showing, she answered in what she hoped was a nonchalant voice, "Surely you're joking? I wasn't even aware you were still here."

To that comment he said nothing, only raised his eyes and smiled in that self-assured manner of his which told her that he didn't believe her. He was not about to let her forget the way their eyes had locked when he first entered the room.

He was standing so close to her now that she could smell the sheer maleness of him—a blend of cologne and rich tobacco. He looked lean and elegant in a casual blue sapphire jacket and matching pants. He deliberately made her aware of him, and the look in his eyes challenged her to admit that she was as attracted to him as he was to her.

Brooke knew beyond a doubt that she was in over her head and would be crazy to accept any kind of challenge from this man. Anyway, how could she be so ridiculous to even consider herself a real candidate for his interest? She also knew she must get away from him before her mixed emotions got the better of her. Her heart was beating so rapidly now that she was sure he could hear it in the quiet of the night.

Making a move to try and get past him to make her way toward Jim, who was diligently searching for her with a drink in his hand, she took a step backward. But she caught her heel on the edge of a flower pot and would have fallen had Ashley not reached out and grabbed her arms to steady her. Even though his touch was firm on her bare flesh, she nevertheless felt the electricity shoot up her arms as a result of their contact.

She knew he felt it too, by the way his eyes narrowed. But she was unable to read what he might be thinking because of the shadows of the night.

After she had regained her balance, he said in a husky whisper, "Please, don't make me touch you again, or I won't be responsible for my actions." He paused, his eyes holding hers captive. "You can forget about your fellow in there. Now that I've finally got you to myself, I'm not about to let you go so soon. And you can quit staring at me with those big eyes of yours. I'm not going to accost you now, unless, of course, you try to run away again." His last remark was made with a softened smile on his face and, at least for the moment, Brooke felt herself relax a little.

"Come on," demanded Ashley, as he grabbed her arm and headed toward the patio steps, "let's go for a walk around the pool. At least maybe there we can have some privacy." Brooke glanced around in time to see Jim Gregory headed straight for them, a determined look on his face. Obviously Ashley had seen him too and was taking no chances in her being whisked away.

Her rather ardent companion of the evening must have gotten the message, because he was no longer in pursuit of Brooke as she and Ashley made their way to the poolside. It was with total reluctance that Brooke went with Ashley. But to have refused would have caused a scene, of that she was sure, considering the obstinate set of Ashley's mouth.

It was a lovely evening. The Hawaiian sky was full of stars and there was just enough breeze to blow the tantalizing aroma of the flowers around them to further enhance the beauty of the night. Not one word had been spoken between them since they left the patio. Brooke was upset and was making no attempt to hide it. She felt that if Ashley said one more thing to her, she would burst out crying. What she could not understand was his pursuit of her. Why would a man like Ashley Graham be interested in a nobody like her when he could have his pick of numerous females? In fact, they were probably waiting in line to vie for his attention. Things were getting out of hand. She was losing control of her emotions, and it really frightened her.

"Have dinner with me tomorrow night." His direct demand cut through her thoughts and the silence of the night like a sharp knife.

"What did you say?" stammered Brooke in a dismayed voice. She was sure he must be aware of how much he was affecting her. Brooke shivered involuntarily.

"I *said,* I want you to have dinner with me tomorrow evening. I'll pick you up at eight o'clock sharp."

Folding her arms tightly around her, she said, "I—er—already have plans for tomorrow evening." Grasping at straws, she attempted to put things back on an even keel. He was just playing with her, because she represented a challenge and she deeply resented it, especially now, when her emotions were already raw. The bottom line was that she was attracted to him and she did not want to be. She had to be careful, however, because she certainly didn't want to aggravate the problem between Jonathan and him if she could avoid it. If only she could dispel that desperate look in her brother's face. It had remained before her eyes all evening and was making her cautious in dealing with Ashley.

"Then tell them you're not interested—that you're going with me instead."

"I'm afraid that's not possible," replied Brooke, striving to keep her voice even. "Did it ever occur to you that maybe I don't want to have dinner with you tomorrow evening, or any other, for that matter?" For the moment she let caution go to the wind.

"I see." But Ashley sounded totally unconvinced.

Brooke was more than a little miffed that he didn't believe her. "Please—the answer's still no." She was trying hard to mask the confusion she was feeling. "Now, if you don't mind, I'd better be getting back inside. . . ."

"I want to take you out," Ashley said quietly, "and I usually get what I want."

"My mind is made up," Brooke replied stiffly. With these words, she turned to go back toward the patio. She had to get away from him. She resented his intrusion into her life. All she wanted to be concerned with now was playing tennis once again. She could not allow Ashley to complicate her life. But she was to have no better luck escaping this time than before. Ashley reacted just as quickly and pulled her up against the hard length of his body. In that instant, Brooke could sense the control he was trying to exercise over himself, but she could tell she had shaken him somewhat with her blatant refusal to go out with him.

"Maybe this will convince you that I mean to have my way." Before she had time to avert her mouth, his covered hers with a hot searing kiss that branded her as his possession just as surely as if she had been marked with a hot iron.

Moaning, she tried to pull her mouth away from his, but he kept tasting the sweetness of her lips and she felt herself drowning in the mastery of his kisses. Blotting out all other thoughts, she gave herself up to the longing he was evoking within her.

As Ashley sensed her surrender, he abruptly pushed her away from him and said in a tight voice, *"Now* tell me that you don't want to go with me tomorrow night."

Brooke was so shocked by her own actions that for a moment she was speechless. When she finally found her voice, she began stammering, "Y—you had no right to do that—no right!" Knowing that tears were near the surface, she turned and ran back toward the house. This time he did not try to stop her.

Chapter Three

Brooke did not know how she made it through the remainder of the evening. The only thing that saved her was the fact that by the time she returned from her encounter with Ashley, the party was breaking up.

After taking a quick look around, she knew no one would miss her, so she hurried to her room and with shaking hands repaired her makeup. It was obvious after taking a look at herself in the mirror that she had been thoroughly and passionately kissed. There was no way she could confront her brother with her lips advertising what had just taken place. She was positive that her and Ashley's absence had been noticed by Jonathan, that he was probably rejoicing, thinking that she had agreed with his plan after all. Well, was he ever in for a surprise! After the moment she had spent with Ashley, she knew that she must firmly but lovingly tell her brother that she would be glad to do anything else for him but not this. She had to keep her fingers crossed that it was just her imagination that there was more to Jonathan's request than met the eye.

When she had finished refreshing herself, she made her way downstairs to find that all the guests had finally gone. Luck was with her, because her brother was alone in the den mixing himself a drink.

"Where's Anne?" Brooke asked hesitantly. She certainly had no intention of discussing what she had on her mind in Anne's presence. If Jonathan wanted to discuss it with her in private, that was his business.

"I persuaded her to go to bed and leave all of this mess for the maid in the morning. She was dead on her feet, so it didn't take too much persuasion."

"Good," stated Brooke, "I was hoping I'd be able to talk to you alone for a few minutes, or have you been drinking too much to concentrate on what I have to say?"

"No, Brooke, I haven't been drinking *too* much!"

The mocking sarcasm in his voice warned her that this wasn't going to be a very pleasant discussion. But she was determined to have her say no matter what!

Sighing, she said, "Okay, Jonathan, I'll come right to the point and won't beat around the bush. Why are you so insistent that I encourage Ashley to ask me out? What kind of trouble are you in that involves him?" Before he could answer, she went on to say, "Ordinarily, I wouldn't be asking you anything personal, but since you've involved me, I feel I have a right to know what's going on."

His mouth tightened angrily as he tried to keep control of his temper. Jonathan had never really grown up and probably never would, regardless of marriage or fatherhood. She could see that now very clearly. If it hadn't been for Anne, he probably would not have made anything worthwhile out of his life.

"Just what makes you think there's anything going on?" he demanded.

Before she had time to answer, however, he went on to say, "In fact, I'm pretty sure I've got everything under control now. So I don't want you to worry your pretty head about it any longer."

"Jonathan, I'm not going one step out of this room until you talk to me. I know there's more going on than meets the eye. You're in some kind of trouble and it concerns Ashley Graham, doesn't it?"

"Now, Sis, I don't intend to delve into my personal problems with you tonight! I'm too tired and besides you're making a mountain out of a mole hill. I'm sure it all boils down to the fact that I asked you to be friendly toward Ashley. Please forget I ever opened my mouth. Just do your own thing as far as he's concerned. If you want to date him, do and if you don't, don't!"

Brooke could definitely tell by the belligerent tone of his voice that he had been drinking far too much to carry on any decent type of conversation. All they would accomplish at this point would be to say things to each other that they didn't really mean and have to apologize for later.

Sighing deeply, more than a little frustrated, she said, "All right! Have it your own way for now, but I intend to have this out with you at a later date." With these words, she quietly walked out of the room and left Jonathan with a brooding and worried expression on his face.

After finally getting her teeth brushed and her nightgown on and crawling in between the sheets, she hoped she could fall asleep immediately, but as soon as she closed her eyes, all of her problems dominated her thoughts. She relived her car crashing into the concrete embankment, as well as a variety of her professional tennis matches.

She sat upright in bed. "Brooke Lawson," she said aloud, "quit being an idiot!" She needed to go to sleep. She must have all her faculties about her tomorrow, because she intended to break her date with Ashley Graham.

Burying her face in the pillow, she willed her eyes to close. But this time voices of the past haunted her thoughts. She tried to block them out, but could not. . . . "Miss Lawson, we caution you against ever becoming pregnant. Conceiving would be a terrible risk. No children."

Dead inside . . . Empty . . .

She finally drifted off into an uneasy sleep.

The next morning her day began just as the previous one had—breakfast with Anne, swimming and lounging around the pool. Then she ate a light but nourishing lunch of shrimp salad, crackers and a bowl of fresh fruit topped with whipped cream.

Being lazy was great fun, except that she could not allow anything to interfere with her workouts. Nor could she keep to herself the fact that she had played tennis in public once already and planned to again soon with Jim Gregory. She must confide in Anne if she was to have the time she needed for practicing. Brooke dreaded telling her, because she knew what Anne's reaction would be.

After lunch she couldn't put off breaking her date with Ashley another minute. At the moment, that was more pressing than playing tennis. Time was slowly but surely running out. Anne and Jonathan had gone to look at baby furniture, so she had no excuse for postponing the inevitable.

Picking up the phone, she dialed information and got the number at the office building where she was sure Ashley would be at this time of day.

When she finally got through to his secretary, a firm but pleasant voice said that Mr. Graham wasn't in his office at this time and would she care to leave a message.

"Yes, please," she stammered. "Tell him Miss Lawson called and will be unable to keep their appointment this evening."

"Thank you very much for calling. I'll see that he gets it, Miss Lawson," replied his secretary.

Now that it was over and done with, she kept waiting for the feeling of relief to hit her. But for some reason, it didn't. If anything, she felt a keen sense of disappointment and frustration.

Deep down she knew she would have thoroughly enjoyed the challenge Ashley Graham was offering her, but she also knew beyond a shadow of a doubt her inability to handle it. She simply refused to allow herself to be any man's plaything. If she ever did succumb to his fatal charm, he would drop her like a hot potato. And furthermore, until she found out a little more about what was bothering Jonathan, antagonizing Ashley would be dangerous. Though she wasn't sure how, the two were closely connected.

Now she had the whole afternoon to practice and exercise. Jonathan and Anne had tried to persuade her to go with them to shop for baby furniture, but she declined, not wanting to intrude on this happy occasion for the two of them.

The afternoon passed too swiftly for Brooke. After volleying the ball for a while off the garage wall, she walked the short distance to the Kailua Raquet Club and practiced for an hour. She was getting stronger every day. Several persons stopped a moment to remark about how good she was.

Brooke had to caution herself, however, not to get her hopes up high—not yet. She still had a long way to go.

By the time she arrived back home, she felt like a deflated balloon. So she grabbed a paperback book she had bought before her plane flight and lay on the chaise longue by the pool until she heard her brother and sister-in-law calling to her from inside the house.

"Hey, you two, I'm out here by the pool," she shouted in return.

"What have you done constructive while we've been gone?" panted Anne as she fell into a chair next to Brooke. "Heavens, but I'm pooped," she said before Brooke had a chance to answer her question.

Laughing, Brooke said, "I take it you got a lot accomplished in one afternoon? By the way where is Jonathan?"

"I'm sure he's mixing himself a drink after what I've put him through this afternoon," laughed Anne. "Poor dear, I'll never get him shopping again with me, baby or no baby!"

"Ha!" retorted Brooke. "I'm sure he loved every minute of it. A first baby is something you only get to share once in a lifetime."

"You're so right, Sis," interrupted Jonathan as he leisurely made his way to the poolside with a drink in hand. "But I can't honestly say I'm looking forward to taking my wife on another shopping spree anytime soon!"

Chuckling, Anne winked at Brooke as she said, "See, didn't I tell you so?"

"Hey," exclaimed Jonathan out of the clear blue. "Why don't I take you two beautiful girls out to dinner this evening. Are you too tired to go, Anne, honey?"

"That sounds great to me! Anne retorted. "How about you, Brooke? I bet you're ready to go somewhere after staying home all afternoon by yourself."

"Sounds great to me, too!" If they only knew the truth, Brooke added to herself. Her small gold wristwatch read five-thirty. Ashley had surely received her message by now, and she was more than a little curious as to how he had reacted to it. That man wasn't used to being turned down by any female. She chuckled to herself just thinking about it. If only she could have been there to see his face when his secretary told him.

"Well, if we're going out to eat, I guess I'd better take a hot bath and soak my poor aching feet so I'll be able to enjoy the evening" exclaimed Anne.

"I had better do the same," chimed in Brooke. "I've been out here by the pool for a while. I'll see you two after a while."

Upon returning to her room she immediately stripped out of her wet bikini and turned on the shower.

She had just stepped out and was toweling her hair dry when she heard the knock on the door. Before walking to the door, she pulled on her terry cloth robe, just in case it was Jonathan.

"It's open. Come on in," she said before reaching for the door handle.

Opening it she found Anne standing there with a puzzled look on her face. "You're wanted on the phone, Brooke, and if I'm not mistaken, it's Ashley Graham."

Brooke could feel the color drain from her face and was rendered speechless for a moment.

"You can take the call on the extension by your bed," said Anne. She was still looking at Brooke with that same puzzled frown on her face mingled with curiosity.

"I'd really rather not talk to him, Anne. Would you please do me a favor and tell him I'm busy and can't come to the phone right now?" She chewed her lower lip in agitation. "I know! You can pretend I'm still in the shower. Please do it for me?" pleaded Brooke as she noticed the indecision mirrored in Anne's face.

"Hey, wait a minute, I am not sure I ought to."

"You just have to do it for me," pleaded Brooke. "I do not want to talk to him again this soon."

Even though her sister-in-law was puzzled, she gave in with a shrug of her shoulders, "All right, I'll do it this time, but don't make a habit of this."

"Oh, thank you." Before Anne turned to go, Brooke planted a quick kiss on her cheek and shut the door quickly before Anne had a change of heart.

Brooke's knees were shaking so badly that she had to sit on the side of the bed for a minute to get herself under control. What would she do if he told Anne she had broken a dinner date with him? No, he wouldn't do that. He was too proud to admit that. Hopefully he would get the message this time for sure that she did not want to go out with him.

Sighing, she pushed her torn thoughts aside and strode to the closet to find something to wear for the evening. She hoped Anne would stick to dressing casually, because she certainly did not feel like even going out now, much less dressing up.

After debating for several minutes, she chose a halter dress made of lightweight cotton with a floral design. The colors were vivid without being harsh.

By the time she blew her hair dry, used the curling iron on the ends and put on her makeup, she knew without a doubt that Jonathan and Anne would be waiting for her. After Ashley's phone call, she couldn't seem to get it all together.

Stepping into her dress was the last thing she needed to do and she would be ready. As soon as that was done she sprayed herself with perfume and was ready to go. She did take time to notice that she had almost gotten too much sun. But even so, she noticed that her shoulders and arms were smooth and beginning to tan a golden brown.

As she was heading out of her room to go downstairs, she heard the sharp peal of the doorbell. Her heart almost completely stopped beating. She knew beyond a shadow of a doubt that when the door was opened, Ashley Graham would be standing on the other side of the threshold. She panicked, but she knew she was trapped.

She heard Jonathan ask Anne from the den, "Who in the world could that be? Were you expecting anyone?"

"No, but I hope it's not company since we're going to have to hurry to make our reservations as it is."

Jonathan opened the door in a hurried manner to see Ashley Graham's grim expression staring at him.

"Hello, Jonathan," stated Ashley. "I've come to pick up Brooke. Is she ready?"

By this time, Brooke somehow had forced her legs to continue moving and had reached the entrance hall just as Ashley came in.

Jonathan hadn't said a word. He just moved aside and looked from one to the other with more than a little confusion on his face.

Brooke finally found her voice and stammered, "It's all right, Jonathan. If you and Anne don't mind, I'd like to talk to Mr. Graham for a moment in private, please."

"Sure," he shrugged. "Anne and I'll just wait in the den."

As soon as Jonathan was out of hearing distance, she exploded at Ashley. "I know you got my message, so why are you here?"

"If my memory serves me correctly," retorted Ashley, "we had a dinner engagement for eight o'clock."

"Didn't you get my message?"

"What message?" he questioned innocently with raised eyebrows.

"You know very well what message! I called and left one with your secretary breaking our date for this evening. You just blatantly ignored it, didn't you?"

In a voice edged with steel, he said, "I intend to do as I said and I expect you to do the same."

Exasperated, Brooke knew she had run up against a brick wall. He refused to acknowledge one way or the other that she had tried to get out of going with him. Short of creating a scene right here in front of Jonathan and Anne, there was nothing else she could do except admit that she had been outwitted. His arrogance was wearing a little thin.

"Oh, all right, you win this time," she said very ungraciously. "Just give me a minute to explain things to Jonathan and Anne."

"I'll be waiting," he said and smiled. Brooke knew that behind the smooth facade, he was very upset. He was one that did not like his authority questioned or bucked in any way. Now the tables had turned, and she was a bundle of nerves.

After explaining to her brother and sister-in-law as best she could under the circumstances, she was at last free to leave. They both would have liked to ask her more questions but she told them she would talk to them later. They could not imagine what was going on.

After seeing that she was seated comfortably in his luxurious Cadillac, the drive to the restaurant was done in complete silence. Brooke tried to force herself to relax but she was uptight and could not calm herself. The one time she glanced in his direction, his expression was more than a little grim. She could see that she was not going to be in for a pleasant evening, not that she ever thought it would be.

When she thought she couldn't stand the silence another minute he said, "We are dining at a friend of mine's new club. The food is excellent and entertainment will be provided with our dinner. Afterward there will be dancing if you would care to do so," he said in a mocking voice. She realized he was still miffed at being stood up, but she chose to ignore him.

The thought of being held closely in his arms on the dance floor made her heart take a plunge. It was definitely a bittersweet one, no matter how much she tried to deny it.

A valet was waiting to park their car as they drove around the circular drive to the front of the building. The restaurant was located on the top floor. Brooke kept her eyes closed the whole way up in the outside elevator. Heights made her dizzy and even though she knew the sight must be breathtaking, she was too frightened to look.

Ashley chuckled close to her ear and whispered, "Fraidy cat!"

When she did not retaliate, he knew she must indeed be frightened, so he put his arms around her and drew her close against him. It was so crowded in the elevator that no one even noticed his gesture. Everyone else was too busy looking at the view.

When Ashley put his arms around Brooke, she made no move to halt his actions. She felt her stomach knot as he tightened his arms closer around her. She was positive he could feel her heart beating against him. But if he did, he gave no indication of it. Everytime he touched her, she felt as if she had been branded *his* all over again.

As they were ushered into the club, Ashley was treated like royalty. The interior was decorated beautifully and elegantly. It was circular in design and the stage and revolving dance floor were centered in the middle. It was completely done in glass from ceiling to floor and the scene was breathtaking.

They were seated on the outside and Brooke felt as if she were suspended in space when she looked out on the sights of Oahu. For a moment she forgot her intimidation of Ashley and exclaimed in an excited voice, "Oh, how lovely! I've never seen anything like this before. But I can see right now," she added, "I won't be able to look down too often. It's making me almost as dizzy as riding in the elevator."

Her eyes were shining and were as big as saucers. Ashley was hard pressed to take his eyes off her to give the waiter their drink order.

She fleetingly noted that he did not bother to ask her what she wanted to drink. He just took it upon himself to order her one of their best drinks, which he explained was a fresh fruit punch laced with rum.

When the drinks arrived, Brooke was a little hesitant about tasting it. She certainly wanted to be in control of her faculties this evening, so she considered it would be in her best interest not to consume too much alcohol. Ashley seemed to know what she was thinking and delighted in teasing her with that all-knowing smile on his handsome face.

It unnerved her to know that not only did his touch send her into orbit, but that he had an uncanny way of reading her mind as well. Was there to be no end to this man's dominance over her?

Laughing, Ashley said, "Don't worry honey, it's not in my plans to get you drunk. In fact, I have quite the opposite in mind. I want your full undivided attention all evening."

She did find that the drink contained very little alcohol and was light and refreshing. At least it gave her something to do with her hands. As she sipped, she looked around the room from time to time, trying to keep her eyes off Ashley.

Although there was a silence between them, it was not an uncomfortable one. Ashley seemed to enjoy smoking his pipe and watching the expressions on her face.

It was a relief when the waiter returned to the table to take their order. Here again, he did not bother to consult her but ordered the house specialty—a salad, a steak and lobster combination and a choice red wine. Brooke felt there was no chance of her being able to eat all that food. But again, it would be useless to say anything to him.

While they waited for their dinner to arrive, Ashley was making every effort to put her at ease. He kept the conversation light and before she knew it she was actually laughing at many of his anecdotes.

By the time their meal arrived, she was much more relaxed and found that she was actually enjoying herself, which was something she had not planned on. She was seeing a side of Ashley that she did not know existed, and if anything, it made him even more dangerously attractive. She again felt the web closing in tighter, but at this moment she was throwing caution to the wind and enjoying herself.

The meal was delicious, and if she had not been so aware of him at every turn, she could have really enjoyed it. Her steak was cooked medium well and was juicy and tender. She could almost cut it with a fork. The lobster shell was split open so that the white fluffy meat was easy to get to as she dipped it in the hot buttery sauce. During the meal, there was mostly silence between them with Ashley silently gazing at her. Staring seemed to be his favorite pastime and it made her uncomfortable.

Following the main course, the waiter brought a bowl of fresh locally grown fruit topped with whipped cream as light as a feather. All Brooke could do was look at it and moan. Even with what little she ate, she felt stuffed.

During their dinner, she had wanted to question Ashley about Jonathan or rather feel him out to see if he knew anything about her brother's trouble and if he were involved in it in any way. But there never seemed to be a time to bring it up, and for a reason she did not even want to admit to herself, she was loathe to bring up anything unpleasant that would spoil this enchantment.

Now, however, it was too late, because the stage was beginning to come alive with the band and entertainment of the evening. Ashley told her that an unknown singer was due to make her debut tonight.

"I've been told she is very good at what she does. I hope we won't be disappointed," he whispered as they were waiting for the singer to make her appearance.

"I'm looking forward to hearing her. I never get tired of listening to good music," she replied.

And true to Ashley's words, they were not disappointed. It was indeed a spellbinding hour for everyone in the room. She bellowed out all the latest in the pop field as well as some of the "oldies" but "goodies" and even threw in a few of the classical favorites.

When she finished, Brooke was so enthralled, she couldn't even applaud. "Oh, but I can't remember when I've enjoyed anything more," she said as she turned toward Ashley, her eyes shining.

The *look* in his eyes as he returned her gaze made her catch her breath. There was passion and tenderness and something else she couldn't quite identify.

She turned away, more confused than ever. Would this man always remain an enigma to her? But before she had time to ponder the question any further, she found herself being ushered out of her chair, Ashley saying huskily in her ear, "Let's dance. I want to hold you."

Brooke felt her legs turn to water and her heart began to beat ninety miles an hour. She knew she should not be letting him say things like that to her. She needed to keep in mind that she had nothing to offer a man like Ashley, but right now she just did not care. This moment was to be savored.

So with only a small show of reluctance, she let him pull her onto the tiny and crowded dance floor. The lights had been dimmed sufficiently to create a romantic atmosphere and the music was throbbing throughout the room.

Ashley made no pretense at talking as he drew her into the center of the floor and pulled her into his arms. They danced cheek to cheek for a moment and she was aware that he must be able to feel her hand tremble as it rested across his shoulders. She kept telling herself she shouldn't be doing this, she shouldn't be doing this. . . .

However, she soon forced herself to relax a little and enjoy the security of his arms, knowing that in a few minutes, he would be escorting her back to their table, when she heard him groan and pull her closer against him. Forcing her to put both arms around his neck, he began intimately sliding his hands up and down her bare back in a caressing motion, finally coming to rest on her hips. He was holding her purposefully next to him, making her wholly aware of his driving masculinity.

"Please, Ashley, don't . . ." stammered Brooke incoherently as she began squirming against him to try and break his hold. This only served to excite him further.

"Hush, honey," he groaned. "I've got to do this. Don't you know I've been half out of my mind from wanting to hold and touch you like this? Just relax, I won't hurt you," he continued in a soothing voice.

For the moment Brooke let him have his way as he continued to hold her close. But when he began to nuzzle the side of her neck, she had reached her limit. She could not take any more. Chills were running rampant up and down her body from his caressing touch.

As she began pushing away from him with real determination the music stopped and the lights suddenly brightened. The band was taking its break. Thank God for small favors, thought Brooke to herself.

Trying to control the trembling in her body, she let Ashley lead her to the table only to refuse to sit down.

"Ashley, I would like to go home now if you don't mind," she said with a waver in her voice.

"Okay." She could tell he was also shaken by their encounter on the dance floor and was as eager to leave as she was.

71

As soon as the parking attendant brought the car around, she collapsed against the plush seat and breathed deeply trying to clear the fog from her brain.

There was complete silence between them all the way home. The tension was so thick she felt it would take a knife to cut it. Brooke just wanted to get home and away from him.

As they pulled up in front of the town house, Brooke turned to Ashley and said, "Thank you for a lovely . . ." She got no further. He moved across the seat like a streak of lightning and pulled her into his arms. Before she knew what was happening, he lowered his head and put his mouth against hers tenderly. The touch of his warm mouth on hers made her bones turn to water. As the kiss deepened, she could sense he was beginning to lose control.

Finally drawing his lips away from hers very reluctantly, he sighed deeply and said, "Honey, I'm going to have to be out of town for about two weeks. And God knows I don't want to go, so if you don't get out of this car right this minute, I may be tempted to kidnap you and take you with me."

Shaking and needing no other encouragement, Brooke opened the door and skirted up the front steps as if she were running for her life, which indeed she was.

The phone rang eight times before Brooke reached it. "Hello!" she choked, gasping for breath.

"Where were you?" she heard Jim Gregory's questioning voice over the phone.

Still breathing unevenly, she said, "I was outside saying goodbye to Anne. She's on her way to the doctor."

"Is she sick?"

"No, no just a routine visit."

"That's good," he replied. "How about you and I playing a mean game of tennis? Think you're up to it?"

She thought for a moment. "I think so, if you'll take it easy on me. I'm still in the early stages of recovery, remember?"

He laughed. "That's a promise. I'll pick you up shortly."

"Fine. I'll be ready."

Hurriedly she put on a short yellow tennis dress and tied her hair back with a yellow ribbon. This outing would be good for her, she mused to herself. Ashley had been gone for two days now and she was at a loss as to how to cope with the feelings he evoked within her. A game of tennis was just the medicine she needed right now.

Jim took her to the country club to play. The tennis facilities were extremely nice and she was anxious to get on the court again.

Today, she played with much more confidence than when she had played with David. Although she and Jim also agreed not to keep score, they still played with a great deal of intensity.

Brooke felt that she would have to be in really good form to beat Jim. He was a superb player in his own right. He made difficult shots look easy and spanned the court with effortless grace.

She moved gracefully on the court herself and felt that old surge of strength returning to her limbs. She smashed the ball across the court several times and aced her serve on two or three occasions. Her lob was so good that at times Jim was kept firmly at the baseline.

At the end of the game, they laughed and shook each other's hands playfully.

"Let's go into the club and have a drink," Jim said. "Is that all right with you?"

She smiled in agreement.

"Are you okay?" he asked, glancing at her. "You didn't overdo it, did you?"

Brooke breathed deeply, shaking her head. "No, I feel great." She smiled. "I'm just a little short-winded, that's all."

"Good. Let's go have that drink now," he said draping his arm around her shoulders.

At this time of the afternoon the bar was not crowded. They chose a table near the glass windows with a view of the pool. Jim ordered a Tom Collins for her and a Scotch and water for himself.

While they waited for their drinks to be served, he asked, his voice hesitant, "Do you and Graham have a thing going?"

Her face clouded. "No . . ." She paused wetting her lips nervously. "Why do you ask?"

He shifted uncomfortably. "Well, I—I just kind of got the impression that there was something between the two of you." He paused, uncertain as to how to continue. "I didn't want to intrude . . ."

Her stomach muscles tightened. "Don't worry, I'm free," she said bitterly, looking down.

Jim compressed his lips, but refrained from saying anything further.

After their drinks arrived, they chatted about tennis, which relieved the tension somewhat. Jim wanted to know about her life as a tennis professional. She delighted in telling him.

All too soon, it was time for him to take her home. He had an evening flight he had to make in connection with his job. As he left her at the door, he promised to call her when he got back and take her sight-seeing.

She had enjoyed herself, but the minute he left, her thoughts once again turned to Ashley. Would he always fill her mind?

Chapter Four

$\mathcal{T}$ he only time Brooke's mind was free of Ashley Graham during the next days was when she was on the tennis court. She kept telling herself that she must get a hold of her emotions and put things in the right perspective. Ashley was definitely not for her and the sooner she forgot about him, the better off she would be. He had no intention of offering her anything permanent. Not that she would be interested, she reminded herself quickly, too quickly. All she needed to be concerned with was becoming a successful tennis player once again. Maybe an affair with Ashley was the answer. But down deep, she knew she could never agree to that, because she knew it would leave her with a lifetime of pain.

She hadn't heard a word from him since he left. Not one word had she heard from him since she jumped out of his car nearly two weeks ago. Ever since he had been gone, she kept thinking that he might call. She was extremely apprehensive, but at the same time, she felt a keen sense of disappointment every time the phone rang and it wasn't Ashley.

Jonathan and Anne had tried to find out about the events leading up to her dinner date and what happened afterward, but she refused to discuss it with them. She knew she had hurt their feelings, especially Anne's, but her relationship with Ashley was still a mystery even to her; so how could she explain it to anyone else?

One morning, after Ashley had been gone a few days, Brooke knew she could not put off telling Anne any longer about her secret workout sessions, especially after the public displays with Jim Gregory and David Ritter.

She and Anne had just finished a leisurely breakfast when she finally got up enough courage to say something. Taking a deep breath, Brooke plunged forth, "Anne, I—er—I don't quite know how to tell you this, but I've been sneaking around and practicing tennis for a while now. In fact, I've played two practice games already."

Before she could say another word, Anne interrupted, "You've been doing what?"

"Please!" cried Brooke in return. "Don't get upset! Just calm down for a minute and let me explain. It's not nearly as terrible as it sounds."

"How can you say that?" cried Anne. "After what the doctors told you? They said you were never to pick up another tennis racket. I'm going to pretend I imagined what you just told me—pretend it was merely a dream." She shook her head.

"Well, it's no dream," replied Brooke, "and I *need* your support and confidence to be able to continue."

"But I didn't think your muscles would even begin to

hold up to something as strenuous as tennis," exclaimed Anne. "I knew you were supposed to swim a little and do other exercises, but to play tennis? It's beyond me!" She sat there shaking her head.

Brooke sighed. "I felt a certain amount of strength and vigor returning to my limbs before I left the hospital. But I didn't tell my doctor because I was afraid it was only my imagination. The big thing there was physical therapy and it really paid off, even I was amazed at my capabilities. Anyway, to make a long story short, I began exercising in earnest and each day I would try to do a little more. It's only been in the last few days that I have really been playing with any expertise. I could only work out when you were gone, which of course, limited my time."

Anne still looked skeptical. "I don't know, Brooke. I'm afraid you'll damage yourself permanently without a doctor's supervision. Please promise me that you'll see and talk to a doctor before you go any further.

Brooke moved her slim shoulders in a helpless gesture. "Oh, Anne, I know what I'm doing. Do you really think I would do anything that would injure me for the rest of my life? Give me credit for having more sense than that."

Anne looked at her with troubled eyes. "Just exactly what are your plans?"

Brooke smiled. "I eventually want to return to the tennis circuit and try to be the player I was before the accident. Oh, Anne, I was really beginning to make a name for myself and I loved the excitement of the people and the traveling. Of course, the money is not all that good unless you're a Billie Jean King or a Tracy Austin, but I had hopes of reaching that goal one of these days."

"What about settling down to marriage and a family?" questioned Anne softly. "Are those no longer important to you?"

Averting her eyes so her sister-in-law couldn't see the pain she said, "All I care about right now is playing tennis to the best of my ability." She squelched the image of Ashley Graham dancing before her eyes. That thought was an impossible dream.

"Okay, my friend, you have my word that I won't do anything to stand in your way if you promise not to overdo it and to relax and spend some time with me. I'm selfish enough to want as much of your time and attention as you'll allow me while you're here."

Jumping up, Brooke hugged Anne and both were laughing and crying at the same time. "I promise you," laughed Brooke "that you'll be sick of me before I'm gone. I don't intend to spend every waking minute on the tennis court."

Brooke kept her word. She and Anne's days had more or less settled into a routine. With Brooke working out early in the morning, that left the rest of the day for being with Anne. They sunbathed, they swam, and Anne even played a little tennis with her at the country club.

Late in the afternoons, after Jonathan got home from the office, they would drive around the island and show Brooke many of the sights she was eager to see. These fun jaunts seemed to pull Jonathan out of his dark moods. He certainly was drinking much more than ever and she could tell by the way Anne acted that she was worried about him, although she pretended otherwise.

It was a fun time for Brooke, too. These outings helped to keep her mind occupied. The beautiful flowers bloomed everywhere, especially on the outskirts of the city. And the beaches were absolutely gorgeous. So far, Brooke had not gone swimming in the ocean, but she looked forward to doing so with enthusiasm.

One morning Jonathan took them to an Hawaiian luau sponsored by his company. It was a private all day affair for employees and any guests they cared to invite. Jonathan warned them ahead of time to be prepared for a long day and evening.

After taking a quick shower and brushing her teeth, Brooke stood in front of the closet, trying to decide which one of her new sundresses to wear. She finally decided on the baby blue print with flowers appliqued along the hem. It had small spaghetti straps with an elasticized waist. She chose her most comfortable low-heeled sandals to wear with it.

After donning her brief underwear, she sat down at the dressing table and began rolling her hair on her hot rollers. She was completing this task when Anne tapped on the door, stuck her head around it and said, grinning, "Good morning. Are you just about ready to go? Your brother is waiting."

Turning, Brooke smiled and said, "Ask him to please give me ten more minutes. I promise I'll be ready. I just can't seem to get moving this morning."

"I know what you mean," groaned Anne as she stepped into the room. "I had the same problem."

Frowning Brooke asked, "You're not feeling sick are you?"

"No," grinned Anne, "just lazy."

"Are you sure?" questioned Brooke intently.

"Scout's honor," replied Anne. "However," she grinned sheepishly, "I will admit I had a little bout of nausea this morning but Jonathan brought me some crackers before I got out of bed. They did the trick. Now I'm fine."

Brooke smiled, her face relaxing a little. "I believe you, but don't think I won't keep my eagle eyes on you today to make sure you don't overdo it."

Anne sighed. "Do you realize that you're spoiling me and that I may never recover from that particular disease." There was a mischievous twinkle in her eyes.

"That's fine with me," exclaimed Brooke. "I love having someone to spoil. It makes me really feel like I belong."

Giving Brooke a hug, Anne said, "Oh, honey, you *are* an important part of this family, and don't you ever think differently! Jonathan and I have decided that you need to stay here permanently."

Embarrassed at her sudden display of emotion, Brooke untangled herself from Anne's arms and said rather huskily, "If we don't quit being so gushy, I'll never be ready, and then Jonathan will be yelling at both of us."

Laughing out loud, Anne said, "How right you are! I'm going downstairs to grab a cup of coffee while I wait for you. Don't forget your swimsuit!" she added as she closed the door behind her.

After putting on the barest amount of makeup, Brooke took the rollers out of her hair and brushed it until it shone like spun silk. Then she pulled it away from her face and secured each side with bright blue combs. Grabbing her dress, she stepped into it and quickly tied the straps atop each shoulder. After slipping into her sandals, she added lip gloss and sprayed herself with Bill Blass cologne. She was ready.

As she reached the bottom of the stairs, her brother came out of the kitchen, coffee in hand and stopped when he saw her. "Where's your bathing suit? You may not use it, but it's better to have it just in case."

"Oh, gee," said Brooke, slapping her hand in agitation. "I forgot it, even after Anne reminded me. I must be losing my mind."

Jonathan merely grinned. "Well, hurry up, run and get it. We still have plenty of time."

Upon reaching her room, Brooke grabbed her tote bag and crammed her swimsuit in it along with a towel, makeup and sunglasses.

Shortly they were on their way. Brooke was finally able to relax in the back seat of the Mercedes with a cup of coffee and enjoy the drive.

The luau was being held at Sea Life Park, about a forty-minute drive from Waikiki. Jonathan was partly in charge of the day's activities so he had to be there early to help supervise the preparations.

The drive took them along the beautiful scenic shoreline. Brooke was enchanted with the beauty of the wild flowers and the blue green water of the beaches unfolding before her eyes.

As they pulled into the park area, Anne turned to Brooke in the back seat and said humorously, "I can't wait to see your face when you see the way they prepare the pig!"

Brooke frowned. "I'm not too sure I want . . ."

"Now, Anne," interrupted Jonathan, "don't make her squeamish before we even get her there."

"I'm just teasing you, really I am," said Anne, a grin on her face.

"I bet you are," chided Brooke playfully.

"No, seriously," laughed Anne impishly, "it's really a treat to watch. Believe me, if I can take it, so can you! You know the condition my stomach is in, especially now!"

Brooke still looked skeptical. "All I can say is that due to my ignorance, I'm in your hands completely."

"Take my word for it," chimed in Jonathan, "you'll enjoy it."

"Okay," answered Brooke reluctantly. "I guess I'm ready."

Anne and Jonathan looked at each other and burst out laughing.

After parking the car, Jonathan came around and opened both doors and escorted them into the building. The banquet hall was brightly decorated and the tables were laden with Hawaiian finery. Everything on the inside was taken care of. Now it was the men's turn to get the food ready by six o'clock.

After Brooke and Anne stored their purses and bags in a safe place, they followed Jonathan outdoors where the food was to be prepared and cooked.

There was a crowd already gathered around a huge oven. Jonathan, after shaking hands and talking to his co-workers, found a place for them to stand where they could see everything. The man in charge was just beginning to explain what he was about to do.

"Listen and pay attention and don't you dare get sick," whispered Jonathan close to Brooke's ear. She jumped.

Turning, she playfully poked her brother in the stomach and said, "You nearly scared me out of my wits."

"I'm sorry," mocked Jonathan, "but I don't want to see your eyes wandering, okay?"

"Yes, sir," she replied ruefully.

As the Hawaiian man talked, Brooke was fascinated with what he was telling his audience. He explained that the main dish of the luau was the whole pig, which he pointed to in front of him. It was to be skinned, eviscerated, scrubbed, shaved and rubbed inside and out with soy sauce and rock salt.

This part was almost too much for Brooke. She heard Jonathan's chuckle from behind. So gritting her teeth, she took several deep breaths and barely flinched when the man skinned the pig. Glancing at Anne, she noticed that she had her eyes tightly welded together and was clutching her stomach. Ha, so much for her brave words, she thought to herself.

Jonathan leaned over and whispered something in Anne's ears and grinned. Her only answer was to nod her head.

The next step was to place the pig on chicken wire and then fill the hollow cavities with red hot stones from the fire. He used tongs to do that. Then the pig's front and back legs were tied together and completely wrapped in the wire. Next he lined the pit with sweet potatoes, bananas, pork and butterfish and placed more corn husks and banana leaves on top of the pig in large quantities in order to keep the steam from escaping. He then covered the fire with wet burlap, and shoveled earth over the top to further insure that no steam could escape. The ceremony was complete.

Laughing, Brooke turned to Anne and said, "Well, how's the tummy?"

Anne looked sheepish. "Fine, how about yours?"

"Ah," said Brooke smugly, "I came through like a champ."

"Well," chimed in Jonathan, "when you two get through patting yourselves on the back, you need to decide what you want to do for the next few hours. I'm going to be busy around here."

After talking it over, they finally decided to spend their time exploring the park. Brooke learned that Sea Life Park was one of the world's finest marine exhibits. They visited first the Hawaiian Reef Tank which was a 300,000 gallon glass tank containing 2,000 ocean creatures. Next they went to the two-hour show in the glass Ocean Science Theater where the sea animals performed both above and below the surface. The porpoises were especially fun to watch.

As she and Anne walked out of the show, Brooke heard someone call her name. Turning she saw David Ritter making his way toward her. "Hi, Brooke" he said, sounding a little short-winded. "I've been looking for you all over this park. Are you having a good time?"

Smiling, Brooke said, "It's been great fun so far. However, I'm not so sure I'll be able to eat the pig I saw being prepared this morning."

Grimacing, David said, "I know what you mean!"

Remembering her manners, she turned to Anne and said, "David, I'd like you to meet my sister-in-law, Anne Lawson. Anne this is David Ritter, whom I met at the public court last week. Remember, the day I disappeared while you were out shopping for my party?"

Laughing, Anne said. "So you're the one that gave her the first workout since the accident!"

"Well, Anne," he said grinning, "I hate to admit it, but even as rusty as she was, she's still a better player than I'll ever be. This girl swings a mean racket!"

"That's enough, David," said Brooke blushing. Changing the subject, she went on to ask him, "What brings you to the luau?"

"Oh, I have some close friends who work at the sugar company and they invited me to come. Now maybe I'll begin to enjoy myself." He looked at her intently.

Brooke sensed what he meant, but chose to ignore his flirting for the moment anyway. But he was determined.

As they strolled toward the main building, David fell

in step beside Brooke. He turned to her and said, "If you don't have any objections, I'd like to have your company for dinner tonight. That is, if you aren't already committed, or if I won't be intruding on your family." He sensed Brooke's hesitation.

Groping for a nice way to turn him down, Brooke stammered, "Well, I . . ."

"Please," interrupted David, "don't say no. Take pity on a poor lonesome soul and keep him company. What do you say?"

Brooke knew a con job when she saw one. But why not? she thought to herself. He had helped her out when she needed it, and he was a nice person.

She looked at him. "Why don't you sit at our table tonight instead?" asked Brooke. "Then you won't be lonesome for sure." Her tone was teasing. The minute, however, she issued the invitation, she looked at Anne for her approval.

Reading the signal from Brooke, Anne said, "Yes, do join us, Mr. Ritter. Another couple is sharing our table, but you'll certainly be welcome, too."

"Great!" he said.

Looking at her watch, Brooke noted that it was already five-thirty. The afternoon had passed in such a hurry. She sniffed the aroma of the meat cooking and realized that she was hungry. Even the thought of actually eating roast pig did not bother her.

"Let's hurry," she said. "I'm starving."

Upon entering the building, Jonathan was waiting for them. Introductions were made and Brooke noticed the grim look on her brother's face when he shook hands with David Ritter. She sensed that he was none too pleased with the extra guest at their table. She could not really understand his reaction. David was harmless enough. Wasn't he?

Pushing Jonathan's unpleasantness aside, she excused herself and beckoned for Anne to go with her to the ladies' lounge and freshen up before they sat down to dinner.

Upon entering the lounge, Anne said, "Did you notice how upset Jonathan got when you told him David was going to sit with us?"

"Indeed I did," exclaimed Brooke. "What's with him anyway?"

Anne shrugged. "Your guess is as good as mine. It doesn't take much to set him off these days as you've probably noticed yourself. I don't know what's wrong with him," she finished, shaking her head.

Brooke said mildly, "Well, let's not worry about it right now," she paused wetting her lips, "maybe by the time we get back, he'll be over whatever was bugging him. You know men. . . ." Brooke rolled her eyes in a helpless gesture, causing Anne to laugh. The mood had lightened.

After freshening up, they returned to the room to find people milling around looking for their seats. Jonathan was standing by his chair waiting for them. Another couple and David Ritter were already seated at their small table.

Venturing a quick look at her brother, Brooke noticed that he did indeed seem in better humor. Anne seemed to notice, also, because her face brightened when Jonathan smiled at her.

Immediately Jonathan introduced her to the other couple. They were Robert and Cindy Grey. She learned that he worked in personnel and she stayed home with their two children. They were a nice-looking couple who welcomed Brooke with enthusiasm.

Although an outsider, David Ritter fit in quite well. He, Robert and Jonathan were involved in a conversation about the economy with Anne glued to every word they were saying. This left Brooke and Cindy free to talk.

The young woman's dark brown eyes flickered over hers with warm admiration and said, "I understand that you're a professional tennis player."

Brooke licked her lips. "Used to be," she corrected. "I haven't played professionally in a long time, but I hope to remedy that situation very shortly."

Smiling sweetly, Cindy replied, "Oh, I hope you can. I'll certainly be pulling for you. I admire anyone who really excels in any type of sport." She spread her hands. "All I do is take care of my babies."

Turning away, Brooke said, "Don't underestimate that job. It's much more important than what I'll ever accomplish." She hoped she kept the bitterness out of her voice, but evidently she didn't because Cindy was looking at her strangely.

Before Cindy had a chance to question her further, however, David turned to her and asked, "Brooke, do you want anything to drink?"

She thought for a moment. "Yes, I believe I would. I'd like a glass of white wine."

Turning, David asked, "How about you, Mrs. Grey?"

She smiled, "What Brooke is having sounds good. I'll have the same."

The buffet table was filled with delicious food. Brooke recognized the salmon dish rather like a small clam which had been marinated in chopped onions and tomatoes. She took a generous helping of that. She also took a large portion of the chicken luau, tender morsels of chicken cooked with taro tops and coconut cream. Anne was next to her in the line. When they came to the pig, they looked at each other and laughed out loud.

Returning to their seats, they all devoured the meal with relish. They were enjoying an after-dinner drink, waiting for the live entertainment, when Brooke just happened to glance in Jonathan's direction only to see a shocked expression appear on his face. His stare was focused on the doorway of the banquet hall.

Turning in the same direction, Brooke saw a man slouched against the doorframe gazing intently at Jonathan. Just as she turned, the man motioned for her brother.

With tight lips, Jonathan leaned over, whispered to Anne and rose abruptly causing his chair to fall backward. The sound echoed like a gunshot. Muttering curses under his breath, he straightened the chair and moved hastily in the direction of the exit without a backward glance.

There was an awkward silence at the table. Brooke could see that Anne was close to tears. She tried hard to keep her lips from quivering. Damn her brother! Didn't he realize what his show of temper did to Anne? Hadn't he realized that her blood pressure was apt to rise and cause insurmountable problems for her and their baby? Or didn't he care? At times like this she wondered about her brother.

Bless David. He took control of the situation, motioned for the waiter and ordered another round of drinks for everyone. At the same time, the hula girls ran out on the stage and began the live entertainment. During the show, Brooke noticed that Anne relaxed somewhat but her eyes kept straying toward the door. It was just as the girls left the stage that Jonathan came back into the room.

The expression on his face was indeed grim as he sat down at the table. Leaning over and touching his arm, Anne said softly, "Honey, who was that man and what did he want?"

Turning Jonathan glared at her a moment and hissed loudly enough for everyone to hear, "Don't bother me, Anne. It's none of your business. It has nothing to do with you anyway. Just leave me alone."

Anne's eyes circled the table. Jumping up with tears pouring down her face, she said, "Oh, Jonathan, how could you?" before turning and practically running out of the room.

The silence at the table was deafening. Brooke was furious and wanted to reach across the table and slap some sense into her brother.

But instead she rose to her feet and said, her voice even, "Excuse me." She felt Jonathan's eyes bore into her back as she went to see about her sister-in-law.

She found Anne sobbing in the ladies' lounge. Pulling her into her arms, Brooke said, "Shhh . . . honey. Stop crying. Think of the baby. You'll make yourself sick if you keep this up." Taking a Kleenex out of her purse, she wiped the tears from Anne's face. "Everything will be all right. Nothing is ever as bad as it seems."

"Oh, Brooke, I . . ."

"Don't worry," interrupted Brooke. "I'll try to find out what's going on, if you'll promise to lie here on the couch and stop crying."

"Okay," Anne said weakly. "I promise."

Brooke squeezed her hand and left.

As she made her way back to the table, she noticed that Jonathan was alone. Thank goodness for small favors, she voiced to herself. She sat down next to Jonathan and came right to the point. "If we weren't in a public place, I'd box your ears, Big Brother. I'm not as easily intimidated as Anne, so let's have it, what's going on?"

Drawing deeply on his cigarette, it was a moment before he replied. "I'm sorry, Sis, but I can't tell you. Believe me, it's something I have to handle on my own." He paused to inhale again. "I know I came down too heavy on Anne and I'm truly sorry. Is she all right?"

"Yes," sighed Brooke. "But no thanks to you. Do you want her to lose the baby?"

"Of course I don't," he barked. "What the hell—"

Brooke compressed her lips, "Well, judging from your conduct I wasn't sure."

He grimaced. "It's just that things are not going according to the way I planned." He paused, as if uncertain how to continue. "For instance, what the hell is that young whippersnapper Ritter doing panting after you. Ashley won't like . . ."

With eyes flashing, she interrupted, "Don't you dare try to put the monkey on my back. And you leave Ashley Graham out of this. He has *nothing* to do with who pants after me, as you so crudely phrased it." The sarcasm dripped from her voice.

Brooke sighed inwardly. Why did he have to mention Ashley's name. She had managed to keep thoughts of him at bay for a little while at least. She refused to admit even now that she missed him and that she wished he were here.

Jonathan's voice jarred her out of her reverie. "Sorry, Sis, forget I said that, please." He gazed at her intently.

Brooke hesitated. "If I thought you really hadn't meant it, I could maybe forget it, but I . . ."

Jonathan cut in abruptly. "Please, let's drop it for

now, okay? I said I was sorry, didn't I?" His face was hidden by the shadows. "Right now I need to go make my peace with Anne. Where is she?"

Brooke shrugged her shoulders helplessly. She had hoped Jonathan would confide in her, but since he would not, then, he definitely needed to see about Anne. With a resigned sigh, she confessed, "She's lying down in the ladies' lounge. Shall I get her?"

Jonathan flexed his neck muscles as if to erase the tension. "Yes," he said, "I'll take her upstairs and talk to her. Then let's go home," he concluded wearily.

After getting Anne and Jonathan together, Brooke made her way back to the table to wait and found David Ritter sitting there. The other couple had obviously disappeared for good.

As she neared the table, he stood up and pulled the chair out for her to be seated. He hesitated. "Is everything all right?"

Brooke shook her head. "No, not really. But there's nothing I can do about it right now."

"Would you like me to take you home?"

Brooke sighed. "Thank you, but no. I think I'd best go home with Jonathan and Anne."

David looked doubtful. "Well, if you're sure . . ."

Brooke smiled. "I'm sure. However, I've really enjoyed your company and I thank you for your concern."

About that time, Brooke turned and saw Jonathan and Anne. They said their goodbyes and left for home.

To Brooke's relief, Anne seemed to have gained control of herself. There were, however, lines of strain around her mouth and Jonathan was definitely still on edge. But the tension between them had lessened enough that the trip home wasn't too uncomfortable.

Brooke, now more than ever, was firmly convinced

that Jonathan was definitely in deep trouble. The strange man's appearance and her brother's odd behavior at the luau confirmed this. However, until he was willing to discuss his problem with her, there was absolutely nothing she could do. She just fervently prayed over and over that Ashley Graham was in no way involved.

She was lying in bed early the next morning mulling over the events of last evening when the sharp ring of the phone startled her. She grabbed it quickly to avoid disturbing Anne and Jonathan. It was only seven o'clock. Who in the world would be calling this early?

Brooke managed to snatch up the receiver after the first ring. Hesitantly she said, "Hello?"

"Good morning!"

The sound of Ashley Graham's soft voice sent a shiver through her body. She clutched the receiver so as not to drop it.

"Who is this?" she asked breathlessly.

She could feel him grinning. "You know exactly who this is. Did I wake you?"

"No," she said quickly. "I mean, yes, you did. What do you want?"

"I thought you were asleep from the sound of your voice," he murmured huskily, not answering her question. "You are all tucked in between the sheets . . . oh, God," he groaned, "I wish I were there."

Her heart missed a beat, and her throat was so dry she could not utter a word.

"Cat got your tongue?" Ashley taunted softly.

She didn't reply.

"I'm holding the phone away from my ear in anticipation of your comeback." He laughed. "Going to disappoint me?"

Drawing a deep breath, Brooke lied, "Actually, I

wasn't too sure who it was at first." She congratulated herself on her detached tone. "After all, I haven't heard from you for a while."

His chuckle vibrated through the phone. "Point taken, honey!" She gasped. But his laughter merely deepened. "I know I told you I'd call, but this is the first moment since I've been gone that I could call my own." He paused. "Surely you didn't want me to call you in front of an audience."

His implication was clear. "Ashley, did you call for a reason?" She refused to let him intimidate her any further. Oh, God, she hated to admit it, but it was good to hear his voice.

"Great, we're back to normal. I can tell by your waspish tone that you're fully awake now." He gave a short laugh. "Still the unapproachable Miss Lawson."

"Ashley, are you suffering from a hangover?" Her patience was growing thin.

"A what?"

"You sound . . . Oh, I don't know . . . different."

Silence.

"I am different . . . but you wouldn't understand," he replied tightly. "So forget it."

"If anything's wrong," she hesitated, sitting up in bed. "Please, tell me."

He waited for a moment before he answered. Then it was almost a groan. "I . . . oh, hell," he said. "Don't you know what's wrong? Brooke, I want you." He paused softly. "I haven't been able to do anything except picture myself holding you, touching you and making love to you." He sighed. "That's what's wrong with me."

"Oh, Ashley, I . . ."

"Don't tell me you don't feel the same," he urged softly.

"Please, I . . ." Tears threatened her. She could not say what she wanted to.

"Forget it," he interrupted suddenly. "Don't mind me. I'm a fool. I've got to go. I'll talk to you later."

She didn't have time to say goodbye.

For several seconds, Brooke lay stunned at his abrupt response. Her hand shook as she replaced the receiver.

The rest of the day was an anti-climax. But she did manage to get some much needed exercise in the pool as well as a good workout session. There was nothing like good healthy exercise to relieve one's frustrations.

It was toward the end of the second week of Ashley's absence, that Brooke again had an unexpected phone call. By mutual consent, she, along with Anne and Jonathan, had agreed to spend the evening at home. Since Brooke's arrival, they had gone and done so much, that they all voted for an evening of rest.

When Anne said that she was wanted on the phone, her heart began to flutter like a newborn bird trying to fly for the first time.

It was Ashley again. She knew it. It just had to be he!

Picking up the phone, she tried to keep her voice as cool and steady as possible. She did not want him to think that she was eager to talk to him, in view of their last conversation. In fact, she wanted him to think the opposite. So in a clear and concise voice Brooke said, "Hello."

"Brooke," said a pleasant but strange voice, "this is Jim Gregory." When Brooke remained silent, he continued by saying, "I didn't disturb you or anything, did I?"

Brooke's disappointment at not hearing Ashley's voice on the other end of the line was so intense it threatened to overwhelm her.

By taking a deep breath, she managed to get control

of herself and answered in as pleasant a voice as possible under the circumstances by saying, "Of course you didn't disturb me, Jim. It's just that I wasn't expecting to hear from you. I was surprised, that's all," finished Brooke lamely.

"You should have known that I would call you. Remember, I said I would," returned Jim Gregory in a warm voice. "I would have gotten in touch with you sooner. Flew in from my trip this afternoon. This job of being a troubleshooter for my insurance company keeps me living out of a suitcase much too often. Calling you was the first item on my agenda."

"Well, it's nice to hear from you." Brooke knew she did not sound very enthusiastic, but she couldn't help it. He was a nice enough person, but she simply wasn't interested in seeing too much of him except on the tennis court.

"How 'bout spending the day with me tomorrow and the evening as well? I guarantee you a good time. We'll crowd as many activities as possible into a whole day!"

"Oh, Jim, I don't think I . . ." began Brooke hesitantly.

With laughter in his voice, Jim interrupted and said, "I forgot to tell you, I won't take no for an answer. I plan to haunt you until you let me have the pleasure of your company off the court," he added, "so it's now or later."

"Okay, you've convinced me! You've convinced me!" repeated Brooke, laughing. "How can I possibly say no when you have such power of persuasion?"

"Is nine o'clock in the morning too early to pick you up?"

"No, that will be fine. Shall I dress for the entire day or will you bring me home to change before dinner?"

"Yes to the first and no to the second. I'm not about to let you out of my clutches until the midnight hour, young lady!"

"Whatever you say," teased Brooke. "I want all the activities you've planned to be a surprise. So don't tell me a thing until you pick me up, okay?"

"Okay by me! I'll see you at nine sharp. Good night! And thank you, Brooke."

After hanging up the phone, Brooke sighed and remained seated in the chair at Jonathan's desk. What had she gotten herself into? When he had asked her to go out with him, she had absolutely no intention of doing so. But she just did not have the heart to turn him down. She had to admit that he was certainly an ego booster and what girl would be foolish enough to turn that down. After all, she told herself, it's only for one day and it would do her good to be away from her brother and sister-in-law and give them a break at the same time. What possible harm could there be in having a day of fun and frolic in the company of a charming young man?

Waking bright and early the next morning, she made her way downstairs very quietly so as not to disturb Anne and Jonathan. When she had first looked at the clock, it had only been five o'clock, so she had turned over and tried to go back to sleep, but at six o'clock she finally gave in and got up.

She was not really excited about spending the day with Jim Gregory. If the truth be known, she actually dreaded it. She hated to admit it, but her thoughts kept centering on the absent Ashley Graham no matter how hard she tried to divert them. After the way she had talked to him, she doubted that she would ever hear from him again *unless* he still saw her as a challenge.

She was positive every female he had ever come in contact with was turned on by him. But, she, Brooke Lawson did not want to be the next in line!

After preparing herself a light breakfast of toast and jelly and coffee, she went back to her room and quickly put on a one-piece tennis suit. She had plenty of time to get a little exercise in before it was time to get dressed. Volleying the ball several times always made her feel better.

When she returned to her room to shower and dress, she found she *was* actually looking forward to the day after all! There were many things that she was still eager to see and do and this was as good a way as any to see the sights of Oahu. She felt really good! Her form and serve were getting better every day. Although she still had to caution herself to take it easy, on the whole, she was pleased with her progress.

She was ready to go in no time and went downstairs to the den to wait for Jim. As she rounded the corner she almost collided head on with Anne.

"Hey, lady," laughed Brooke. "We'd both better watch out where we're going. A little more and we would both have been picking ourselves up off the floor. What's your hurry, anyway?"

"Oh, Brooke," wailed Anne, "I just wish I knew what was bothering Jonathan. He's so short and snappy, especially since that episode at the luau. He bites my head off for the least little thing. He's mad at me now for buying some maternity clothes. He insists that I take all but one or two outfits back. He's never said anything about what I bought until now."

Brooke tried to cover her dismay at hearing her worst fears put into words. But trying to cover up her concern, she merely said, "I'm sure he's probably just having a rough time at work, especially since Ashley's been gone for nearly two weeks. Just try to bear with him."

Brooke was at a total loss as to what to say in regard to the clothes. She was positive that Anne would decline an offer from her to pay for them. If her brother were haggling about a few items of clothing, he must indeed be in more trouble than she imagined.

Soon she would *have* to pin Jonathan down and make him talk to her. She could not put a showdown off much longer. However, all she could do right now was try to calm Anne.

"Honey, just take it easy. Everything will work itself out, you wait and see. Come on, let's go sit down in the den."

"I'm so glad you're here, Brooke. You always know how to make me feel better. Heaven only knows, I'm not the easiest person to live with nowadays myself. I'm not too sure being pregnant in the summertime is going to agree with me."

"Hush," chided Brooke. "It's not your pregnancy that's your trouble right now, and we both know it."

Anne sat down heavily on the couch, her hands knitted in her lap. Her lips trembled. "Do you know what's wrong with Jonathan?" she asked, looking up at Brooke.

Brooke chewed her lower lip. "No—I don't." She sighed. "But, I aim to find out just as soon as I can."

"The Lord only knows," said Anne wearily, "how hard I've tried to get Jonathan to confide in me. But he just brushes it off as nothing, or he jokes and tries to make me think everything is fine. He was that way at the luau and for a while, I believed him. He simply doesn't want to upset me because of the baby." She was weeping in earnest now.

Brooke sat down on the couch close to her and

patted her hand. "Shhh. Dry those tears right now! Do you hear me. Crying never solved anything. Remember the baby and your blood pressure."

Anne sobered and the tears ceased.

"Keep in mind that Jonathan loves you and that sooner or later everything will straighten itself out. Nothing is ever as bad as it seems. Just trust me, okay?" Brooke gave her a brilliant smile and held her close for a moment.

"Okay," gulped Anne, smiling tremulously.

Swallowing the lump in her own throat, Brooke asked, "While I'm out with Jim, what do you intend to do?"

"I'm going to eat lunch at the club and then play bridge all afternoon," she replied. "You go ahead and have a good time and don't worry about me. I'll be fine. It seems I cry at the drop of a hat lately, anyway." She grinned.

Brooke's eyes twinkled. "They say it goes along with the condition. . . ."

Before Anne could reply, the doorbell rang loud and clear. Telling Anne they would talk more later, she went to the door. Jim was right on time. His eyes had the same mischievous gleam in them.

"Hi, come in," she said.

"Okay, but only for a minute. I've got a busy day planned, and we're going to have to play hard to get it all in. No tennis this time. Just you and your beautiful face."

"Well, I'm ready," laughed Brooke. "Just let me tell Anne I'm leaving. I'll only be a moment."

The day spent with Jim Gregory turned out to be one of pure enjoyment. The first thing on their agenda was a drive along the North Shore which took in Oahu's famous Sunset Beach and Waimea Bay. Jim explained to her that in the winter the international surfing championships took place here and this event attracted hundreds of tourists. The waves were the largest in the world rising thirty feet before crashing to the smooth sand.

The beaches were absolutely gorgeous even now with the tourist season in full swing. Jim promised later to show her some of the small inlets off the main beaches where they could swim and sun in more privacy than the over-populated main beaches.

Next, they went across the highway to the Waimea Falls State Park. Before coming to Oahu, she had read about this park and had been looking forward to visiting it. She wasn't disappointed in the least. Thank goodness she had worn shoes that were comfortable to walk in, because in order not to miss anything, walking was definitely a must. They hiked down the winding lush pathway that led to the 50-foot waterfall. Surrounding the fall were primitive bridges made of rock leading to the outdoor cafe.

Looking at Jim, Brooke shook her head. "I'm not—you don't really expect me to cross that thing do you?"

"Of course," laughed Jim, "where's your sense of adventure, young lady?"

"I guess I was born without any," Brooke responded.

"Oh, come on, I'll hold onto you. Look at all those other people. They wouldn't be crossing if it weren't safe."

Much to her regret, she let Jim talk her into going across. She kept her eyes closed the whole time, knowing she would never make it if she didn't. Brooke felt the bridge sway any number of times before she safely reached the other side.

During their meal, they watched the peacocks roaming freely on the sunny deck. It was a completely new experience for Brooke and she was thoroughly enjoying every minute of it.

After leaving the park later in the afternoon, they drove back to Paradise Park which was not far from Waikiki. Native Hawaiian villages were set on the fifteen acres of lush valley floor. Since there was so much to see and not nearly enough time to see it all, Brooke was content to gaze at the fields of wild orchids and watch the tropical birds. Abruptly, Jim pulled the car off the road and stopped. Turning to Brooke, he said, "What are you waiting for? There's not a woman alive who would pass up the chance to pick a handful of orchids."

Laughing, Brooke opened the door and ran in her eagerness to pluck the beautiful plants. After gathering as many as their hands would hold, they climbed back into the car.

"Wow," said Brooke. "I can't believe anyone can just help themselves to these beauties. Do you realize how much these would cost back home?"

After walking around the park a little while, Brooke was beginning to feel exhausted. She knew that she not only felt tired, but knew she looked it too. Jim was so busy entertaining her that she hadn't really had a moment to herself. They had been going virtually nonstop since nine o'clock that morning.

Finally, around seven o'clock, he suggested that they go and have a few cocktails and a nice quiet leisurely dinner at the exclusive supper club in the Hilton Hotel. She tried to tell him that she was not dressed for such a fancy place, but he was determined to take her there anyway.

Upon arriving, she excused herself and went to the ladies' lounge to wash her hands and repair her makeup. She sat down on the couch and slipped her shoes off and laid her head back to rest for a moment. The day in Jim Gregory's company had been thoroughly enjoyable and she had made an extra effort not to let her thoughts of Ashley Graham ruin her mood. But the fact that he was due to return home tomorrow was never far from her mind.

Afraid Jim would be worried about her if she stayed too long, she ran a comb through her hair and added a light touch of lip gloss and a quick spray of cologne. She was looking forward to the before-dinner drink that Jim had promised. Since lunch, they had not even stopped for a drink of water until now.

Jim was waiting for her at the entrance to the bar. They were escorted to a table next to the glass and were able to look out over the twilight at Waikiki Beach and had a perfect view of Diamond Head crater.

Brooke chose a Tom Collins to drink and Jim ordered a Scotch and water. While waiting for their drinks, Brooke gazed around the plush restaurant. It was beautifully decorated and the soft music coming from the piano in the corner created a warm atmosphere.

Although she was not dressed to match her elegant surroundings, she didn't feel out of place. There were others more casually dressed than she. They drank their drinks in companionable silence. She was thinking once again what a nice and considerate person Jim was. Although he had never said anything, Brooke knew that he was interested in her. She could tell by the way she caught him looking at her when he didn't think she was aware of it. She hated to hurt him, but she knew there would never be anything between them other than friendship.

"What would you like for dinner?" asked Jim smiling, breaking into her thoughts. "I know you must be starving to death."

"I am rather hungry," laughed Brooke. "You're a real slave driver. Did anyone ever tell you that? I can't begin to tell you how much I've enjoyed myself."

"I'm glad," he said huskily, reaching across and squeezing her hand. "I have in mind many more of these kinds of days and soon too, if I have my way."

The waiter interrupted, and at the most opportune time, too. She lightly disengaged her hand and said, "Please order for me, Jim. I'd like to try one of the island specialties, but I'll leave the choice of which one up to you."

He ended up choosing a traditional fare—a saimin, which he explained to her was an Oriental concoction of noodles and vegetables, along with mahi-mahi, a delicious fish fillet, lightly coated with batter and grilled over an open fire. These dishes were followed by bowls of fresh pineapple chunks topped with whipped cream.

The conversation between them during dinner was sparse. The food was absolutely delicious and to her amazement she found that she had devoured everything on her plate. After one more drink each, he beckoned for the waiter and after signing his American Express ticket, he escorted her to the front where they waited for his car.

Although he had kept everything on a strictly friendly basis, except for briefly squeezing her hand, Brooke was dreading going home with him in case he felt that she owed him something for the time and money he had spent on her. She knew she was probably misjudging him, but she was uneasy nevertheless.

When they pulled up in front of the house, Jim turned to her and it was all Brooke could do to keep from jerking the door open and running. It brought back all the memories of the last time she drove up to this exact same spot and Ashley's strong handsome face began to swim before her eyes. Swallowing, she tried to calm herself before she made a complete idiot of herself in front of Jim.

He seemed to sense that she was upset about something all of a sudden, but didn't say anything. He merely looked at her with a puzzled frown on his face and reached for her hand and brought it to his lips.

"Please, Jim," stammered Brooke. "I just want us to be friends, nothing more."

"I thought we were friends," he said with indulgence in his voice and continued playing with her hands.

Sighing, Brooke said, "But that's *all* I want us to be," and firmly, but gently, withdrew her hand.

"Why?"

"Because that's all I can handle right now. I've had a lot of problems lately. I don't want to bore you with the details right now. But I could sure use a friend, if you're willing."

"Okay, Brooke. I'll go along with that for now. Just let me know when you change your mind. I'll be waiting."

Reaching over, he kissed her on the cheek before getting out of the car and coming around to open her door. After seeing her safely inside the house, he flicked her chin and said, "Maybe later." With these words, he jumped back into the car and was gone.

Brooke knew he was disappointed in her behavior, as well as angry. But she couldn't help how she felt and did not intend to apologize for it. She noticed a light still burning brightly in the den. Jonathan was sitting with a drink in his hand, staring into space.

"Brooke, is that you?"

"Of course, Jonathan. Who else were you expecting at midnight?"

"Are you alone?" he questioned further, completely ignoring her sarcasm.

"Yes, why?"

"Come in and sit down a minute."

"All right, but only for a minute. I'm tired and as usual, you've been drinking too much."

"Please don't patronize me. I only wanted to tell you that Ashley came by this afternoon, *to see you*. He was more than a little upset when I told him you were out with Jim Gregory sight-seeing. He had already heard about Gregory and your rendezvous on the tennis court."

Brooke felt her face drain of every ounce of color. She had been anticipating Ashley's return, but not like this. She had known he would find out about Jim. But she would rather have told him herself.

"What exactly did he say?" questioned Brooke hesitantly.

Frowning, Jonathan said, "Well, he appeared to be outright jealous of Gregory, but when I made the remark about tennis, his jealousy switched to concern. He must have questioned me twenty minutes or more about your tennis workouts. Heaven knows how he found out. The club, maybe?"

Brooke struggled to keep her voice even before answering, "I certainly hadn't planned for you to say anything to Ashley about Jim or anything else for that matter!"

"I'm sure from his reaction, he'll have something to say to you."

"No doubt," returned Brooke sarcastically. "Just to set the record straight, I did not play tennis with Jim today. We went sight-seeing and nothing more. So you caused an uproar for nothing."

Brooke was upset. She was terribly disappointed that she had missed Ashley. Part of her desperately wanted to see him and the other part was infuriated because he assumed that all she had to do was wait for him. She could not, however, squelch the glow of happiness that she felt as a result of his concern.

Breaking into her thoughts, Jonathan said, "What the hell did you go off with Gregory for, if you knew Ashley was coming home? What's with you two anyway?"

A feeling of intense irritation gripped her as she listened to her brother's slurred questions. As usual of late, he was in no condition to talk rationally.

"There's no point in talking to you now," said Brooke sharply. "I'll see you in the morning." With those words she went up to her bedroom and quietly locked the door, lay down on the bed and let the tears flow.

Chapter Five

𝒥t had been a long day, yet, Brooke found it impossible to sleep. She had cried until there were no tears left. Before she even attempted to go to sleep, she took several aspirins and later during the night she got up and took two more. She must have fallen into a drugged sleep, because when she opened her eyes again and looked at the clock, it was after eleven o'clock.

Forcing herself to get out of bed, she stumbled to the bathroom and splashed cold water on her face and quickly brushed her teeth. Maybe after a shower and a cup of coffee she would feel better.

She was certain that it was not her physical health that was her problem right now. But nevertheless, she felt it was time to visit the doctor here in Honolulu whom her doctor in Houston had referred her to. After all, she *had* promised Anne. She needed to have physical examinations on a continual basis since the accident and she knew she was long overdue for one, especially now that she had been playing so much tennis. Her physical well-being was the essential part to making a successful comeback. The strain she had been under lately with Ashley Graham and her brother's strange and moody behavior did not help matters any.

As she showered, she wondered if Ashley would call her today or try to see her. Her heart began to flutter at the thought of him being angry because she had had a date with someone else. What could that possibly be a sign of? Was it conceivable that a man of Ashley's caliber could be interested in her? The ramifications of such thoughts made her giddy.

She kept remembering his passionate kisses in the car and how she had responded to him. No man's touch had ever affected her in that way. Also, she kept remembering his phone call. Just thinking about it now, sent her pulses racing. She knew she was asking for trouble, but she wanted to see him again.

When she went downstairs, the house was unusually quiet. Jonathan was at work, but where was Anne? When she poured herself a cup of coffee, she noticed a note beside the coffeepot from Anne. She had gone to the doctor and was going to meet Jonathan for lunch.

Brooke had just sat down to drink the coffee at her leisure, when the doorbell rang. As she set the coffee cup down, she stared at her shaking hand. She wanted it to be Ashley very badly, but there was no way she was going to let her thoughts be known. So with as much composure as she could muster, Brooke methodically opened the door to a scowling Ashley.

Without giving her a chance to ask him in, he frowned and moved into the den before she knew what was happening. Sighing, she closed the door and very gingerly followed him. She knew that this was definitely not going to be a pleasant encounter. This brooding

Ashley was certainly not the one who had been haunting her thoughts day and night for the last two weeks.

Ashley was staring at her as she walked into the room. Without any preamble, he demanded in a tight voice, "What are you trying to do to yourself *and* to me?"

"I don't know what you mean," retorted Brooke with uncertainty in her voice. Just being in the same room with him made rational thinking impossible.

The sight of him affected her as she knew it would. She felt as if she had been kicked in the stomach. He stood quietly in the center of the room, his blue eyes raking over her with a thoroughness that made her tremble.

He was dressed casually in a pair of gray slacks with a pale yellow knit shirt. The outfit accented the hard masculine lines of his broad chest, shoulders and slim hips. He looked very much the macho male with his deeply tanned face, hard, rugged and arrogantly handsome. Beneath his jutting brow, his eyes were piercing as he waited for her answer.

"Ashley," she finally stammered, "I *really don't* know what you mean. Your question makes no sense . . ."

But she did not finish the sentence. He moved like a panther and hauled her into his arms. As his lips descended to hers, he growled. "Maybe this will make sense to you." He kissed her long and passionately, drugging her senses and leaving her weak and frightened.

"And I come back to find you've been entertained royally by Jim Gregory," he muttered. "What's your next trick? To walk over my body with spike-heeled shoes?"

Jerking herself out of his arms, she said in exasperation, "What right have you to say anything about what I do or with whom I do it? You only bothered to call me once the whole time you were gone. Now you have the audacity to come here and act like you own me. I don't know what kind of game you're playing, but I'm certainly not going to be any part of it."

After she uttered the harsh words, she wished she could retract them. This was not at all like she had imagined their reunion—the kisses yes, but not the harsh words. She was so afraid of being used by Jonathan and she didn't know what Ashley's intentions were. To say the least, her thoughts were chaotic.

He stared moodily. "Right now, my main concern is your health and your lack of good judgment. The very idea of playing tennis without your doctor's release? What in the world caused you to behave so foolishly? Answer me that."

His voice was sober now, with an undercurrent of possessiveness that left her weak and trembling.

Averting her eyes, she whispered, "I want so much to play tennis again that I—" She choked on a sob and could not say another word.

Ashley nodded and grimaced. "I guess there's nothing left for me to say." He began walking toward the front door.

Brooke went after him, wanting to say she was sorry, that she cared what he thought. Instead she said, "Oh, Ashley," in a broken voice.

He merely looked at her for a moment. Slowly he bent down and very gently erased the tears with his lips. Then he drew her close within the circle of his arms. After holding her for a moment, he led her back to the couch and pulled her into his arms once again. She opened her lips to him. Each kiss deepened with his tongue, exploring, tasting and probing.

"I want you," he said, his voice laced with emotion, "but not like this. . . ."

Breaking away was not what Brooke had in mind when Ashley stood up. He turned his back to her and she felt more confused than ever.

"For God's sake, don't look at me like that. I want you so badly right now, I'm crazy. When I take you, Brooke, it won't be in your brother's den, fully clothed."

For long moments he waited without speaking.

"Would you like some coffee?" she asked in a small voice.

He smiled. "Can you make coffee?" Sensing her hesitation, he went on to say in an indulgent voice, "I would love a cup."

Brooke didn't need any more encouragement. With cheeks aflame, she almost ran to the kitchen. What in the world had come over her? she chided herself. She had acted like a complete wanton, practically begging Ashley to make love to her right then and there. What must he be thinking, that she was easy and experienced? She hoped not, because nothing could be further from the truth. Ashley was the only man she had ever wanted to be truly intimate with. Cody had never made her lose control of her emotions like this.

With shaking hands, she tried to pour two cups of coffee, but ended up pouring more on the counter top than in the cups. "Oh, damn," she muttered out loud.

"Need any help, honey?"

Brooke turned and found Ashley leaning rather nonchalantly against the doorframe, an indulgent smile on his face. Again Brooke felt the tears threaten to burst forth. It wasn't fair for anyone to have so much charm, she fumed to herself.

Sensing her mood, Ashley said in a teasing voice, "A

man could die of thirst, woman! Let me help. Two hands are better than one." Grabbing both cups of coffee, he headed back to the den. There was nothing left for Brooke to do but follow.

They drank their coffee in silence, lost in their own thoughts. It was past noon. Anne would be returning from the doctor, and Brooke dreaded having to explain Ashley's presence to her. Oh, what a complicated web we weave, she thought to herself.

"Let's go somewhere quiet and have a bite to eat. You're nervous as a cat on a hot tin roof." When she hesitated, his voice grew grim. "You're not afraid of me?" he questioned.

"No, not exactly, but I'm not at all sure I should continue seeing you. I'm about as confused now as I've ever been in my life. Things are going too fast, I guess that's what I'm trying to say," finished Brooke lamely.

"Will you believe me if I tell you my intentions toward you are honorable? After all, wasn't I the one that called a halt right here on this very spot?"

"I'm not proud of that fact. Please don't remind me of that again!" Brooke bristled. Damn his arrogant tongue!

He sighed heavily. "Let's not fight again. If you'll just listen to what I have to say for a minute, I'll leave."

Brooke did not want him to leave, but she had no intention of begging him to stay, now or ever. They couldn't even carry on a conversation with each other that didn't turn into a slinging match.

"I want you to fly to Kauai with me first thing in the morning. I should have already been there, but I stopped here first to see you. We'll be gone about two or three days depending on the problems I have to deal with when I get there. My grandfather will enjoy your company!"

"What!" exclaimed Brooke in a loud voice. "Surely, you're joking. Your grandfather?"

"No, I'm not joking," returned Ashley uneasily. "What's wrong with my grandfather?"

Brooke knew he was hurt and was trying to keep his emotions under control. His mouth was drawn in a tight line and a muscle was flexing in his jaw.

"Well, I . . ." stammered Brooke. "I mean, going to someone's house . . ."

"Are you going to come? Your kisses tell me you want to be a part of my life and when I try to make you a part . . . Exactly what kind of game are you playing?"

"I can imagine why you take women to your house," she returned hotly. "I should be the one asking *you* what kind of game you're playing?"

"For God's sake, Brooke. Just be ready at eight in the morning. I don't intend to sit here and argue with you another damn minute!" With those choice words, he left the house, slamming the door behind him.

The rest of the day Brooke ran around completely disoriented. One minute she fumed to herself that she definitely was not going. Then the next minute she found herself standing in front of her closet trying to decide what she wanted to take with her to wear. Finally, after what seemed like an eternity of vacillating back and forth between not going and going, she sat down to rest a minute and drank a Coke.

This is where Anne found her when she came in from the doctor.

"Hey, kid, what's happening?" laughed Anne as she eyed Brooke staring off into space.

"Oh, hi, Anne," sighed Brooke in a dejected voice.

"Is something the matter, honey?" questioned Anne with concern. "Are you feeling all right?"

"No, no, nothing like that," Brooke assured her quickly. "It's just that I thought I was leaving my problems behind in Houston, but it seems that since coming here, I've picked up new ones."

"It's Ashley this time, rather than Jonathan, isn't it?"

"How did you know?" responded Brooke sharply.

"Now calm down, Brooke. It's obvious that something is going on between you two. Would it help to tell me about it?"

"There's nothing to tell really, except that Ashley wants me to fly to Kauai with him tomorrow and stay a few days while he takes care of some business."

"Are you serious?" cried Anne. "As long as I've known Ashley, I've never known him to take any woman to his home—to his apartment, yes, but home to his grandfather's, definitely not."

"Well, I'm not so sure I'm going either!"

"Does he care about you?" asked Anne.

"Of course not!" declared Brooke. "At least not in the way you mean!"

"How do you know which way I mean?" questioned Anne, raising her eyebrows.

Brooke turned and gazed sharply at her sister-in-law. Then she saw the twinkle in Anne's eyes and knew instantly that she was teasing her.

"Oh, you . . ." laughed Brooke. The mood had lightened.

"I'm sorry, honey," repented Anne. "But at this point, I'm not at all sure you even know your own mind."

Sighing, Brooke agreed. "You're right. I don't." She paused and poured herself more Coke. "I seem to always be groping in the dark where Ashley is concerned."

Anne's eyes narrowed. "You don't have to answer

this if you don't want to." She hesitated. "Just exactly how far have things gone between you two?"

Brooke sighed. "Well, not far enough to suit Ashley, that's for sure." Bitterness crept into her voice.

"It's you I'm concerned about, not Ashley," said Anne. She searched her features.

"I know, and I appreciate it," she whispered, avoiding Anne's penetrating gaze.

"Well," sighed Anne, "if you don't want to talk about it, just tell me. I'll understand."

"Oh, please," cried Brooke, "don't pay any attention to me. It's just that . . ." She licked her dry lips. "I haven't let my emotions get out of control *yet,* if that's what you mean. But I can't honestly say I haven't been sorely tempted."

"I know it can be hell when you find yourself in that situation," she sighed. "Temptation wears many colors, my friend."

"Tell me about it," said Brooke dejectedly.

"I'm thinking," declared Anne, "that I've depressed you far more than I've helped you." She rose abruptly to her feet and began pacing the floor.

Brooke frowned. "Oh, no, you haven't! Don't ever think that! It helps just to have someone to talk to."

Anne nibbled at her lower lip. "I'd like to think I'm paying you back a little for all the times you've let me cry on your shoulders."

Brooke laughed. "Well, consider it paid in full. By the way," she added on a serious note, "I still intend to have that chat with my brother. I know you're worried and so am I."

"Thanks," replied Anne, as she leaned back in the chair. Her voice was husky.

Changing the subject, Brooke said, "I'd like to know about Ashley's grandfather. Do you know him?"

Anne hesitated. "No, not really. Only what I've been told."

"And what was that?"

Anne gave a teasing grin. "Only that when the old man says jump, Ashley asks him how high."

Rolling her eyes upward, Brooke said, "Be serious! *If* I decide to go, I need to know what I'll be walking into. So, come on now, tell me what you know."

Anne wrinkled her nose. "Actually I don't know much . . ."

"Quit stalling and tell me what you've heard. Please . . ."

"Okay," said Anne, shrugging her shoulders, "but you're going to be disappointed because I actually know very little." She paused. "Gossip is that Ashley has never found anyone he thought would please his grandfather. Now, just why that's important to Ashley, I have no earthly idea." She spread her hands. "They say he's a crusty old gentleman, hard to get along with. And that the only person other than Ashley who can cope with him is Ashley's aunt who lives there and takes care of him."

"Do you know if Ashley has any other relatives?" questioned Brooke.

"No, not that I know of." She wrinkled her brow. "Jonathan knows Ashley pretty well, but he said Ashley keeps quiet about his personal affairs."

"Well, I guess that's that!" said Brooke, shrugging her shoulders.

"I told you that I didn't know very much. If anything, I probably made you more curious than ever. Right?"

Turning, Brooke laughed a little anxiously. "All I can say is that if I decide to go, I'll find out how Little

Red Riding Hood must have felt when the Big Bad Wolf chased after her."

"You may be right, honey. So watch your step," laughed Anne. "He's a great looking hunk of man and his kind of charm is hard to ignore. *But,*" continued Anne with a grin and a twinkle in her eyes, "I still think you should go—if for no other reason than to find out what he has up his sleeve."

"A lot of help you are," laughed Brooke. "I know when I'm being fed to the wolves. But you're right. Down deep I want to go and probably intended to all along. What's that famous quote about a fool being born every minute?"

Anne's laughter followed Brooke all the way up to her room where she spent the rest of the afternoon and evening packing.

Brooke was up bright and early the next morning. It promised to be a beautiful clear day. She was glad of that because she was leery about island hopping in a small plane.

She wore white straight-legged pants with a cuff at the bottom and a lime green and white terrycloth V-necked top, which barely accented the softness beneath. She arranged her hair on top of her head and kept the loose tendrils confined with vivid green combs. She was beginning to tan just slightly and she looked healthy once again, her responses more alert, sensitive and fluid.

Her brother was delighted that she was going to Kauai with Ashley. He had stopped by her room last night to tell her he heartily approved of the whole idea. Brooke told him he was reading much more into the visit than was actually there. But for the first time, she noticed that some of the strain had been lifted from his face. His eyes had a twinkle to them like the old Jonathan.

She had been tempted to question him about his affairs and just exactly what role Ashley played in them, but she didn't. She was simply not up to a fight.

She sensed that Jonathan's restored good humor was because he thought she was pursuing Ashley just as he had planned. Of course, nothing was further from the truth. But at this point, she was too confused about her own feelings and too tired to convince him otherwise. Just let him think what he wanted to right now. His disillusionment would come soon enough.

With her heart and mind set on regaining her professional momentum and the fact that she was not to have any children, there was *nothing* she had to offer a man of Ashley's caliber and background. Depending on her to come through with Ashley was a grave mistake on Jonathan's part. Maybe she was wrong in *not* telling her brother and sister-in-law all that the doctor had told her, but it was still too painful to think about, much less to talk about.

As soon as she finished dressing, she made her way downstairs to wait for Ashley. She joined Anne and Jonathan in the kitchen for a cup of coffee, and was taking her first sip of the hot liquid when the doorbell rang. Glancing at the kitchen clock, she saw that it was eight o'clock sharp. Ashley was exactly on time.

Jonathan rose and said, "Keep your seats, girls, I'll get the door."

When Jonathan left, Anne leaned over and whispered to Brooke, "Are you nervous, honey?"

Breathing deeply, Brooke said, "I'm so nervous that I'm sick to my stomach." Her face was as pale as a sheet.

Anne frowned. "Hey, I was really just teasing you,

you know, when I asked you that. If you change your mind and don't want to go, *no one* is going to make you."

Fingering the gold chain around her neck, Brooke said haltingly, "Oh, I'm not at all sure I want to go. But I'm going anyway." She paused. "I think the die was cast a long time before now."

Anne gave her a questioning look, but there was no time for any further conversation. Ashley had preceded Jonathan into the room.

Looking up at him, Brooke felt her senses spin. The effect this man had on her was overpowering. The expensive scent of his cologne subtly permeated the room as did his presence. Their eyes locked for a moment and she read possession in them as his glance stroked her body.

She felt trapped!

Brooke's eyes darted around the room looking for a way out. But Ashley leaned negligently against the doorframe. There was a tense expression plastered on his face.

Sensing that something was wrong, Brooke turned in her brother's direction. His face was devoid of color. What had passed between the two of them out in the hall? Angry words perhaps? Accusations? She did not know, of course, what had actually been said. But she was positive that some type of unpleasantness had been exchanged.

Anne was completely oblivious to the tension in the room. She indicated the chair next to hers and smiling said to Ashley, "Surely you don't have to be in such a hurry that you can't sit down for a quick cup of coffee."

Before Ashley could reply or move, Jonathan's voice chimed in, his tone agitated, "Honey, of course he's in a hurry! I know for a fact he has a lot to do when he gets to Kauai." Jonathan was clearly upset.

Ashley's only reaction for a moment was to tighten his lips. Then he nonchalantly walked over and sat down next to Anne. "No," he said rather lazily as he made himself comfortable in the chair, "we have plenty of time."

Jonathan flushed. He shuffled uncomfortably for a moment before sitting down himself.

Brooke was appalled at her brother's behavior. Anne, too, was aghast. It was obvious that he was uncomfortable with Ashley's presence all of a sudden. Why? To cover the silence that had befallen the room, Anne jumped up, grabbed the coffeepot and began refilling their cups.

When she poured Jonathan's, she accidentally spilled the coffee. He snapped, his voice terse, "Dammit, woman, can't you even pour coffee right?"

Anne's lips trembled. She turned and went abruptly to the sink where she began putting dishes in the dishwasher.

Ashley's steel voice broke the quiet. "Don't you think you came down on her a little hard?"

Jonathan was definitely feeling repentent. Sighing deeply, he ran a hand over the back of his neck and walked to where Anne was sobbing openly. "I'm . . . sorry, I . . ."

Brooke could hold her tongue no longer. "You should be!" she cried, staring coldly at her brother. "Whatever possessed you to talk to Anne like that? I . . ."

Ashley interrupted. "Enough, Brooke! Keep out of it. Let me handle it."

Brooke was furious! Who did he think he was,

talking to her like she was a two year old? After all, Jonathan was *her* brother.

Before she got the chance to voice her opinion however, Anne said unsteadily, "Please . . . let's not . . . quarrel anymore." Her eyes were pleading with Jonathan.

Brooke was still fuming. It was obviously all Ashley's fault. Whatever he had said to Jonathan caused him to smolder like a volcano. Maybe as soon as she and Ashley left, Anne and Jonathan would make up. They were already making progress in that direction. Anne's expression had lightened somewhat, much to Brooke's relief.

Rudely breaking into her thoughts was Ashley's demanding voice, "If you're through daydreaming, we'll go."

Obviously, while she had been deep in thought, he had made peace with Jonathan and Anne, at least on the surface. Her brother, though still a little tense, shook his hand and Anne kissed his cheek.

If it hadn't been for the unpleasantness that had gone before, Brooke would have put Ashley Graham in his place. He was definitely out of line. Brooke stood scowling at him. He must have read her thoughts because his face darkened even more.

Turning, she gave Anne a brief hug, ignored her brother, grabbed her purse and quickly headed for the front door.

Ashley's face grew black with anger, but he said nothing. He merely followed and opened the door for her and saw that she was comfortable before putting her luggage in the trunk.

As they pulled out of the driveway, Brooke remained silent and so did Ashley. But her thoughts weren't silent. What had transpired between him and her brother? The question was gnawing at her insides. If she asked him, would he tell her?

Several times, Brooke felt his eyes upon her. But she completely ignored him, looking neither to the right nor left.

He chuckled. "Are you going to pout all the way there, honey?"

She bristled and glared at him. "You've—you've got your nerve! You're the one who started all this. I . . ."

"Started what?" he asked mildly. His blue eyes danced.

"You—you, know what!" she sputtered.

Ashley lifted his dark brows. "No, I don't," he stated innocently. "Suppose you tell me."

Brooke halted, but her brown eyes met his directly. "You talked to me as if I were a child in front of Anne and Jonathan and . . ."

Ashley's laugh stopped her in mid-sentence. "Is that all you're upset about?"

"No!" she cried. "And you know it isn't! That's only part of it. What I really want to know is what you said to Jonathan to cause him to behave so rudely?"

She waited breathlessly for his answer.

His eyes narrowed speculatively on her face. "What makes you think I said anything to him?" he asked quietly.

Brooke wanted to scream, but she dug her fingernails into her palms and hissed, "Why can't you just answer my question, instead of answering with one of your own?"

He smiled. "Temper, temper, temper."

She looked at him in disgust. "Don't think you can use the old psychology trick on me. It won't work!"

Ashley's eyes probed hers. "Honey, would it make you happy if I said I was sorry?" he questioned softly.

She frowned. "It depends on what you're sorry for." She held her breath. Surely now he would tell her what she wanted to know about her brother.

Silence.

They had arrived at the airport and he was taking his time parking the car. After completing this task, he turned to her, his gaze warm and said huskily, "Will you trust me for now, honey, and not ask any more questions?"

When he looked at her like that, he wove a magic spell around her and she could deny him nothing.

But what was so surprising, even to her, was that she did trust him. Anyway she was tired, and it was much too beautiful a day to keep up the verbal boxing match with him.

Sensing the return of her good humor, he looked directly at her and said, "I forgot to tell you how lovely and fresh you looked this morning."

Before she could say a thing, he leaned over and planted a firm kiss on her lightly glossed lips. She felt his touch all the way to her toes. "That's just the beginning of what I'd really like to do to you," he whispered huskily.

Flushing, Brooke continued to stare at him with a confused look on her face. One moment he treated her like a child and snapped at her like a bear with a sore paw and the next, he was charm personified. Would she ever be able to figure this man out?

"Get a move on. Our plane is waiting," laughed Ashley.

Brooke had no idea that Ashley himself would be piloting the small Cessna. But she should not have been surprised. There seemed to be nothing he could not do. He winked at her as he climbed into the cockpit and began checking the instruments.

"Relax, honey. I've been doing this for many years. A plane in the sugar cane business is an absolute must! You're in good hands, believe me. All you have to do is concentrate on the scenery."

Once they were airborne and Brooke knew that Ashley was definitely a competent pilot, she relaxed and began to look at the lush valleys and mountains far below. When they passed over something of importance, Ashley pointed it out to her. For most of the time, he left her to her own thoughts. She closed her eyes for a moment, and took several deep breaths. She was nervous and worried about spending time alone with Ashley as well as meeting his grandfather.

All Ashley had to do was get anywhere near her and her bones turned to water. When he touched her, she lost all sense of reality. This irritated her beyond words. She wanted to be in complete charge of her emotions and keep them intact at all times. But when Ashley was around, she was unable to do this.

He got under her skin as no one else ever had and she was at a loss as to how to cope with it. Now, she had to encounter his grandfather, who she felt was probably just another version of Ashley, only older. How could she ever bear two Ashleys? She almost cried aloud in panic at the thought.

What would the crusty old gentleman think of her? According to Anne, he was the only person in Ashley's life whom he considered to be superior to himself.

Did his grandfather want him to ever marry? If so, why couldn't Ashley find anyone he thought would please the older man. Surely out of all the beautiful women Ashley had been involved with, one would have met his grandfather's standards.

Something was wrong with the whole situation. But what she did not know, hopefully, did not concern her. What did Ashley expect from her during this trip?

She shuddered, but not from anticipation. . . .

Flying time from Honolulu to Kauai was only about thirty minutes. She was jolted from her reverie when she felt the small plane begin to descend for the landing. She assumed they would be landing at the airport in Lihue, the largest city on the island, but again she was wrong. Shouting once more at her above the engine's noise, he told her that they had their own airstrip on the plantation and that was where they would be landing.

As they taxied down the small runway, there was a station wagon waiting for them by the maintenance building. A couple of workers leaned leisurely against the doors and the moment the plane stopped, they hurried toward it.

Ashley jumped out of the aircraft and shook their hands. After helping Brooke alight, he introduced her to the two grinning Hawaiian workers.

Transporting their luggage from the plane to the wagon only took a moment. Before she had a chance to notice her surroundings closely, they were speeding away toward what Brooke assumed was Ashley's home.

She took deep breaths to try to quell the nervousness which was causing her stomach to churn. Once again she questioned her sanity in making this trip. She was only hurting herself. Ashley needed sons to inherit all the beauty and wealth of the empire that was unfolding before her eyes.

Everywhere she looked there was beauty. She had

read that Kauai was called the "Garden Island" because of its rich natural greenery and beautiful gardens. It was covered with sugar plantations and banana plantations as well, Ashley's being the largest of the working sugar plantations.

Ashley was busy listening and questioning the workers about what had happened while he had been gone. This left Brooke time to compose herself before they arrived at the house. He had an uncanny way of reading her thoughts and he knew she was uneasy. Although he did not talk to her, she felt his eyes upon her from time to time with a tender look in them.

Before they actually reached the house she could see it nestled in the midst of lush flowers and tall swaying palm trees. As they drove up the circular drive to the front of the house, Brooke's eyes were as large as saucers. It was magnificent. It had been in the family for years and had been kept in perfect condition with a lot of tender loving care. The house itself was built with whitewashed stone. The second-floor verandah circled the entire house. Glass had been added to give it an open effect. The grounds around it were immaculate and the fragrance coming from the perfectly groomed flower beds was overwhelming. In the distance the tranquility of the beach sparkled in the sunlight.

"Well, what do you think?" questioned Ashley as he helped her out of the car.

"It's lovely, Ashley, truly lovely!"

"I'm glad you like it," he returned in a warm voice. When he talked and looked at her like that, she wanted to hold him and never let go. That was not to be, she reminded herself once again.

There was a tall and elegant older woman waiting on the verandah with a smile lighting up her face. Brooke knew she had to be a close relative of Ashley's from the close resemblance.

Ashley put his arm around her and planted a kiss on her firm cheek. Drawing Brooke into the circle of his arm, he introduced her. "Brooke, this is my aunt, Madge Conway." He grinned. "She is the 'Keeper of the House' in its truest sense of the word. Without her, Eli and I would never make it."

"Oh, pooh, don't believe that," she said as she viewed Brooke closely. A smile lighted her eyes. "I'm so glad to meet you, Brooke. Welcome to our home. I know you must be tired and want to freshen up a little. Ashley, why don't you show her to the green guest room and then go see Eli before he has another stroke. He heard the plane and is anxious to see you."

"How's the old man been feeling lately, Aunt Madge?" he asked with real affection and concern in his voice.

"Not good, Ashley, not good at all. I'm worried about him. He simply refused to do as the doctor tells him. Maybe you can beat some sense into that stubborn head of his! Lord knows, I can't."

"Is your grandfather that ill, Ashley? Perhaps I shouldn't have come," suggested Brooke hesitantly.

"Eli has been sick for a long time, honey. He's nearly ninety and the stubborn old cuss just refuses to do anything the doctor advises. Just like someone else I know," he whispered for her ears alone. "Half the time he won't even take his medicine. I think you being here will help him more than all the medicine combined."

Brooke gave him a puzzled look at hearing those words, but he ushered her into the house and up the stairs before she had a chance to question him.

The house on the inside was just as lovely as the

outside, from the quick glimpse she got of the downstairs.

Ashley opened the door to a large airy room that was done in different shades of green. The furniture was made of dark, heavy wood. But with the bright wallpaper and matching bedspread and curtains, the room was elegant. To the right was a bathroom all her own with a sunken bathtub.

"When you've freshened up, I'll meet you in the living room, and then I'll take you up and introduce you to Eli." With a quick kiss he was gone. Kissing her was becoming quite a habit with Ashley. However, she could not say she did not enjoy it.

Repairing her makeup only took a few minutes, so in order to kill a little time, she walked out onto the verandah and sat down and looked at the ocean. Beauty was a mild word for what was before her eyes. One could stay here forever and never want for more, she thought.

Growing restless, she ventured downstairs to meet Ashley. When she crossed into the living room, he was at the bar in the corner mixing drinks.

"I know you must be thirsty for something cool to drink. I know I am. How about a glass of Aunt Madge's special fruit punch drink—guaranteed to make a new woman out of you!" Ashley said grinning.

"Sounds great. Bring it on! I didn't realize I was so thirsty until you mentioned it," laughed Brooke.

"Aunt Madge is giving the cook instructions to prepare us a light lunch. Afterward we'll take a tour. That is, after you meet Eli." He paused. "Hopefully, he'll be able to join us downstairs for dinner this evening."

"That's quite all right with me. I can't wait to see this

gorgeous place. You must be the happiest person alive, owning something like this," exclaimed Brooke, still very much in awe of the house and all its surroundings.

"You're wrong. I'm still missing the one thing that I need to complete my circle of happiness," Ashley said gruffly while looking at her with a strange light in his eyes.

Brooke's heart took a plunging dive. He was referring to a woman, of course. Obviously, he had not as yet convinced his mistress to marry him and come and live on this enchanted island. Once again she chided herself for being his playmate until the one he really wanted gave him the magic "yes."

Noticing the darkening of her expression, Ashley looked at her rather anxiously and said, "Are you sure you don't need to rest a while? It's that damned tennis that keeps you pulled down. I hope you can see how foolish it is to continue with a sport that is hazardous to your well-being."

Trying not to show her irritation, Brooke said, "I'm just fine," completely ignoring his last comment. She really could use the rest, but she wouldn't admit that now. He obviously never intended to forgive her for wanting to pursue her career. Did he think she would give up her dream so easily? She had to admit that it was not as bright as it had been since she met Ashley.

The days spent with him here at his house would be the end, however. She intended not to see him anymore. They weren't right for each other and she could not bear to see the disappointment on his face.

Lunch was an enjoyable and casual affair. Aunt Madge seemed to enjoy her company and asked her numerous questions about Houston and her home. She explained about the death of her parents. She didn't mention her accident, but Ashley did.

"Brooke's been injured quite seriously, in a car collision. She's here recuperating with her brother and his wife."

"Oh, I'm sorry to hear that, my dear," said Madge with concern in her voice.

"I'm fine now, really I am," said Brooke.

Sensing her reluctance to talk about herself, Madge tactfully changed the subject. The rest of the time passed quickly.

After lunch, Ashley took her upstairs to meet his grandfather. She knew she shouldn't be nervous about meeting the old man, but she was. In the back of her mind, the conversation with Anne kept haunting her. However, the minute she met him, her fears were overturned. He didn't appear to be the hard-nosed person that gossip labeled him. He was truly a charming old gentleman. Although frail, and some of the time bedridden, he nevertheless demanded respect and attention from anyone who came in contact with him.

He was indeed an older edition of Ashley. But the twinkle was still there and there was absolutely nothing wrong with his mind.

"You make this boy of mine treat you right now, you hear, young lady. Make him toe the line and mend his devilish ways. I can see you'll be just right for the job."

"Now, Eli," responded Ashley quickly.

"Hush, son. Let me have my say and then you two can go along about your business. Just humor me a moment."

Brooke felt her face turn red with the old man's words. What in the world did he think was going on between the two of them? He obviously thought that she was the latest of his mistresses, or better still, a prospective wife. Although she probably would not see Eli again after she left here, she could not let him think she was either one. He acted as if he would be delighted to see Ashley brought to heel. She was more confused than ever now. She smiled at Eli uncertainly.

"I'm sorry, Mr. Graham, but I've just recently met your grandson and I have no intention of trying to make him do anything," she finished lamely after seeing Eli raise his bushy eyebrows.

"Well, we'll see about that, young lady," smiled Eli weakly and in a patronizing tone.

Brooke felt her face begin to turn red again, not from embarrassment this time but from confusion. However, before she could say anything, Eli waved his hand at them and said, "If you two want me to join you for dinner tonight, you best get out of here and let this old man rest."

As they were leaving the room, Brooke caught Eli's eyes and he gave her a conspiratorial wink which added to her confusion even more. She liked the old man, but he was reading too much into her and Ashley's relationship.

The afternoon passed in one of complete harmony for Brooke. Ashley took her on a complete tour of the house and the grounds. The beauty of his home was never ending. It dawned on Brooke how much wealth and power were in the palm of his hand. The people who worked for Ashley adored him. The workers would stop and talk to him. He took time to say a personal word to each and inquire about their families.

As they continued their leisurely pace around the grounds, hand in hand, Brooke noticed several pineapples that had dislodged and were laying on the ground. Could she hold another morsel of food? She thought to herself how good one of those would taste.

Licking her lips, she turned to Ashley and said,

"Mmmmm! I can just imagine what one of those fresh pineapples would taste like."

Looking at her in astonishment, Ashley said, "Surely you're not still hungry, honey?"

"Not for food, only for one of those juicy tidbits," she said, pointing to the pineapples.

"Well, your wish is my command. Never let it be said I didn't come to the rescue of a damsel in distress." Ashley laughed in a lighthearted manner. After pulling out his knife, he pared a succulent wedge of the golden fruit.

"Want it?" he said grinning, holding it just out of reach.

Standing on her tiptoes, Brooke lifted her lips, then twisted her mouth. "That's not fair!"

His eyes twinkled merrily. "Who said anything about being fair? If you want it, come and get it." He backed away from her.

Placing her hands on her hips in mock agitation, she said, "I don't want it *that* badly."

Smiling smugly, Ashley said, "Oh, but I bet you *will!*" He proceeded to drop the tasty bite in his mouth. "Mmmmm—that was good!" He paused, licking his fingers one at a time.

Brooke wrinkled her nose. "You're a devil, Ashley Graham!"

"Oh, really?" He grinned, appearing unconcerned.

"Yes, you are. And you know it!" she returned crossly.

Ashley laughed outright. With softened eyes, he said, "All right, honey, you win." He came closer. "After all, it was your idea, wasn't it?"

She flashed him a smile.

He immediately sliced another piece of the juicy fruit

and still in a teasing manner, touched the tidbit lightly to her lips.

Brooke sank her teeth into its pulp before Ashley changed his mind. He grinned as a second later, he replaced it with another.

The more he peeled, the faster she crammed the pieces into her mouth. When she felt the juice begin to trickle down the sides of her mouth, she laughingly reached for Ashley's handkerchief.

Ashley stilled her hand. In that moment their eyes locked. The teasing expression was gone.

Brooke held her breath.

He leaned forward and slowly with his tongue, licked the juice from her mouth. Her eyes misted at the beguiling sweetness of his touch.

She trembled.

Ashley too was affected. He groaned, drawing her closer and placing his lips tenderly upon hers. The kiss was like none they had ever shared, intimately deep and moving.

Upon pulling apart, they were both visibly shaken. No words were necessary as he smiled and reached for her hand. Brooke wanted to cry with the passing of such a tender moment.

Once they reached the car, it did not take long to reach their destination. As Ashley parked the car, he said, "No one should be allowed to leave Kauai until they've taken the Wailua River boat trip. You'll see what I mean in a minute." He looked down at her. "Are you ready?"

She nodded.

"Good, let's go." He grabbed her hand and folded it into his large one. This insignificant gesture on his part made Brooke's stomach muscles tighten.

The three-mile trip by motor launch up the river

from Wailu Marina was a tropical daydream. The guide explained the history and romance that surrounded the areas they passed, telling his passengers that the kings and royalty of the island lay buried in the caves on the bluff. The riverbanks and valley walls were a tangled mass of lush vegetation dominated by pandanus trees and the rare pili grass that was once used for Hawaiian houses.

After landing upstream, Ashley secured her hand in his and helped her out of the boat. Brooke caught her foot accidentally and would have fallen had it not been for Ashley's tight rein on her arm. "Watch it, honey." He grinned. "I'd hate like hell to have to fish you out of the water."

She gave him a playful punch in the stomach before they joined the others on the trek through the dense jungle. Oh, why, she mused to herself, couldn't things always be this way between her and Ashley. If only . . .

She was jerked out of her reverie. They had arrived at their destination, the Fern Grotto. Since Ashley had told her very little about it, she really didn't know what to expect. But whatever her mind had conjured up was nothing in comparison to the sight she encountered.

The Fern Grotto was a cool, damp cave draped with lush maidenhair ferns. Brooke had never seen anything in her entire life to compare with it. The ferns hung from the rocks. There had recently been a rain shower, so a transparent curtain of raindrops continued to fall across the wide mouth of the cavern. The water came from the plants which were relinquishing the water they had gathered.

As the crowd stood close to the cave's entrance, a Hawaiian couple from within sang "I'm Waiting for Thee."

Ashley put his arm around her, drawing her close

and said huskily in her ear, "Did you know that this song is better known as the Hawaiian Wedding Song?"

He disarmed her. "No . . ." She hesitated, licking her suddenly dry lips. "I didn't."

Ashley moved his head back to look at her. "Mm— well, I guess we'll just have to see what we can do about furthering your Hawaiian culture and education. Can't have you living here in ignorance, now, can we?"

She flushed uncomfortably. When he was in this kind of mood, she didn't know quite how to take him. She quivered when she thought about being just another spider in his web.

"Hey," he said, tapping her playfully on the nose. "I was just teasing. I wouldn't change one hair on your head, or anything else about you." His tone had grown serious now. "I like you the way you are. . . ."

Their eyes met, with each one hiding what secrets lay behind them.

Soon the trip came to an end, but it was all Ashley said it would be and more. Brooke was delighted that he wanted to share it with her.

Their time after they returned was so limited, Ashley did not have an opportunity to take her on a tour of the sugar mill. He promised to do so the next day, if time permitted.

Brooke was only able to grab a few minutes of rest before having to dress for the evening. She chose a simple but clinging black jersey dress to wear for dinner. It showed off her curves to the fullest but without being too suggestive. With her hair clean and shining, she knew she looked good. However, a little extra makeup was needed to hide the tired lines under her eyes.

When she made her way downstairs, Ashley was alone mixing himself a drink.

"I didn't expect you down quite so early. You could have rested a little longer," he chided.

"Well, I don't really feel all that tired," returned Brooke flushing. She was touched by his continued show of concern for her but was still unsure of how to deal with it.

"You're looking extremely lovely tonight," he added, as he strode closer to her to hand her a drink.

Being so close to his big, hard, muscular body without being able to touch him was a bittersweet pain for Brooke. Her senses were reeling from the potency of his nearness.

Unconsciously, Brooke stepped back to try and break the spell that had descended upon her.

She heard his indrawn breath before he said gently, "Honey, as much as I'd like to touch you, I'm not going to. Although, if I had my way, I'd skip dinner entirely and have you as my dessert. The fresh sweet smell of you makes me so hungry . . ."

Looking up at him now with eyes wide and frightened, she shivered. "Please don't say . . ."

However, she got no further. The rest of the family chose that moment to enter the room. A stoic calm descended upon Ashley's face as he turned toward them.

Ashley's grandfather enjoyed the evening. Although he remained in his wheelchair for the short time he joined them, he was in fine form, teasing Madge until it brought a flush to her kind face. He asked Brooke several pointed questions about the world situation and the nation's economy to which she gave her opinion and offered no apologies for doing so. This appeared to please the old man, although why, Brooke did not know. Maybe it was because she was not afraid to speak her mind. Or maybe it was because she would not let him intimidate her. The fact that she and Eli liked each other seemed to satisfy Ashley also. This too, added to Brooke's puzzlement.

When it finally came time to retire for the night, Brooke was more than ready. The strain of being around Ashley was beginning to tell on her nerves. She knew her thoughts should not be turning in that direction, but she could not seem to stop herself. She was physically attracted to this man and the kisses they had shared burned brightly in her mind at all times. Yet she knew she was playing a dangerous game in which she was sure to be the loser. With these unhappy thoughts, she shed her clothes, crawled between the silk sheets and fell into an exhausted and dreamless sleep.

Chapter Six

*B*rooke felt great as she stretched and got out of bed at seven o'clock the next morning. She was not sure what Ashley planned for them to do today, but it didn't really matter as long as she was with him. She was an utter fool and she knew it for letting herself fall under his spell. It's only a matter of two days at the most and she would have to exclude him from her life altogether. She was still sticking to her plan of not seeing him anymore after she returned to Honolulu. She was not exactly sure how she was going to accomplish this, because of her brother. But nonetheless, she did not plan to be deterred.

Sighing, she made her way to the bathroom where she washed the sleep out of her eyes and brushed her teeth before jumping into the shower. She had just put on her underwear and was combing her hair when she heard a soft knock on her door. Thinking it was the housekeeper, Mrs. Lupokini, she called, "Come in."

In walked Ashley, but he stopped in his tracks when he encountered Brooke standing there staring at him half naked. They were both too stunned at the moment for either one of them to move or say anything. Ashley was devouring her with his eyes and Brooke was powerless to move under his burning gaze.

"My God," finally groaned Ashley indistinctly, "you're beautiful!"

Brooke felt her legs turn to jelly and she still could not move. The naked desire she saw in Ashley's eyes kept her rooted to the spot.

When Ashley did make a move in her direction, she somewhat sensed the danger she was in and reached for her robe lying at the foot of the bed.

"No!" muttered Ashley thickly and reached for her and pulled her into his arms. His mouth clamped down on hers and he kissed her with such intensity that there was no doubt about the state of his arousal. He began to run his hands down her back, each time drawing her closer to his taut muscles. Brooke knew that it was up to her to call a halt to this madness. Ashley, she sensed, was already over the brink.

When she felt his hand gently squeeze her breast, she began to struggle and push on his chest to try and break his hold on her. Finally, she was able to pull her mouth away from his and pleaded, "Ashley, please don't, I won't let you do this to me." She couldn't say any more because the tears were rolling down her cheeks faster than she could stop them.

When Ashley saw the tears, he pushed her away from him. "Why are you crying? Do you enjoy getting under my skin? You must lie awake at night thinking of ways to annoy me. Hasn't anyone ever told you what happens when you push a man too far?"

"But I didn't mean to . . ."

"Are you sure?" Ashley's tone was dry now.

"Well, I'm sorry if I gave you that impression. I certainly had no intention of doing so. You just caught me off guard, that's all!" finished Brooke lamely.

He made a face.

"You keep telling yourself that."

Brooke knew Ashley was perturbed and if the truth be known, he had every reason to be. She should have demanded that he get out of her room immediately instead of standing there like some half-wit dummy. No wonder he thought what he did.

To his retreating back, Brooke said with a waver in her voice, "I'm sorry, I didn't mean to . . . What I'm trying to say is that I . . ."

She got no further before he interrupted and said, "Forget it. I have!" Brooke stepped back as if he had slapped her. Refusing to let him know how much he had hurt her, she asked, shrugging her shoulders nonchalantly, "Are you planning to work today or . . ."

"I had planned to take you swimming and on a picnic," stated Ashley, "but I suppose that plan's down the drain now."

"No, not if you still want me to go," stammered Brooke, her tears threatening again.

Turning, he looked at her and said thickly, "You know I want you to go. However, please do me a favor and put some clothes on that lovely body of yours and quickly, too, or next time I won't be responsible for the consequences. Now hurry, I'll wait for you downstairs."

Blushing, Brooke hugged her robe closer to her body. "Yes, sir, your wish is my command!" she said, relieved that they were on safe ground once more.

As soon as Ashley left, Brooke sat down on the side

of the bed too weak to move. She knew she was asking for trouble by going with him for the day, but she was going to throw caution to the wind and go anyway.

Ashley was waiting for her in the kitchen dressed in a pair of white tennis shorts and a light blue knit shirt.

"How about a cup of coffee and some toast before we go," said Ashley.

"Just coffee for me, please. It's too early for anything else."

"In that case, you can take it with you and we'll be off and running."

"Okay, let's get going," Brooke replied, sensing that he was going to make an all out effort to see that she enjoyed the day. Maybe, just maybe, they could keep from arguing with each other for the remainder of the day.

After they had been riding for only a few minutes, Ashley told her that he was taking her to Lumahai Beach on the opposite side of the island. He planned for them to have a leisurely swim and then sight-see and enjoy the picnic lunch his cook had prepared.

The rest of the drive was spent with Ashley pointing out various points of interest to her, including several banana plantations as well as small sugar plantations. All along the way the perfume from the tropical flowers penetrated Brooke's nose.

Ashley kept the conversation on an impersonal level. There was a lot about Ashley that Brooke was curious about but was afraid to ask him. He never mentioned his parents, so she assumed they were dead. Also he never mentioned anything about a brother or sister. But it didn't really matter as their time together was limited to the next few days. She had to keep reminding herself of this.

However, just before they arrived at their destination, Ashley broke into her thoughts and said, "How well do you know your brother, Brooke?"

She felt the color subside from her face. "I guess I know him as well or better than the average sister knows her brother. Why?"

"I was just wondering, that's all. Forget it!"

Before she could question him further, they had apparently reached their destination because he was getting out of the car and coming around to her side to open the door. She knew there was a reason behind his question and it frightened her. She was convinced now that her brother's unhappiness and problem were very definitely linked to Ashley. Barring no complications, maybe she could find out just how involved Ashley was with Jonathan before they left.

When Brooke got out of the car, she was overcome with the lovely beach. The white sand and the huge waves were very inviting. The mountains and the cool greenery surrounding them made the whole area look like a picture on a postcard.

"Well, what do you think?" inquired Ashley with a smile on his face.

"It's beautiful! I can't wait to hit the water. This will be the first time I've been to the beach to actually swim since coming to Hawaii."

"Since we seem to virtually have it to ourselves, you can change into your suit behind the car." Seeing the hesitant look on her face, he went on to say, "Don't worry, honey. I'll turn my head."

Brooke knew he was teasing her but she didn't really care. She crouched down behind the trunk of the car and put on her new bikini. She almost wished she had brought the one-piece suit she had left back home in the drawer. Although this one completely covered her, it did not leave much to the imagination. Sighing, she guessed she could just as well swim in her panties and bra.

By the time she finished changing, Ashley was spreading a pallet on the ground for them to lie on between swims. He turned and watched her as she strode toward him.

Again Brooke could see the same desire and passion leap into his eyes, but this time he turned away from her and finished the task he had started. Even though she had put on a little weight since coming here, she was still as slender as a reed, her curves still in the right places and her breasts as large and firm as ever. She could feel them strain against the material of her suit just from the naked lust mirrored in Ashley's eyes.

Trying to make things appear as normal as possible, she said, "Do you think the waves are high enough for me to learn to body surf?"

"Are you sure you want to try it? It's not really a sport for beginners."

"Oh, please, Ashley," she pleaded. "I'll just pick a little wave and try it, okay?"

"All right, maybe later," he said indulgently, "but first let's get some suntan lotion on you before you burn to a crisp."

"Hand it to me, and I'll put it on myself," exclaimed Brooke, reaching for the bottle.

Instead of handing her the bottle, Ashley reached up and grabbed her hand and pulled her down beside him. "What's the matter, you don't trust me? Or is it yourself you don't trust?" he questioned coolly.

Angrily, she said, "I just don't want to get anything started!"

"Honey, we got something started the minute we laid eyes on each other and we both know it. So just let me put this stuff on your back and then I'll let you return the favor."

Sighing, Brooke did as she was told. Did he always have to have the last word? But she knew he was right. The first time they had come into contact with each other the sparks had flown.

Right now with his hands on her body, she was finding it hard to do anything, even breathe. He had made her lie on her stomach and was literally caressing, not rubbing the lotion into her body. She gasped however, when he unclasped the hook on her top, but when he finished, he clasped it back. Then he rolled her over onto her back and began doing the same thing on her stomach. She wanted to tell him to stop, but the words wouldn't come.

"Relax," he murmured. "I'm not going to hurt you."

"Oh, Ashley," she whispered fearfully, "why are you doing this to me?"

"Because, dammit, I want you," he ground out harshly.

Suddenly, with him half pulling her, she had no choice but to follow as he ran toward the waves. Her legs, however, were so wobbly she could hardly stand up, much less run.

By the time they hit the water, he was making every effort to put things back on an impersonal basis. Brooke knew that he was by no means in complete control of himself. There was still that line around his mouth and a haunted look in his eyes. How could she have let herself get into this situation?

They swam and played with a ball in the water; then she floated on her back for a while, closing her eyes. Before she knew it, Ashley was back on the beach, hollering for her to come and eat some lunch. Watching him lug the heavy ice chest from the trunk, she noticed the muscles in his arms and legs. In his bathing trunks, or in anything else for that matter, he had to be the best looking man she had ever seen. Vigor and vitality radiated from his hard, tanned body. The silver in his hair danced in the sunlight and made him that much more attractive. To think that she, Brooke Lawson, unschooled as she was in the art of lovemaking, could turn this man on, amazed her.

"Quit your daydreaming and come on," shouted Ashley.

"I'm coming, I'm coming, just hold your horses!"

Swimming always made her terribly hungry and apparently it affected Ashley the same way. His cook had packed a various assortment of lunch meat, chips and dips, pickles, fried chicken and several different types of cheeses and bread. In the ice chest was beer and wine.

After consuming so much food, all they could think about was resting for a few minutes. She knew Ashley would not let her try to body surf on a full stomach, so she rolled over on her side and closed her eyes. The next thing she was conscious of was a tickling feeling on her nose.

"Wake up sleepyhead. You've been asleep for an hour and if you plan to do any more swimming today, you had better get your lazy body up from there and hit the water!"

"Why did you let me sleep so long!" pouted Brooke.

"I hated to disturb you. You were sleeping so peacefully. After all, aren't you supposed to be taking it easy and recover from your accident?"

"Well, yes, but not here on a lovely beach when I'm on a picnic," Brooke responded saucily. She strove to keep her tone light.

Sensing her withdrawal at the mention of her accident, he quickly reached for her hand and pulled her up against his firm hard body. He held her there a moment longer than necessary, and then turned and pushed her toward the water.

Trying to learn how to body surf was easier said than done. Brooke had never done any kind of surfing in her life. Although there was a beach about thirty miles away from her home in Houston, she had never really taken advantage of it. Body surfing, Ashley patiently explained to her, was nothing at all like surfing with a board. There was nothing involved except learning to meet and ride the waves with one's body.

About midafternoon, the waves seemed to loom larger and larger, making the surfing that much more fun. The object was to hit the waves at exactly the right moment. After working with her a while and showing her the techniques, Ashley was more than a little apprehensive about letting her try without him right along beside her.

However, Brooke soon convinced him that she was capable of conquering the waves just like an old pro. So very reluctantly he waded back to their pallet with an indulgent smile on his face and waited for her to perform.

She was having a good time, boldly meeting wave after wave at just the right angle so that she was able to ride the crest. It gave her a feeling of being airborne. But it wasn't long before she encountered a wave that was so large that she couldn't meet it properly and it tumbled her. She was in the process of trying to regain her balance and clear the water out of her lungs when she heard Ashley yell at her. It was too late. She was hit from behind by what felt like a ton of bricks. The force of the huge wave knocked the breath completely from her lungs, picked her up and slammed her into the rocks close to the shoreline. She grabbed and held onto the rocks for dear life.

Ashley reached her about the time she had landed against the largest rock and hauled her into his arms. Brooke was too stunned to speak. All she could do was hang onto Ashley as if she never intended to let him go.

All the time he was holding her tightly, he kept saying, "Are you all right? What the hell are you trying to do to me? Please, Brooke, talk to me? For God's sake, woman, answer me!"

Finally Brooke was able to answer him, "I'm all right," she croaked, "Please just help me to the blanket."

Ashley picked her up and carried her. She was too weak to protest, not that she would have anyway. She felt safe and secure in his arms.

It was after Ashley laid her down and began pushing her tangled hair out of her eyes that she noticed her bikini top was down around her waist. Ashley became aware of it at the same time, because his hand stopped in midair and his eyes darkened at the sight of her breasts with their tender pink nipples.

He reached for them first with his hands. He began caressing the nipples with his thumbs and then with all of his fingers. Brooke was powerless to move.

Sensing that she did not intend to stop him, he leaned down and touched one with his tongue and then moved to the other one. By this time, both nipples were taut with desire.

From her breast, he left a trail of kisses upward until he reached her mouth. Using his tongue again, he forced her mouth open to receive the hot passion of his kisses. Each time he kissed her was deeper than the last. She was returning kiss for kiss with tongues intertwined.

Somehow they had drifted down on the pallet until they were lying side by side. Brooke could feel the hairs on his chest rubbing against her breast as he continued his fiery assault on her mouth.

Finally, breaking away enough so he could talk, he muttered, "Dear, God, Brooke, I've wanted to do this since I first saw you."

"You don't know what you're saying!"

"Don't tell me what I mean," he groaned. "You've wanted it too!"

Before she could answer, Ashley began running the tip of his tongue on the inside of her mouth. The touching began all over again. Brooke loved the feel of his hairy chest and the hard muscles of his back. But most of all she loved the feel of his mouth and tongue as it burned into hers.

Brooke could feel the tautness of his desire and knew he had reached his limit as he put his leg over hers and began to pull at the elastic waist of her bathing suit.

"Ashley," she whispered fearfully, "please don't."

"What are you afraid of, honey?" he asked softly.

"You, me, the two of us together."

"Why, Brooke?"

"Because I just am."

"I'm not going to hurt you or do anything you don't want me to."

"Then please let me up," she said with a quiver in her voice.

"You don't really mean that." Ashley's voice was husky.

"Yes, I do," returned Brooke with more force and confidence in her voice. She tried to push him off her.

"No," groaned Ashley stilling her with the rock hardness of his body. "I won't let you do this to me again." He began all over to assault her swollen and tender lips with hard determined kisses.

Brooke began to fight in earnest now. She did not mind losing her virginity; she would have gladly given herself to Ashley had she thought there could ever be a future for them. But she knew there never could be. She was aware that once she gave herself to him, she would never be able to say goodbye. Then she would learn about the other women who had succumbed to his charms. She would not beg for his favors, and she could not bear to be the last in line.

Brooke's continued struggle and unwillingness finally penetrated Ashley's fog of passion and he pulled away. "I don't have to rape a woman to get what I want," he said bitterly. After he threw a towel over her, he walked in the direction of the car without looking back.

Her whole body was beginning to shake with pain and horror at what she had done. There was no doubt about it; he hated her now. The contempt she had seen in his eyes when he had thrown the towel at her would remain in her memory for a very long time.

It was all she could do to get the top pulled up and back in place. Brooke then got up and began picking up the remains of their picnic. She ventured to look in Ashley's direction. He was sitting in the car smoking a cigarette and staring out across the water. She knew what she had done to him and she was not proud of herself. Twice in one day was too much.

Brooke was beginning to fold the pallet when she looked up and saw Ashley coming toward her. She noticed that he looked as if he were in complete control of himself once again. The hard mask was back in place. To look at him now, one would never know he had been consumed by passion almost to the breaking point just a little while ago.

Ashley helped her clean up and together they loaded the trunk of the car. Still he had not spoken. The silence was beginning to grate on her nerves. Why didn't he shout at her and get it over with? She knew he would never do that. The great Ashley Graham felt he owed nothing to a mere woman. She was probably the first and only woman to ever turn him down. If the joke weren't on herself as well, she would have scored a victory.

Breaking into her thoughts, Ashley said coolly, "If you would like to change out of your bathing suit, you can use that clump of bushes." Not even bothering to see what she said in return, he once again turned his back and walked to the car.

Shrugging her shoulders, Brooke strode off to change her clothes. The trip home was definitely going to be a long one. As soon as they reached their destination, he would probably demand that she get her things ready so that he could fly her back to Honolulu tomorrow. She knew it was inevitable, but the thought was tearing her apart inside.

During the entire drive home, there were no words exchanged. The few times Brooke eased a look in Ashley's direction she noted the look of disaffection on his face.

If only he knew that she would make no man a suitable wife. The fact that she should never try to have children would make him flee as if he had been stung by a cluster of bees. But marriage was probably the farthest thing from his mind right now. All he wanted her for was a bed partner and after a while, he would be ready to move on. If she would keep this in mind, she would survive.

Although Brooke was not familiar with the area around Ashley's home, she knew that they were not quite there when he pulled the car off the road to an out of the way spot. Once more the silence was almost deafening. The only sound was coming from the beat of Brooke's heart. She felt sure Ashley could hear it.

The only movement from within the car was Ashley reaching for a cigarette and lighter. He then began to slowly inhale. It was as if he were playing some kind of deadly game with her. She literally thought she would scream if he didn't tell her why they had stopped.

But when the explanation came, she almost fainted from shock.

"Will you marry me?" asked Ashley in a cool and unemotional voice.

Chapter Seven

He couldn't be serious! But as she stole a glance in his direction, he was staring at her with a look that radiated complete self-assurance. No, he knew exactly what he was doing! It was impossible to hide the bewilderment and uncertainty she was feeling at this moment, so she didn't even try.

Ashley could not help but be amused at the look on her face. Her face had lost all of its color and her eyes were huge as she gazed at him.

Raising his eyebrows and smiling, he said, "Have you lost your voice?"

"As a matter of fact I have," said Brooke in a dazed voice. "I can't believe you're even halfway serious."

Before Brooke could say anything else, he continued, "Oh, but I am serious. I have never asked any woman to marry me. It's something I definitely don't take lightly."

"But, but," sputtered Brooke, "why on earth would

you want to marry me? I'm just an ordinary girl with no money and no important family. What do we possibly have in common?"

Ashley's fingers gripped the steering wheel, "I'd say we're physically attracted to one another. That's a start," he replied.

Brooke felt the color invade her cheeks. "That's hardly enough to build a lasting marriage on," she flung back at him.

"Well, it's a hell of a lot more than most people have."

"But you don't know anything about me. We are in no way compatible. We're together only a matter of minutes and we're at each other's throats. What brought all this on anyway? From what I've heard, you're not the marrying kind!"

"I want you, Brooke," stated Ashley quietly. "I want to take you to bed and feel your naked body next to mine morning, noon and night. Now is that plain enough language for you? And if I have to marry you to do that, then so be it!"

"You shouldn't say things like that to me," stammered Brooke in a whisper. She was shaking all over and her insides were melting.

She longed to throw herself in his arms and let him love her. Then maybe, just maybe, she would be able to satisfy the gnawing hunger she felt for this man once and for all. But she knew no matter how much she might want him, she was aware that she would be the one destroyed and left to pick up the pieces. As it was right now, she was already striving to rebuild her life and career after the accident and broken engagement. She *had* to remain firm and not let her emotions override her good sense.

It was Ashley's caressing fingers that brought Brooke back to reality. He was running his fingers down her arms and then into the palm of her hand. Before she could tell him to leave her alone, he began to run his fingertips around the outline of her lips. From there they roamed down to her throat and then to her breast. Brooke could feel her nipples hardening in anticipation of his touch and she knew she was drowning once again in the sheer sensuality of his caress.

Waiting breathlessly for his lips to claim the sweetness of hers, she felt a coldness descend upon her when he abruptly turned away and moved back to his side of the seat.

"I'm flying you back to your brother's tomorrow, and I'll give you twenty-four hours to get your things together."

"Ashley, I'm not going to marry you."

"Oh, yes you are," he said flatly.

Brooke felt her face flushing. "You can't force me to," she exclaimed. "Anyway, you haven't told me the *real* reason why you're so anxious to marry me!"

"I've already told you why," he said, growing impatient.

"I believe wanting me is only part of it. I feel there is more to your proposal than you're telling me! Not that it's going to make me change my mind," she finished belligerently.

Ashley's mouth tightened visibly in the wake of her statement before saying, "Let's just say I have my reasons for wanting to marry now, the main one being *I want you.*"

"Is there another woman?"

"I didn't say that."

"But that's one of your other reasons, isn't it?"

"Brooke, honey," said Ashley, gently reaching over to grab her hand. "Why can't you just accept this thing we have between us and give in to it? I promise we'll have a good marriage. When I make a bargain, I stick to it if that's what's worrying you."

Swallowing the lump in her throat, she said in as clear a voice as possible, "I'm sorry, but the answer is still no. I can't marry you now or ever."

"We'll see about that," said Ashley in a tight voice. "I suggest when you get back home you have a talk with Jonathan. Maybe then you'll come to your senses."

"What do you mean by that? What does Jonathan have to do with my marrying you?" Her voice was shaking.

Ashley ran his fingers through her hair. "I've said all I'm going to say for now!"

Brooke's emotions were so raw and exposed that she didn't know if she could make it back to the privacy of her bedroom at Ashley's house before she burst into tears.

Her one main thought was to get away from Ashley and back home to talk to her brother. If Ashley were involved, she aimed to get out of the picture completely and let the two of them work it out. She refused to be caught in the middle any longer.

She was frightened, but she kept telling herself over and over again that there was no way she would or could be forced into marrying him. Ashley had no way of knowing the heartache that would follow.

All she had to do to end this madness was tell him the truth—that she could never have children, but she was much too vulnerable to expose herself in that way, since she didn't intend to marry him anyway. Children or no children, she felt she would never be able to hold a man like Ashley Graham for long.

The last evening she spent at Ashley's home wasn't worth remembering. After they arrived from the beach, she and Ashley had parted in silence. Brooke remained in her room until it was too late to avoid going down any longer. She had missed the cocktails before dinner on purpose because she just didn't want to be around Ashley at all. But she liked Eli and she knew he might try to come down to dinner because it would be her last evening there.

She decided to dress up for the evening hoping that it would give her self-confidence, something she badly needed in Ashley's presence. She still could not for the life of her figure out why marrying Ashley was somehow connected with her brother.

The dress she chose for the evening was a simple beige silk, slim fitting with a slit up the front. It had a scooped neck and long loose sleeves. With it she put on high wooden heeled sandals. The height of the heels added to her confidence. She wanted to look her very best for Ashley since this would be their last time together, although she did not know why she was punishing herself. But she wanted him to look at her with desire one more time.

However, the Ashley she encountered when she went downstairs was a cool stranger. Brooke felt he would have ignored her completely if it hadn't been for his grandfather. The conversation at dinner bounced back and forth among Brooke, Eli and Ashley's aunt. Madge was such a calm person that it helped having her there to act as a buffer. Ashley remained silent throughout most of the meal with a grim expression on his face. The only time he spoke was when his aunt or grandfather asked him a direct question. Brooke could read the puzzled expressions on their faces and could have kicked Ashley for the way he was behaving.

She tried her best to ignore him. She even tried to pretend he was not in the room with her. But that was virtually impossible to do. His masculine smell drugged her senses. His broad shoulders completely dominated the room. He was casually dressed in an expensive suit with an opened-necked shirt showing his bronze skin underneath. The few times she was forced to look in his direction, her breath caught in her throat.

When dinner was over, Ashley's aunt suggested they return to the den for an after-dinner drink. Even Eli felt up to doing this. Brooke could not very well refuse.

Ashley only remained a short while. He had some paper work he had to attend to before leaving in the morning, he said. The only direct words he spoke to Brooke were to tell her they would be leaving at eight sharp the next morning. Shortly after Ashley's retreat, everyone else called it a night.

The next morning Brooke awakened early and before going downstairs for even a cup of coffee, she showered, dressed in jeans and a T-shirt and packed her bag. She certainly did not want to add to Ashley's displeasure by his having to wait for her. By seven she was on her way downstairs. After having some coffee, she hoped to say goodbye to Eli. She liked him very much and was really sorry she would not get to see him anymore.

Trying to shake the depression that had settled upon her, she breezed into the kitchen with a forced smile on her face and said to Aunt Madge sitting at the table, "Hi, how are you this morning?"

"Just fine, my dear and you? I trust you slept well."

"Oh, just fine, thank you."

Brooke knew she had not fooled Ashley's aunt. She couldn't help but see the dark circles under her eyes that makeup had not been able to cover. Also, with her nephew acting so strangely, she knew something was amiss. Aunt Madge was too tactful to ask, but the concern was there nevertheless.

"Sit down and let me get you a cup of coffee."

"Oh, please, keep your seat, I'll get it," Brooke responded.

As she sat down with her steaming cup of coffee, she noticed the plate of pastries and fresh fruit in front of her. Not being able to stand the temptation, she helped herself to some of each. She had not eaten much for dinner the previous evening and she just now realized how hungry she was.

She asked in a hesitant voice, "Have you seen Ashley this morning?"

"No," said Madge. "As far as I know he hasn't made an appearance yet." She went on to say, "I just don't know what drives Ashley so. I don't recall ever seeing him so uptight. He seemed to be having to really make himself keep a lid on his temper. It's time that boy settled down."

Brooke knew she was hinting, but there was nothing she could contribute to the conversation. She knew that she was to blame for Ashley's emotional upheaval but not entirely, that was for sure. You had to love someone very much before they could penetrate your emotions to that extent. Desire her, yes, but love her, certainly not!

Excusing herself, she went to the den to wait for Ashley. She did not have to wait long. Promptly at eight o'clock he appeared, looking superb as usual in a casual pair of slacks and an open-necked sports shirt.

It dawned on her at that moment that she was in love with Ashley Graham. She did not know when it had happened, but it was a fact that she could no longer deny. Knowing that she would not be seeing him again after today, except perhaps on a casual basis, was practically killing her.

Looking at Brooke with a veiled expression on his face, he said crisply, "You look terrible!"

"Thanks," she said bitterly, "that's exactly what I needed to hear."

Sensing her state of mind, Ashley's expression softened as he said, "Are you ready to go?"

Refusing to meet his eyes, she said, "Yes," in a terse voice. She was not ready to forgive him his unkindness of a moment ago, nor his ungracious behavior of last evening.

It was still a mystery to her how she could have let herself fall in love with this self-assured man. Why couldn't she have fallen in love with someone who had the same interests in life? Making a comeback in her profession was still important to her.

It only took a minute to say goodbye to Madge. Ashley was obviously in a hurry, so it was not long before she found herself airborne.

There was virtually no conversation between them again as they headed back to Honolulu, due to the noise of the engines. Brooke was glad she didn't have to make polite conversation. She couldn't help but think that maybe he had changed his mind about wanting to marry her. He had not mentioned it again. Apparently he had accepted her answer and was looking forward to dropping her off at the house.

However, as they pulled up in front, Ashley said,

"I'll be back in the morning to make plans for the wedding."

She was stunned! Leaning toward her he planted a hard kiss on her parted lips before leaping out of the car to get her luggage from the trunk. He deposited it on the front steps, and came back and opened the door for her in one fluid motion. She hesitated and drew several deep breaths. Here she was thinking that he did not want her anymore. It would have been better had he changed his mind. She still could not marry him.

Anne was waiting on the steps to greet them.

She gave Brooke a quick hug and said, "What in the world were you doing sitting in the car so long?"

"Oh, just too lazy to get out in a hurry I guess," she responded lightly.

Brooke was trying hard to overcome the jolt from Ashley's statement. Her thoughts were chaotic.

Anne smiled, "You two come in and I'll fix us some fresh coffee."

"Thanks, Anne, but count me out," said Ashley, smiling. "I've neglected things at the office long enough. I'll take you up on that coffee tomorrow, okay?"

Turning to Brooke, he planted another solid kiss on her startled mouth and then sauntered down the steps to his car, acting as if everything were going his way.

Anne raised her eyebrows. "What's going on between you two?" she questioned.

Brooke's expression was grim. "Is that offer of coffee and a shoulder to cry on still available?"

"You know it is. Come on," said Anne as she put her arm through Brooke's and steered her toward the kitchen. Brooke kept silent until the coffee was through dripping in the coffee maker and Anne had brought each of them a cup to the table.

"Okay, let's have it, my friend. You look like death warmed over. Apparently you've kept everything bottled up inside long enough."

"Thanks," said Brooke emotionally, "that's the second time I've been told how bad I look. It certainly doesn't help my feelings any!"

"Hey," quickly responded Anne, "you know I didn't mean it to sound as if I was criticizing. I'm just terribly concerned about you and want you to have the very best of everything."

"Anne, Ashley asked me to marry him," said Brooke in a quivering voice.

"He did what?" yelled Anne, and then clamped her hand over her mouth when she realized she was shouting. "I'm sorry," she continued, "I didn't mean to burst your eardrums—it's just that I'm so shocked."

Smiling, Brooke said, "Well, I know the feeling, because I couldn't believe it myself. But he did ask me and meant it too. In fact, he refuses to take no for an answer."

"Do you mean to tell me you actually turned him down!" wailed Anne.

"Oh, Anne, I didn't want to, but I had to," cried Brooke. "There's a lot that's happened to me that makes it impossible for me to marry Ashley." She paused. "And besides, I'm sure he had some ulterior motive for wanting to marry me and I won't be used by him now or later."

"What makes you so sure he's not really sincere?" questioned Anne.

Shrugging her shoulders, Brooke said, "Well, you were shocked that he would ask someone like me to marry him. Your actions told me that I have absolutely nothing to offer a man like Ashley."

"That's not true," retorted Anne. "You have a lot to

offer Ashley or any other man for that matter. I just couldn't believe that he actually wants to get married. But what's important is whether you love him or not."

"Oh, yes I love him," stated Brooke, "but as I said before I can't marry him."

"You said there was something in your past that is stopping you?"

"That and the fact that I couldn't take it if he were to ever tire of me. I can't honestly believe that he will remain satisfied with one woman for long."

"Honey, I'm not so sure you should pay attention to all the gossip concerning Ashley. He's been pretty well tied down to his latest mistress, Toni Lattimer, for a good while now. A lot of that junk they print about him is simply not the truth."

"But he does have a mistress!" Brooke said bitterly, "I could never share him with anyone, ever!"

"What is your other concern? Is it tennis?" asked Anne, worry written on her face.

Brooke looked distressed, "Please, Anne, don't ask me any more questions. But, I can assure you it's not tennis. It's something that I can't talk about right now. The wound is still too raw. All I can say is that Ashley doesn't need my problems, nor I his."

By now the tears were streaming down Brooke's face and she made no attempt to stop them. Maybe a good cry was what she needed.

"To make matters worse," gulped Brooke, "Ashley's coming over tomorrow to make plans for the wedding. What am I going to do?"

Striving to show a calm she was far from feeling, Anne said, "I want you to talk to Jonathan. He knows Ashley a lot better than I do. Maybe he can shed some light on all of this. Right now," continued Anne, "I think you should go upstairs and try to sleep for a while. As soon as your brother comes home, I'll send him up to talk to you. Things have a way of working out for the best, if we just keep the faith."

"I don't know what I'd do without you," said Brooke with a waver in her voice.

"Ha!" laughed Anne. "You've come to my rescue more often than I've come to yours."

As soon as Brooke reached her room, she lay across the bed intending to blot out everything and try to sleep, but she could not do it. She dreaded the encounter with Jonathan very much. She felt that whatever light he could shed on the matter would not be to her liking.

She did not know how long she had been laying in that same position when she heard a knock on the door. "Brooke, are you awake?" questioned Jonathan softly.

Hesitating only a moment, she said, "Yes, you can come in."

Brooke was trying to put her clothes and hair back in some semblance of order when her brother walked in the door. She should have been used to his haggard appearance and the desperate look in his eyes, but every time she saw him, she became more upset.

His eyes flashed over her face. "Anne left some cool drinks on the patio table for us. I thought maybe you would like to talk by the pool. She went to the grocery store and won't be back for some time."

"That sounds great. I'll just follow you down then."

After they sipped their drinks for a moment, Brooke said rather hesitantly, "Jonathan, I've been wanting to talk to you for some time now. I know you don't really want to confide in me, but I think the time has come for you to do so."

"I don't know where you got the idea that I can't handle my own affairs," he said grimly. "Just mind your own damn business. Anyway, I thought you needed to discuss an urgent problem having to do with yourself!"

Sighing impatiently, but managing to hold on to her temper, Brooke said, "I do have a problem. But I think our problems are tied together, so please tell me why you've changed so during the last couple of weeks? You're not the same Jonathan that picked me up at the airport."

"Oh, for God's sake, don't . . ."

"Please, Jonathan," cried Brooke, "let's not fight or say things to each other we'll be sorry for later. I don't mean to sound as if I'm criticizing or deliberately trying to cause problems. But *I* know you're in some kind of trouble and it worries me."

"All right, Sis," said Jonathan in a defeated voice. "I might as well tell you the whole sordid story. It doesn't really matter now because sooner or later everyone is going to know about it anyway."

To have her inner fears confirmed was a blow to Brooke. Thinking something is wrong and knowing it are two different things. What she really wanted to do was run and not listen to anything he had to tell her. She was so tired of problems that she could scream. After all, she had more or less forced him to confide in her, but she knew she could not desert Jonathan now. He had been spoiled a long time ago and the weakness in his character was forever rearing its ugly head.

Squaring her shoulders and breathing deeply, she finally said, "Okay, let's have it."

"Well," he said bitterly, "there's not much to tell, except that I borrowed a large sum of money from the company retirement fund, and to date haven't replaced what I borrowed."

"Do you mean to tell me," cried Brooke in a shocked

voice, "that you actually took money from Ashley's company for your own personal use? No," continued Brooke, shaking her head, "I just can't believe that you were ever that desperate for money that you could ever do anything that stupid."

"Well, I assure you I was and still am," he retorted harshly.

"Oh, my God!" whispered Brooke more to herself than to Jonathan.

He chewed his lower lip. "When I borrowed the money, I fully intended to put it back immediately. But the house cost more to build than I expected and I've been involved in a few poker games that got completely out of hand." He paused and wet his lips nervously. "Also, I owed a great deal of money to a certain party that I didn't dare keep waiting. Now Anne's pregnant and if she finds out about all of this, she will probably lose the baby and that will be the end of my marriage."

"For heaven's sake, now is not the time to feel sorry for yourself," snapped Brooke. "That's your main problem—thinking about yourself before Anne or anyone else. Or maybe your main problem is that you didn't think at all! How much did you take from the fund and how have you managed to cover it up thus far?"

"It's been easy up until recently. But now I'm trying to move up a couple of notches in the company. I won't be in the finance department if I get the vice-president's job. As head of finance, I knew I could get by with it until the next audit which isn't for two or three months. But if I leave, someone will surely catch the fact that the money is missing! Believe me, Sis, I didn't mean for this to get so far out of hand."

"How in the world do you think you can become

Ashley's right-hand man when you've been stealing from his company?" asked Brooke in an exasperated voice. "I'm fully convinced you've completely taken leave of your senses, Jonathan."

"I thought I had the money last week to pay it all back. But at the last minute the deal fell through. Remember the guy at the luau? He was supposed to bring the money to me."

"More poker money?" she interrupted sarcastically.

He flushed, ignoring her question, and continued, "That's why I thought maybe if you and Ashley started dating you could intercede for me and tell him that I meant no harm. That it was just a loan I fully intended to pay back."

"Exactly how much money are we talking about? I have a little money in savings. . . ." replied Brooke.

"I borrowed fifty thousand dollars in all," said Jonathan in a flat voice.

Upon hearing this, Brooke felt a sense of frustration equal to the time when the doctor had visited her room after the accident. She had hoped that she would never have to face anything like that ever again. But here she was being faced with another problem that was just as bad, only in a different way. She was not sure at this point how much more she would be able to take. She had come to Hawaii in hopes of recovering both emotionally and physically and now she was about to be beaten down again with a crisis that was not of her own making, but one she was apparently going to have to help solve.

Fighting to keep the tears back, Brooke said with a waver in her voice which she could not quite conceal, "I don't even begin to have that much money, nor do I know anyone that does. The only way *you* can ever begin to get out of this ungodly mess is to go and talk to Ashley and," she halted in mid-sentence, looking stunned, *"does Ashley know?"*

Jonathan looked extremely uncomfortable. "I don't know." He licked his lips. "The day Ashley picked you up to go to Kauai, I let him in. Remember?" Brooke nodded. "Well, out in the hall, he told me a team of top-notch auditors was due to inspect the books. And did I have them in order?" He paused. "As you well know, I panicked." He began pacing the floor. "So I really don't know if he just thinks something is wrong or whether he actually knows . . ."

"What you have actually done is a criminal offense for which you could easily spend the rest of your life in prison. Who knows, maybe Ashley will let you continue to work until you've paid it all back," she continued in a defeated voice.

His mouth became straight and firm. "I came so close to winning the money to pay the company back with no one the wiser and then the vice-president's position would have been mine," exclaimed Jonathan harshly.

She stared at him in disbelief. "There's absolutely no way to do what you did and not pay the consequences," stated Brooke, disgust in her tone. "I can't believe that you thought you could just pay the money back and everything would come up smelling like roses. Don't you realize exactly what you've done, not only to yourself and your future, but most of all to Anne and to your child?"

He nodded, avoiding her gaze.

Taking a deep breath, she continued, "Please, just don't involve me anymore. You ought to know that my dating Ashley will make no difference whatsoever when he learns about this. Right is right and wrong is wrong. And Ashley will look at it in exactly those terms!"

By now tears were streaming down her cheeks and she made no pretense of even caring. How in the world was Jonathan ever going to get out of this mess? She could visualize him going to prison, Anne losing the baby, and herself caught right in the middle.

Then Ashley's image danced before her eyes and her blood turned to ice water. Did Ashley know what Jonathan was up to? Of course he did, she reminded herself. That was why he told her to talk to her brother before she said no to him. That was why he asked her earlier exactly how well she knew her brother. The best clue of all was when Ashley had warned Jonathan about the auditors.

Was he going to use blackmail to force her to marry him? Why did Ashley really want to marry her? Surely not just because of what Johathan did? That was too farfetched. Somehow, none of it made any sense.

"Sis, please," begged Jonathan, "don't look like that. I promise I'll take care of it. I've got another deal pending and if it doesn't work out, I'll tell Ashley myself."

Brooke shivered, wrapping her arms around her body. "I have a feeling it's already been taken out of our hands," she said in a dull voice.

Pushing back his hair in an agitated manner, Jonathan said, "I don't know what you mean."

"You will, my dear brother, you will."

Chapter Eight

$\mathcal{W}$hen Brooke came downstairs the next morning, she was exhausted. With all that she had on her mind, sleep had been impossible.

Noticing that it was still early, she hoped she would have a while to collect her thoughts before Anne and Jonathan joined her. She put the coffee on to drip and sat down to wait. But she was too restless and upset to remain still.

What she really needed was some exercise. Picking up the tennis racket always expelled much of her tension. So, without even waiting for the coffee, she ran lightly upstairs to her room and grabbed her gear and headed for her favorite spot at the back of the garage.

She had been volleying for quite some time, when she sensed she was not alone. Glancing to the side, she saw Ashley standing with his arms folded, watching her every move.

She stopped and turned to face him.

His eyes bore into her, and she could feel herself going hot all over. "What are you doing here this time of morning?" she asked hesitantly.

He raised his eyebrows mockingly. "I told you I would be here today, didn't I?" he questioned softly.

She looked at him in disgust. "I know but . . . ."

"But what?" That unnerving smile touched his mouth.

He was taunting her and she refused to rise to the bait.

Shrugging, she said, "I told you, you're wasting your time. Please, just leave me alone."

He gave a short laugh. "I think not."

She flushed, whirled around and began volleying once more. Maybe if she ignored him, he would go away. While her body responded to her actions and relaxed, her mind refused to cooperate.

She thought, listening to the thump of the tennis ball against the backdrop that she had seen times when life hardly seemed worth living. One was when the doctor came into her room at the hospital and told her there would be no more tennis and probably no children as well. She had been totally devastated. Now she was being forced into marrying a man in order to save her brother's reputation. This was the worst.

When she could no longer see through the tears, she halted her play and averted her face away from Ashley's piercing gaze. Brook felt his presence behind her. She stiffened.

His hand slid caressingly down her arm to catch her

hand and slowly turned her around to face him. Gently, his hands brushed the tears away.

"Brooke, honey, look at me," he said softly.

She shook her head.

"Brooke?"

She looked up at him, her eyes shimmering.

"What are you afraid of?" he probed, caressing the sides of her neck with his thumbs.

She trembled. His superior height made her feel small and fragile. What she really wanted to do was throw her arms around his neck and beg him to make the hurt go away.

"Where do you want to be married?" he questioned rather thickly.

His question brought her out of her reverie. She pulled away from him abruptly and moved in the direction of the patio.

He grabbed her arm and turned her around to face him. "I know about Jonathan!"

There was a tense silence.

Brooke knew her heart was going to break, it was beating so hard and fast. Then she felt her shoulders sag.

"God, I'm sorry," he muttered, rubbing his hand over his chin. "I didn't mean to tell you like that." He expelled a sigh. "I wasn't even sure that you knew what I was talking about until I saw your face."

"Please, I can't marry you," sobbed Brooke. She had to try one last time.

His mouth hardened. "If you don't marry me, I promise you that Jonathan will go to prison."

She swallowed with difficulty. She was defeated. "You leave me no choice, then," she whispered.

He made a weary gesture. "That's right. You have no choice. This is the way it will be," he said.

172

She said nothing. She knew it was true. This *was* the way it would be.

Brooke sat silently in the corner of the den chewing her lower lip. The last place she wanted to be was here, involved in the confrontation between Ashley and her brother. There was total silence in the room as she and Ashley waited for Anne and Jonathan to join them.

She dreaded what was going to happen. Her brother deserved whatever Ashley gave him but not Anne. Hopefully Ashley would take her condition into consideration and handle her with care.

Brooke knew her sister-in-law would be as shocked as she herself had been when Jonathan had told her. To have Ashley present was almost unforgivable. But there had been no choice, he had taken it out of their hands.

Had it only been a matter of hours since she had promised to marry Ashley in exchange for her brother's freedom?

It seemed like a lifetime ago.

After she had made the commitment to him, he informed her that as soon as he could get the license they would be married. Her worst fears had finally come home to rest. But she couldn't let her brother go to prison.

Much to her dismay, Ashley had insisted upon following her immediately into the house and talking to Anne and Jonathan. He wanted everything straightened out before they married.

When they entered the cool quiet of the house, Jonathan was coming down the stairs. He raised his eyebrows when he saw Ashley following her. Without wasting any time or words, Ashley had told Jonathan that he wanted to talk to him and Anne.

Jonathan's face whitened. He had said, "You know, don't you?"

Ashley nodded.

With a dejected air, Jonathan had turned and slowly went back upstairs to get Anne.

Shortly they came into the room, Anne followed by Jonathan. Their expressions were tense. Brooke, looking up at them, felt her stomach churn.

After sitting down on the couch, Anne looked first at Brooke and then at Ashley. She spread her hands in agitation. "I'd like to know what's going on. Jonathan won't tell me, so maybe you will." Her eyes were on Ashley.

Ashley didn't hesitate. "I'm sorry Anne, it's not my place to tell you anything at this point. But Jonathan *will* tell you." Although his tone was gentle, his expression was determined.

All eyes turned toward Jonathan.

If Brooke hadn't been so hurt herself, she would have felt sorry for her brother. But she hardened her heart. He deserved this.

Wetting his lips, Jonathan said haltingly, "Anne—I have something to tell . . ." His voice broke and he stopped.

"Go on," demanded Ashley, his voice edged with steel.

Anne's eyes were as big as saucers as she turned to stare at her husband.

Taking a deep breath, Jonathan plunged forth and did not pause until he told Anne the whole sordid story in detail, including his gambling, the man at the luau and his conversation with Brooke.

The only sound in the room was Anne's quiet sobbing.

After a moment, Ashley ran a hand around the back of his neck and stepped into the middle of the room. "Jonathan, here's what I propose to do." He paused. "I'll loan you the money to repay the company *and* pay off your gambling debts as well."

Brooke held her breath. Would he tell them now?

"But," Ashley continued, "you will have to pay every cent of it back. It will be deducted out of your monthly paycheck."

Jonathan looked stunned. "Do you mean to tell me that you're not going to file charges against me?" He mopped the perspiration from his forehead.

"No," Ashley replied without rancor. "Nor am I going to fire you." His mouth twisted, "In fact, I'm going to give you a shot at the vice-president's job." He paused letting what he said soak in. "In that position, I can keep an eye on you. You've been a damn good hand. I rarely give second chances so make the best of it, my friend."

Anne gasped. "You're not serious!"

A slow smile warmed his face. He then turned his eyes in Brooke's direction.

She groaned. Here it comes, he's going to tell them now!

She tried to avert her eyes, but the burning intensity of his gaze kept her from doing so. His eyes held her for a moment and then he turned back around to Anne and Jonathan. She found it difficult to breathe.

Confusion was mirrored on both their faces. Before Ashley could say anything else, Jonathan jumped up, his face still ashen, and shouted, "Good God, Ashley, don't keep me in suspense any longer." He paused, lowering his voice. "What the hell is going on? Why *aren't* you going to fire me?"

Ashley looked satisfied. "Because," he drawled, "it wouldn't look too good for my brother-in-law to be in prison, now would it?" He grinned.

Silence. Then Jonathan and Anne both started talking at once.

Brooke closed her eyes for a second, clenching and unclenching her fists. She had no idea what measures Ashley planned to take regarding the embezzlement, so the turn of events was as much of a surprise to her as it had been to her brother and sister-in-law.

She was absolutely furious at Ashley for using her in this manner. He was ruthless in obtaining what he wanted, and he wanted *her*. Jonathan was virtually getting off scott free, except for paying the money back, while she was committed to a marriage that would never be successful.

"Brooke?"

Hearing her name, she looked up to find that Ashley had crossed the room and was standing in front of her with an outstretched hand. His eyes burned into hers, causing her to catch her breath. She saw passion as well as another emotion she couldn't quite identify mirrored there. Was it understanding, perhaps?

"Honey," he said, "your family is waiting to congratulate us."

Without hesitation, she placed her slender fingers in his and he pulled her up to stand beside him. His touch seared through her thin shirt and caused her heart to melt. Was he aware of how he affected her?

Two shocks in one day were almost too much for both Jonathan and Anne. They looked washed out but undeniably happy, for themselves as well as Brooke and Ashley. Brooke played her part. She allowed them to hug and kiss her and scold her for keeping it such a secret.

Brooke was glad that Anne seemed to be all right. Thank God Ashley had followed the bad news with good news. Anne's blood pressure could have risen sky-high and caused even more trouble. She noticed the tender looks that passed between Anne and Jonathan. Seeing the worried look disappear from her brother's face almost made the sacrifice worthwhile.

And if she were perfectly honest with herself, she wanted desperately to marry Ashley, but she was afraid of the heartache it would cause her later.

"Brooke," called Anne, "let's go prepare some breakfast." She laughed. "I'm starving and I know the men are too."

"Now that's a good idea!" said Ashley, his eyes narrowing in laughter. "My stomach thinks my throat's been cut."

"Okay, you've made your point. We'll hurry," answered Brooke, smiling at him, his eyes holding her captive until finally she tore her gaze away.

When she and Anne were alone, Anne bombarded her with questions not only about what had made her change her mind about marrying Ashley but also about Ashley's lenient treatment of Jonathan as well. From now on, Ashley would be Anne's knight in shining armor.

"Come on now, you might as well confess. I'm not going to let you off the hook until you tell all, my friend," Anne's smile deepened. "Well?"

Brooke poured herself a cup of coffee and sipped the hot black liquid, stalling for time. "Let's just say Ashley made me an offer I couldn't refuse." She tried to inject the correct amount of happy emotion into her voice.

Anne grabbed the bacon out of the refrigerator. She turned and looked at Brooke sharply. "Are you really happy, honey? That's what concerns me." She hesitated. "I know there were reasons why you said you couldn't marry him." She paused as if uncertain as to how to continue. "When did you get everything straightened out? This morning?"

Brooke flashed her a brilliant smile. "He was here bright and early and we had quite a chat outside before we came into the house."

She was determined that Anne must never know the circumstances that brought about her agreement to marry Ashley. At all cost Anne must be protected from the fact that Brooke was blackmailed.

Chatting nonstop, they soon had the meal ready and the men and Anne ate with hearty appetites. Brooke picked at her food. She was not hungry. Ashley played the concerned fiancé and tried to cajole her into eating. When he teased her in this manner, she found herself responding to him like a fly to honey.

Shortly after the meal, he said his goodbyes to Anne and Jonathan and Brooke walked him to the door.

"I'll call you later, honey," he said huskily. He then leaned down and planted a firm kiss on her soft mouth. She was definitely caught in his tangled web.

The last week passed in a daze for Brooke. In two more days she would become Mrs. Ashley Graham. She could not believe she was actually going to go through with this marriage, but she was. She had no other choice.

She had been caught up in a whirlwind of wedding plans. Her sister-in-law was so full of energy that she kept Brooke running from daylight till dark. They were to be married in the backyard of Jonathan and Anne's home. At home, in Houston, it was referred to as a garden wedding.

Ashley hired a band and all the food was to be catered. All week workmen had been hanging lanterns around the yard and bringing in lawn chairs, a podium and other essential equipment that would be needed.

Brooke saw very little of Ashley. She talked to him a couple of times on the phone, but that was all. When she could escape from Anne, she went to the country club and worked out. She was getting stronger and stronger every day. Since she no longer had to practice in secret, she had cultivated a lot of friends who were avid tennis players. She played with a different person almost every time she went to the courts.

Ashley continued to ignore the fact that tennis was a real part of her life. He never mentioned it, nor did she. Her career was definitely in jeopardy due to her impending marriage.

Tonight Ashley was taking her out to dinner and unknown to him, she still planned to try to make him change his mind. There had to be another way for her brother to get out of his predicament.

Since Anne and Jonathan had successfully put the pieces of their lives back together they were delighted with the turn of events. If they thought Brooke was rather quiet and on the unhappy side, she said it was the premarital jitters.

Brooke was hoping that Ashley would choose a restaurant that was not too crowded, so they could talk. Even though she dreaded the evening ahead of her, her pulses quickened at the thought of seeing him again. The physical power he held over her was overwhelming.

Brooke had the house to herself after Jonathan and Anne had left to go out to dinner with some friends. It was quiet without Anne's constant chatter, but it was nice to have a few moments alone. While she waited, she mixed herself a Tom Collins and had only taken a couple of sips when the doorbell chimed.

Setting her drink down, she went to open the door for Ashley. At the sight of him, her heart skipped a beat. Although her smile wavered somewhat, she managed to appear calm. She didn't intend for him to ever be aware of just how attracted she was to him.

Brooke was contemplating asking him if he cared for a drink, but squelched the idea when he said, "I made our dinner reservations early so we wouldn't have to wait."

"I'm ready then, let's go," smiled Brooke.

Ashley must have read her mind because he chose a little out of the way restaurant, far away from Waikiki.

When they left the restaurant, it was dusk and the smell of flowers and ocean filled her senses. She would love to stay here forever, but she knew she couldn't. She still had the awesome task of telling Ashley that she could not go through with the marriage. If he had really and truly loved her then, maybe, there would be a chance for a union between them to work. But as things stood, Brooke knew that their marriage could never last.

Leaning her head back against the velour headrest, Brooke closed her eyes. With the cool air, the comfort of the car and the strains of music, she actually felt drowsy.

The next thing she knew the car had stopped and she felt Ashley's warm breath on her cheek.

"Hey, sleepyhead, I wondered how long it would take you to wake up," he whispered as he began to nuzzle her neck with his mouth and tongue.

Sighing, she turned to be completely encircled with his arms. She had to be close to him this one last time.

"God, honey," groaned Ashley, "if you encourage me too much, I won't be responsible for the consequences. You go to my head like potent wine."

"Please, Ashley, I . . ." But she never finished her sentence. His lips possessed hers and she felt herself drowning in his kisses. Her lips parted of their own free will at the insistence of his probing tongue. The kiss lasted what seemed like an eternity and when they finally separated, they were both breathless.

When Brooke finally got her breath back, she put her fingers against Ashley's lips and said, "You have got to listen to me. I cannot marry you. There are certain things about me you don't know."

She knew Ashley was not paying any attention to what she had said. He was kissing each one of her fingertips as they rested against his mouth.

Brooke managed to get her hand back and moved to the far side of the car. She had never felt so unhappy or frustrated in her life.

Sensing she was really upset, Ashley said quietly and gently, "Honey, forget about the past—we have all our tomorrows to learn about each other."

Then moving across the seat next to her, he began removing the tears from her face with his mouth and tongue. The intimate gesture made her weak. When all traces of tears were gone, he cradled her in his arms and said, "I'm taking you home now. Thank God, the day after tomorrow you'll be mine and mine alone."

Brooke knew that no matter what the outcome, she would become Ashley's wife. She couldn't fight him any longer. She only hoped they didn't both live to regret it.

The morning of the wedding dawned bright and clear as only days in Hawaii can. Brooke managed to steal a few quiet moments to herself and took a good look at the beautifully decorated yard. There beneath the lanterns, she lay down on the grass, closed her eyes and tried to relax. But her brain refused to remain idle. For some unknown reason, flashes of her younger years paraded through her thoughts. Her childhood had been a happy one. She wished more than ever that her parents were still alive to share this day with her.

She was frightened of the future and what lay ahead of her as Ashley's wife. Although she loved him deeply, all the hidden deceits would tarnish their marriage vows as well as their life together.

Why couldn't things have been different? Even though she still loved her brother, she couldn't lean on him any longer, if she ever really could. And to think, they had shared so much together and had had so many good times. She could still remember vividly, even now, the time Jonathan swung her in the hammock in their backyard. She kept yelling at him, "Higher, higher, brother, swing me higher." Laughing loudly, he proceeded to do just that. In his enthusiasm, he swung her way too high, flinging her out of the hammock onto the hard ground.

For a moment, she had been completely stunned and disoriented. Jonathan had run over to her and cried, "Brooke, Brooke are you hurt? Please, please say something." He had grabbed her shoulders and had shaken her trying to make her tell him she was all right. She had had the wind knocked from her and had had no broken bones. Ever since that incident, Jonathan had more or less been her protector. A closeness had developed between them from that day on.

But the pendulum was swinging. Now she was the one bearing the burden for him. She hadn't told Jonathan that Ashley had blackmailed her into marrying him. But Jonathan knew. She saw it in his eyes every time she looked at him.

Where had it all gone, the closeness she and Jonathan had shared? He didn't care anymore. He knew about Ashley, and he hadn't even said he was sorry.

The salty taste of tears brought her back to reality. She blinked them back, jumped up and brushed the debris off her clothes.

Her time alone was already at an end. The ceremony was to take place at six o'clock in the evening, followed by a short reception. There were still a few items left to attend to, and Anne was beckoning. No rest for the weary, she mused to herself.

Ashley told her on the phone he wanted to leave before dark. They were flying to Kauai to spend their honeymoon. They had a long drive to his secluded cabin nestled in the lush greenery of the island, and he didn't want to be too late arriving there. He was taking care of everything and Brooke was content to let him do so.

After those early moments to herself, the rest of the day was spent in Anne's company being pulled and pushed in every direction. Now that she was about to become Ashley's wife, she found that she was more frightened than ever before. What if she could not please him? She kept asking herself this over and over. But only time would tell. . . .

The dress she selected to be married in was simple in design. It was made of white silk and molded to Brooke's figure in all the right places. She wore nothing on her head, just brushed her hair until it shone to perfection. She carried a cluster of orchids.

She remembered very little of the actual ceremony. Brooke knew she repeated her vows loud and clear, as did Ashley. Not even Ashley's quick but passionate kiss seemed to penetrate her daze.

Now that the wedding was over, Ashley led her back down the aisle. All she could do was stare at the circle of gold with a two-carat oval diamond mounted on top that he had placed on her slender finger.

There was no turning back. She was now Mrs. Ashley Graham for better or worse. Maybe during her honeymoon she would be able to tell Ashley her secret. Guilt was ever present in her mind. In all fairness to herself, she had tried to tell him, but he had refused to listen. His words from the night before kept echoing through her mind—"We have all our tomorrows to learn about each other." She just hoped that would be true.

Upon reaching the end of the man-made aisle, they were bombarded by Anne and Jonathan and the closest of Ashley's friends. Only a select few of his friends and business associates had been invited. Due to his position, it had been inevitable. Brooke would have liked it to have been only their families in attendance but there again she had left the plans to Ashley so she had to go along with them.

When everyone had congratulated them, Brooke went inside the house to refresh her makeup and catch her breath. Ashley was waiting for her at the foot of the stairs.

Smiling at her, he said, "Are you tired?"

"No, just thirsty and maybe a little hungry. I haven't eaten anything since early this morning."

"Come on then. I'll fix you a plate and talk to you while you eat."

"Why don't you join me. Aren't you hungry?"

"Oh, yes, I'm hungry, but not for food," said Ashley huskily.

"Oh, you, you," sputtered Brooke. She could feel her face turning red. Several people were milling around inside who turned and grinned in the direction of the newlyweds.

Shortly after they finished eating, Brooke and Anne slipped up to Anne's room to change Brooke's clothes.

All the time she was changing, Anne was chattering nonstop about how happy she was for the two of them. Brooke was beginning to feel panicky on the inside. Soon she would be completely under Ashley's dominance.

When she and Anne made their way downstairs, Ashley was again waiting for her at the foot of the stairs. Jonathan passed them, insisting on loading Brooke's luggage while she said her goodbye to Anne.

There were tears in both their eyes as they hugged and kissed each other. Anne even planted a firm kiss on Ashley's grinning face.

Finally, managing to get Brooke halfway down the front steps, he laughed and said, "Girls, you two beat anything I've ever seen. We're only going to be gone two weeks, maybe three at the most."

"I know," wailed Anne, "but I'm so used to having her around. It's going to be so lonesome."

"I promise I'll spend as much time with you as I can when we get back," said Brooke.

A very impatient Ashley finally got them loaded and away from the house.

"Well, how do you feel now, Mrs. Graham?" asked Ashley, as he sped toward the airport.

"I still can't really believe it all, if you really want to know," said Brooke with a waver in her voice.

"You will, my darling, you will," responded Ashley as he leaned over and squeezed her hand. "And it will be in the most satisfying way, I promise," he finished huskily.

The rest of the journey, including the plane trip and

the long drive to Ashley's cabin, was accomplished in a companionable silence. Brooke was a bundle of nerves on the inside, but she refused to let Ashley see this. She kept forcing herself to take deep breaths and relax.

It was dark by the time Ashley pulled up in front of the small cabin nestled at the foot of a mountain. Even though it was dark, the full moon shone brightly enough so that Brooke could see the surroundings. Ashley came around and helped Brooke out of the car. She stood quietly listening to the sounds of the night while Ashley unloaded the trunk and carried their luggage inside.

When he came back out, he wordlessly swept her into his arms. Not wishing to look or even open her eyes, Brooke buried her face in his shirt. The door slammed shut when he kicked it with his foot. Brooke felt her stomach muscles tighten as he carried her straight to the bedroom where the king-size bed dominated her attention.

Her heartbeat jumped up into her throat now that the time had come to face her husband. Putting her down, he stepped to the opposite side of the room and opened the drapes. At once soft moonlight flooded the room. Walking to the window, she pressed her flaming cheek against the cool glass and listened to the waves. His steps behind her blended with the swish of the waves outside.

He turned her and gently folded her into his arms. "Oh, God, honey," he groaned. "I want you the way I want air to breathe. Abruptly, hungrily, he lowered his mouth down on hers. Her senses began to spin. The warmth of his kiss seeped into her bones. His hand began caressing her hair, only to pull her closer against his shoulder while he slowly tasted the delights of her mouth.

Brooke felt as if she were on a roller coaster that was moving much too fast. She had no control. She was scared.

"Please—Ashley," she whispered, trying to push him away.

Ashley groaned, "Please don't fight me, not now. Poison, you're just like poison in my bloodstream."

She was sinking fast into the quicksand of no return. He was pulling her under. She screamed to herself, *No, I'm not ready*. But to him she said, her eyes pleading, "Ashley, I can't. Not yet . . ."

"No!" he groaned thickly, pulling her back into his arms. "I won't let you do this to me. Don't you understand, I worship you. I want to undress you slowly, reverently, and take you down a path of pure delight."

He was the victor. She could not fight him any longer.

Brooke had no mind or will of her own as Ashley led her to the side of the bed. There he began removing her clothing, never taking his eyes off her body as he stripped one item at a time from her.

When he finished, he removed his own clothing and joined her on the bed. His hands, tongue and mouth all became busy at one time. She felt his tongue trace around the inside of her ear. Then he nibbled kisses on her mouth. There he plundered deeply. While she drowned in his kisses, his hands were busy playing with the already firm peaks of her breasts pushing against his hands. When he kissed first one breast and then the other, Brooke felt like she would die. She was on fire from head to toe. After a while, there was not one part of her body left untouched by Ashley's burning mouth.

"God, you're beautiful. The smell and touch of you

is driving me out of my mind." His voice was harsh with desire.

"Oh, Ashley darling, I want you too," whispered Brooke, "but I'm still scared. . . ."

"Don't be. I won't hurt you," he said gently. He took her hand to his mouth and kissed each finger before placing them between his knees, trapping them there.

She pulled back.

Her struggle caused Ashley to tighten his hold. Her hand burned against his flesh like a flame. He said hoarsly, "Touch me."

Like a puppet on a string, she had no will of her own. Her caress was timid as it touched the leanness of his thigh, upward to his chest, across the flatness of his stomach.

Finally, he couldn't take it any longer. And she couldn't fight him any longer.

He kissed and touched until she felt the first pain of possession. So great was her pleasure that she was lost in its intensity.

Afterward they lay with legs entwined and exhausted in an ecstasy which she never dreamed of experiencing. From the way Ashely was still holding onto her like she was a china doll, his hands gently stroking her, she knew he felt the same way.

She feel asleep in the crook of his arm, but it was not long until she was awakened by his whispered words, "Will you let me love you again?"

Brooke's answer was to turn in his arms and place her mouth on his. They loved again but this time longer and fiercer than before.

It was not until the bright sunlight flooded the room that she opened her eyes. She could not quite get her bearing for a moment and then she noticed the imprint of Ashley's head on the pillow next to hers and she smiled contentedly.

It was about that time she heard the splashing of water and knew Ashley must be in the shower.

Not stopping to think, Brooke rolled out of bed and walked across the floor to the bathroom to say good morning to him. Thinking he would be closed in behind the shower curtain, she marched right in. She stopped just inside the door. Ashley was standing under the shower rinsing off with the curtain wide open. They stared at each other. With passion darkening his eyes, he stepped out and gently pulled her into the shower with him.

Brooke's groan of loud protest was silenced by his mouth clamping down on hers. After that she didn't want to protest any longer. He began washing her body from head to toe. They giggled, nibbled, kissed and got acquainted with each other's bodies all over again.

Not even bothering to dry off, Ashley carried her back to the bed and made fiery love to her with both their bodies dripping wet. It was late afternoon before they got up, dressed and fixed themselves something to eat. His small but efficient cabin had all the comforts of home and was exactly right for two people. It already felt like home to her.

From that day on their honeymoon was idyllic. They went hiking through the lush mountain terrain around the cabin. Brooke picked wild orchids and birds of paradise and wild ginger until her heart was content. Each evening a new flower decoration adorned the table for their candlelight dinner. Ashley did most of the cooking on the outside charcoal grill, cooking steaks, chicken and hamburgers to perfection.

After sleeping late one morning, Ashley insisted that they drive to the little village of Haena to Ke'e Beach.

From there he told her the Na Pali Cliffs were visible. The afternoon was a perfect time to see them.

Also he wanted them to swim in a secluded area of Ke'e Beach. Brooke was a little apprehensive about this venture, since she had nearly drowned body surfing. Ashley realized this and he wanted her to get over her sudden fear of water.

As they drove to the coast, Brooke sat close to Ashley. Her hand rested on his thigh and was conscious of his muscles. At this moment, Brooke was perfectly content. As Ashley turned down the road leading to Haena, he said, "Now, honey, this is the last village before the Na Pali Cliffs. The village itself is at the end of the road and where the road ends, the cliffs begin."

Brooke looked around eagerly. "I can't wait to see it all." Lightly tapping his leg, she went on to say, "Can't you drive a little faster?"

Ashley laughed. "If I go any faster, Brooke my girl, we'll end up in the cliffs instead of looking at them."

She wrinkled her nose at him. She knew he was teasing her, but he made his point.

He parked the car just inside the Haena Park Area. From there, they walked down the beach where the view of the cliffs was much more impressive. Brooke stopped in her tracks. Not only was the beach beautiful and serene, but the wild and magnificent cliffs that rose above it were truly awesome.

Ashley kept his eyes glued to her face. "I told you it was something to see, didn't I?" His eyes twinkled.

She grinned. "That's an understatement!" She stood looking above her at the untouched beauty, the breeze deliciously cool on her bare arms.

Ashley, standing close, casually draped an arm around her shoulder and pointed out the great valleys and other indentations nestled within the cliffs. The cliffs rose 2,000 to 3,000 feet from the sea.

"Come on," he said, "let's walk for a while."

They strolled barefoot along the beach, the warm sand oozing between their toes. Hand in hand, they walked a while and then rested at the water's edge, allowing the cool ripples to curl about their toes.

Brooke began to kick playfully through the shallow water, enjoying the beauty of the early afternoon. She accidentally kicked a little high, not paying attention to what she was doing, and splashed Ashley with a shower of water. In mock retaliation, he kicked water over her. She turned and bolted away from him, laughing helplessly. For a few minutes they played like children, chasing one another all over the deserted beach.

Finally they fell down exhausted onto the softness of the white sand.

"You don't play fair," Brooke said, in a petulant voice. "Look at me, I'm wet all over!" She pulled at her wet clothing plastered to her skin.

Ashley grinned. "Why don't you take them off, then?" he drawled, leaning back on his elbow, watching her closely.

Her heart raced. "I will if you will," she said breathlessly.

"Oh, I will," he replied in a lazy voice, "but you go first."

She saw the passion leap into his eyes as she slowly removed her shirt and shorts leaving her clad only in the skimpy bikini she was wearing under her clothes. After casting aside her wet clothing, she sat down beside him. His eyes roamed her body as he slowly traced a finger up her arm to her earlobe. She trembled. Then he leaned over her and laid his mouth upon hers. She moaned to herself at the sweet taste of his lips. She was dizzy from its impact. His tongue, touching hers made her feel warm all over.

She slid her arm around his back drawing him closer. They were lost in a world of their own.

Suddenly, the sound of laughter nearby penetrated their heightened senses forcing them apart.

"What the hell . . . ?" demanded Ashley.

Turning, Brooke's eyes centered upon two bright-eyed Hawaiian children standing close to them, staring. Looking beyond them, she could see their parents further behind, not paying attention to their wandering offspring.

Upon encountering Ashley's harsh stare, they turned and ran.

He shrugged, his face still on the grim side. "Well, so much for the privacy I promised."

Brooke looked at his stern expression and grinned. He grinned sheepishly. Then they both burst out laughing and kept it up until their sides ached.

When he caught his breath, Ashley said, "Honey, I can't say I don't know what it feels like now to get caught with your . . ."

"Shush!" she interrupted, clamping her hand over his mouth. "Don't say it out loud. We're still *not* alone."

Ashley groaned and rolled over. His expletive caused Brooke to grimace.

The bright-eyed children were back. This time their parents were nowhere in sight.

Realizing they were fighting a losing battle, they grudgingly got to their feet and walked back along the beach to the park. Here they had a light snack of cheese and crackers, fruit and soft drinks. Ashley would not allow her to eat a lot since they were soon going for a swim.

They milled around the park area for a while, letting their food settle. Ashley went to the car and retrieved their gear.

When he returned, he grinned and said, "This time I aim to keep my promise and take you to a place where I *know* we won't be disturbed."

The section of Ke'e Beach he took her to was a paradise all its own. Very secluded, it was enclosed by lush greenery and hanging foliage. The beach was perfectly calm and uninhibiting. Brooke was not nearly as frightened of the water as she had feared. Maybe it was because Ashley was near her this time.

After spreading their blanket, Ashley pulled her beside him and together they plunged into the water. They swam as one for a while. He made sure Brooke's nervousness had passed before he allowed her to venture out on her own.

During the remainder of the afternoon they swam and played in the water until they were exhausted. Finally dragging their tired bodies to the blanket, they fell onto it. After resting until her breathing was back to normal, Brooke turned to Ashley and said shyly, "I've had such a good time this afternoon. I hate to see it end."

Ashley leaned over and gently pushed her hair away from her face in a caressing motion. "Oh, honey," he said huskily, "I promise you that our time of sharing is just beginning."

"I hope so, oh, I hope so," she whispered. But inside she screamed, my darling, if you only knew the deceit I'm carrying around with me. . . . I'm scared, scared of the future.

She must have whimpered aloud, because a concerned look flashed across his face. He stared at her intently, watching the early evening twilight dance over her face capturing her moment of torment.

"What's the matter?" he questioned gently. "Are you hurt someplace?"

She smiled up at him tremulously. "No, everything's fine. I guess I'm a little sore from so much swimming," she lied.

"Brooke—Brooke," he shuddered, "do you have any idea how beautiful you are and how much I—" He broke off.

"I know," she whispered, sharing his agony. She touched his cheek gently, and he turned his lips into her palm.

"And I can't or won't deny myself your sweetness any longer," he said, his voice unsteady.

She looked up at him hesitantly. The evening light cast a shadow over his face. "Here . . . ?"

"Yes, here," he ground out.

"Are you sure?"

"Shhh, you talk too much."

What started out to be a gentle sweet touch soon turned into one of fiery passion as he molded her supple body against his lean strength. She could feel his passion and knew she was past the point of no return. Feeling the consent of her body, Ashley proceeded to slowly remove her brief garments, followed by his own. There on the sand two naked bodies were joined as one as the darkness enveloped them.

As their time together slowly came to an end, the only cloud in her silver lining was the fact that no words of love had passed between them. She did love Ashley with all her heart and would continue to do so no matter what. But the words, I love you, had never been spoken. She almost told him on many occasions that she loved him but the guilt buried deep within kept her from doing so. She hated hiding anything from Ashley, or anybody else for that matter. She had always been an open and affectionate person and disliked any type of deceit.

She shuddered to think what would happen to her newfound happiness if she told Ashley the truth now. If only he loved her, that would supply all the courage she needed. Brooke knew beyond a shadow of a doubt that she could make Ashley happy, children or no children, if he would be willing to let her do so.

The only other mark on her bright horizon was that Ashley had not mentioned the fact that she was playing tennis. Brooke was sure now that they were married, that Ashley expected her to forget about tennis. She knew she would probably never return to the circuit, but she wanted to prove that she could at least hold her own in a few professional matches. Sooner or later, she and Ashley would have to settle this contention between them.

Trying to push these unhappy thoughts aside, she concentrated on getting dressed. This was their last full day together and Ashley was taking her snorkeling this morning and to Waimea Canyon this afternoon.

They had both been a little quiet and pensive since yesterday morning. Ashley was enjoying their times together as much as she. He no longer looked tired and was full of vigor and vitality. He never seemed to run down, and he, too, hated to see it all come to an end. No matter what the future held for them, she would never forget their time here.

"Hey, honey, are you ready?" called Ashley as he came inside after getting their gear together.

"I'm coming, just one minute." Hurriedly she fastened the silky strands of her hair on top of her head. Slipping into her tongs, she ran down the stairs.

Grabbing and kissing her quickly, Ashley said, "Let's go!"

He had been promising to take her snorkeling since the first day of their honeymoon, but they were just now getting around to it. Ashley told her that if a person can kick his feet, he can snorkel. All the equipment she would need was a snorkel to breathe through and a pair of fins.

The waters of Brennecke's Beach Bay were calm and peaceful and relatively shallow, which made it a perfect place for snorkeling. They had the whole area to themselves this early in the morning.

Ashley showed her how the snorkel fit on her face and then helped her put her feet in the fins and they were ready to go.

It was an exciting world for Brooke to witness while leisurely floating five to twenty feet above the ocean floor. Ashley held her hand when possible and led her to the beautiful coral structures where small octopus and exotic coral creatures often nestled. There were literally thousands of brilliant fish that seemed to be unaware of their presence.

As soon as Ashley felt she had been down long enough, he motioned for her to follow him. When they surfaced, her eyes were shining. "Oh, Ashley, that was beautiful. I can't tell you how much I enjoyed it," she finished breathlessly.

Ashley gave a short laugh. "This will just be your first of many times. There are a million places on every island suitable for snorkeling."

Upon returning to the cabin, they changed their

clothes, grabbed sandwiches and set out for Waimea Canyon. It didn't take long to reach the canyon by car and Brooke was enthralled with the sights along the way. They took Route 55, the Kokee Road, to the deep gorge that cut into the Kokee Plateau.

Upon reaching the lookout site, Brooke had never encountered such beauty. The crisp invigorating mountain air was unbelievable. It resembled the Grand Canyon in size and character, but with the added attraction of the lush vegetation of mossy greens and blues. These were complemented by the reds and browns of the exposed volcanic rocks. Clouds were hovering just about the rim, calling further attention to its vastness. Ashley insisted they move onto a higher elevation of 4,000 feet to Kalalau Lookout. From there they could see the green-carpeted Kalalau Valley with the sparkling blue sea at its mouth.

By the time they began their descent, it was late in the afternoon. After all the exploring and looking, Brooke was exhausted. But it was a contented and pleasant fatigue.

Ashley was quick to sense her moods and to react to them. She was always next to him, she belonged to him and he wanted everyone to be aware of it.

As they drove up to the cabin, it was dusk. It dawned on Brooke once again that this would be their last night here. She should have been looking forward to leaving here and creating a real home for Ashley but for some reason she was afraid something was going to happen to break the slender thread of happiness that bound them together. She was not looking forward to rejoining the real world.

Ashley grilled fish on the outside pit and they drank

champagne to celebrate. Brooke was beginning to feel very lightheaded when Ashley insisted they call it a night and go to bed.

Reaching their room Ashley opened the drapes to let the moonlight shine upon them as he began to kiss Brooke slowly and tenderly. He leisurely began to unbutton her knit shirt and when that was done, he flung it to the floor. Soon, his hands were roaming freely over the burgeoning fullness of her breasts. He nestled, caressed and bit them until she was moaning from the sensations he was arousing deep within her. She found her hands moving up to grasp his shoulders and then up around his neck pulling his mouth onto hers. His tongue intertwined with hers and the kiss was full of sweetness, longing, hunger and desire. She realized again just how much she loved this big man in her arms.

By now they had migrated to the bed and she lay with half closed eyes while he began removing his clothing with deliberate slowness. When he finished, she could not take her eyes off his lean but powerful frame. When he rejoined her, it only took him a minute to remove the rest of her clothing.

During their numerous times of making love, Ashley had taught Brooke how to please him just as he pleased her. He was trembling as her hands roamed his body and he began kissing her with an intensity never present before. His lips could not seem to get enough of her sweet tasting mouth or her full and taut breasts. There was a deep moving urgency in his lovemaking tonight, as if he were desperate for her. She clung to him with the same driving need and when he rolled onto her, she met his burning desire with a force of her own and they scaled the heights together.

Afterward, Brooke lay satisfied and exhausted in the close circle of her husband's arms. The last thought that flashed through her mind before she drifted off to sleep, was that tomorrow they would be going back to civilization. And then what?

Chapter Nine

One month later, Brooke was still in a state of marital bliss. From their honeymoon, they returned to Ashley's apartment in Honolulu and things settled down to a routine. While Ashley was gone, she practiced at least an hour every day at the country club. In the late afternoon, when Ashley arrived home from work, they would take long walks along the beach and take a swim if the mood hit them. Evenings were spent listening to music quietly in the den. Occasionally they played a game of cards. Brooke learned that her husband could be very good company; even their silence was companionable.

Still underlying all the comradery they shared was a constant awareness they had of each other. It seemed as if the atmosphere became too intimate. Their nights were filled with long hours of lovemaking. Ashley knew all the hidden delights of Brooke's body and made no secret day or night of his desire for her.

They had only quarreled once since returning home. Ashley had stopped by the club early one afternoon to meet a man concerning his sugar company. It was while he and his companion were enjoying a drink that he noticed Brooke and a young man playing tennis. Under the circumstances, Brooke thought he handled himself well. He was furious with her for playing tennis and at the same time jealous of the laughing young man at her side.

Brooke knew he was tempted to forbid her to continue her workout but he refrained from doing so. However, she was positive she had not heard the last of this.

Their first quarrel, if anything, brought them closer together. It was during these companionable times spent together that they talked about their pasts. Although it was Brooke who did most of the talking about herself, Ashley was interested in learning everything about her, including the details of her car accident. When she finished relating the facts, his concern was evident in the tightening of his jaw.

They entertained only when Ashley felt he had to do so. Her cooking skills had improved since her marriage and she enjoyed entertaining his friends in a grand style. Ashley, however, resented these intrusions upon their privacy. He did not like sharing her with anyone, even his friends. Just this morning he had said to her, with a gleam in his eye, that if he had his way he would lock her in his heart and throw the key away.

Those words were the closest Ashley had ever come to telling her that he loved her. Brooke longed to hear those words from him, but she kept reminding herself that the fact that he acted as if he loved her was more important than the words. Many times during their passionate lovemaking, she had come so close to telling him she loved him, but something always kept her from doing so.

Nevertheless, Ashley's statement had brought a special glow to her heart and with more energy than usual, she was getting the house in order so that she could meet Anne at the country club for lunch.

Since their return, she had been redecorating Ashley's apartment. He had given her permission to change it any way she desired. Anne was volunteering her help for which Brooke was glad since she had never undertaken a job of this type before and had been a little leery about her talents.

The apartment was already lovely, but was a little too masculine. It was one of the high-rise apartment buildings in downtown Honolulu with a breathtaking view. The only area in the apartment she was leaving unchanged was the indoor swimming pool and the surrounding area. Trees and flowers had been planted around it which made them feel like they were swimming at the beach except the water was unsalted.

During the short period of her marriage, the memories of this pool were vivid in Brooke's mind. Many times they had swum nude in it only to end up in the bed exploring each other's bodies until they were both exhausted.

Anne had enjoyed helping her with the decorating and Brooke had certainly needed her help. Today they were celebrating a job well done. The rooms in the apartment all had an airy lived-in look now without the large heavy furniture and oppressive drapes. Brass urns with plants were sitting in various places with mini-blinds and woven wood shades replacing the drapes, letting the sunshine fill the rooms. New carpets had also been added. Ashley was pleased with her efforts and that made Brooke even more proud of what she had accomplished.

It was now one o'clock and she was due to meet Anne in about an hour. Having finished watering the plants, she was on her way upstairs to shower and change her clothes when the peal of the doorbell stopped her.

She wondered who it could be. Lano, Ashley's handyman, butler and valet all wrapped into one, was out doing some errands for him, so Brooke made her way back downstairs to answer the door.

Opening it, she was puzzled to see an elegant young woman standing on the very top step. Before Brooke could say a word, the woman passed swiftly and rudely by her into the entry hall.

"Are you Brooke, my dear?" she asked sweetly.

"Yes, I am, and who might you be?" questioned Brooke coolly.

"My name is Toni Lattimer."

Brooke frowned. She knew she had heard that name but at the moment she could not recall where.

"Miss Lattimer, I—"

"He belongs to me!" the woman announced with a slight tremor to her firm, feminine voice. "No matter whom he's had in the past, he's always come back to me."

With these words she marched herself into the den as if she owned the place and subsided into one of the comfortable chairs. She crossed her shapely legs and waited for Brooke to follow.

Brooke could hardly put one foot before the other. She was shaking all over, partly as a reaction to the woman's words and partly from sheer anger. It had finally dawned on her who this Lattimer woman was.

She remembered her sister-in-law casually mentioning the name as Ashley's latest but longest association. At the time, it had not meant much to her, but now . . .

Toni was in the process of taking a cigarette out of her purse with her long, carefully manicured hands. It gave Brooke a chance to study her and she was not at all pleased by what she saw. Toni Lattimer was a tall shapely redhead with beautiful skin and eyes. But Brooke could see immediately upon looking closely that there was nothing truly soft or feminine about her, unless it was her voice. She appeared to be cold and calculating and dangerous.

Striving for control, Brooke ground out furiously, "How dare you come into my house and say these things to me!"

In an unperturbed voice, Toni purred, "I dare, because what I just said happens to be the truth."

Brooke compressed her lips, "I don't believe you," she stated flatly.

"You have no idea why Ashley married you, do you?" Toni asked sarcastically.

She would have liked to shout at this vile creature that Ashley married her because he loved her, but she knew she couldn't say it. Ashley didn't love her; he just desired her.

Seeing the apparent confusion and uncertainty on Brooke's face was all Toni needed. "I'll tell you exactly why he married you!"

Brooke rose abruptly to her feet. "I don't intend to sit here and listen to anything else you have to say! You are unwelcome in this house!" She felt her legs tremble beneath her. She had every intention of showing her unwanted guest to the door.

"Ha! You'll listen all right, because *you* do not know

why he married you and it's eating you up on the inside."

Brooke knew what she said was the truth even though it killed her to admit it even to herself.

"All right," hissed Brooke, "say what you have to say. It won't do you any good though because he married me, and I'll never let him go!"

"Oh, yes you will!" declared Toni.

Brooke was stunned by the audacity of this woman. Evidently nothing she could say would penetrate her ego. The sooner she heard what Toni had to say, the quicker she could get rid of her. Apparently she was not going to leave until she had her say.

"Ashley married you for one reason and one reason only. That was because his grandfather wouldn't turn over complete control of the sugar company and all his other assets until Ashley settled down and married and had a child. Ashley really loves me, you know, and would have married *me* except Eli didn't think I was good enough for his precious grandson!" she lashed out bitterly.

"But make no mistake," she continued, "he'll soon tire of you, and when he does, I'll be waiting to take him back! He'll find a way to get around the old man yet. He always does. As soon as you have a brat, he'll drop you, just wait and see!"

Brooke fought back the hot tears that stung her eyelids, and tried to pull herself together. She tried to assimilate the shattering knowledge of why Ashley had ramrodded her into marriage. But the first thing she had to do was get rid of this woman. She refused to break down completely in front of her.

There was a look of triumph on Toni's face as she rose to let herself out. She had scored and she knew it.

"Don't worry, darling, I'm sure it won't be necessary for us to meet again. Goodbye."

Brooke heard the door close quietly as the world fell apart. The pain in her chest was so intense she was not sure she would be able to bear it. She hurt too much to cry. Brooke was not even aware of how long she had been sitting there until the shrill ring of the phone cut into her thoughts.

As if in a trance, she went to answer it. "Hello," she said hesitantly.

"Brooke, is that you?" anxiously questioned her sister-in-law. "Why didn't you meet me as planned? Is something wrong?"

"Please, Anne," stammered Brooke. "I just forgot, that's all."

"You forgot! I don't believe that! Something's wrong. I can tell by the tone of your voice. I'm coming right over."

"No, no, don't do that!" cried Brooke. Striving to calm herself, she went on to say, "Everything's fine, really it is. The truth is that I don't feel well. I woke up with a terrible headache this morning and I haven't been able to shake it. I'm going to take a couple of aspirins and lie down for a while. I'll call you later."

"Okay, if you're sure that's all it is," Anne said anxiously.

"I promise that's all it is. I'll talk to you in a little while."

After hanging up the phone, Brooke knew she would never be able to rest. Her head was throbbing, so she hadn't told Anne a story after all. What she felt like doing now was crawling off by herself to nurse her wounds. She knew that her marriage to Ashley was over before it had really begun. "Marry in haste, repent at leisure," kept running through her mind as she paced back and forth until she felt she would go crazy.

Maybe if she got out of the apartment for a while, she would be able to think more clearly. Taking time to swallow a couple of aspirins, she grabbed her purse and sunglasses and headed out the door.

Upon their return to Honolulu, Ashley had bought her a small sports car to drive. She did not use it a lot except to go to and from the tennis court, but right now she was thankful she had it. She certainly did not want Lano to have to drive her around in the Cadillac.

Letting the wind blow her hair free, she drove, not paying any attention to where she was going. She obeyed all the traffic signals and speed limit signs, but she was oblivious to anything else at this point.

Brooke was hopelessly disillusioned with herself, her life and most of all, her marriage. She was extremely hurt and angry at Ashley for being deceitful about his reason for marrying her. Although he had never actually said he loved her, she had nevertheless hoped that he really did. She had convinced herself that hearing the words was not important. She had only been kidding herself.

The fact that she was not to have a child loomed larger and larger. Brooke was completely and utterly shattered that Ashley had only married her to please his grandfather and to sire a child. The idea that he would even attempt to use her like that was appalling!

But one question kept popping in and out of her thoughts. Why wasn't she pregnant? They told her she would never play tennis again, but she did. Since she had recovered the full use of her limbs, then why couldn't she also have a baby?

Yet the weeks passed and she was no different than before. . . .

By the time she returned home, it was quite late, past time for Ashley to be home. But when she turned into the drive, she noticed his Cadillac was not in the garage. She was glad. She didn't know what she was going to say to him. She did know, however, that she must leave him. She could not bear to let him touch her again after learning his reason for marrying her. Her pride would not let her remain just an outlet for his lust. There had to be much more for her. Now that she knew the truth, her heart would wither up and die like a garden with no rain if she stayed with him.

When she walked inside, Lano informed her that Ashley had called and said he would be late coming home and for her not to hold dinner for him. Being too tired to care, Brooke made her way to their room and took off her clothes and put on a long terrycloth robe. By now she was completely numb. She knew that she should eat something, but the thought of food made her stomach upset.

Gazing at the clock on the bedside table, she noticed that it was after eight o'clock. She had been lying in a daze for over two hours. Forcing herself to get up, she went to the bathroom, brushed her teeth and mechanically discarded her robe for a shorter gown.

Not even bothering to remove her makeup, she crawled between the sheets hoping to be sound asleep before Ashley came home. Sleep escaped her as she knew it would.

Where was Ashley? This is the first time he had been late coming home since their marriage. Could her visitor of this afternoon be the cause of him being late? She knew she should not be punishing herself this way but there was no relief to her torturous thoughts.

She heard him when he very gently opened their

bedroom door, although she pretended to be sound asleep. Brooke remained perfectly still, hardly daring to breathe.

Not hearing another sound for a moment, she felt her ruse had worked. Then the next instant the bedside lamp was switched on and her eyes flew open as Ashley lowered his heavy form beside her on the bed.

He leaned forward. "I had a feeling you were awake. Why are you in bed so early? Are you sick?"

Her nerves were on edge as she stared up into Ashley's tired face, taking in his lean jaw with the shadow of a beard, his dark hair flecked with gray at the temples and the lingering smell of his cologne.

Brooke was so acutely aware of the sensual masculinity radiating from his body that she felt her senses begin to stir in the way she knew so well. What she wanted to do was throw herself into his arms and beg him to tell her that what Toni had said was a lie, but she knew she could never do that.

"Come on, honey," he continued, "tell me what's wrong. You look like you've been crying." While he was speaking softly to her, his hand was caressing her arm very gently.

"Don't you dare touch me ever again," she wept, drawing as far back away from him as she could.

She closed her eyes to the shocked look and the pain that fleetingly crossed his face before he exclaimed rather violently, "What the hell's the matter with you?"

"I want a divorce."

"Brooke, please," pleaded Ashley, "tell me what this is all about. I'm trying hard to hold on to my temper to get to the bottom of this. But, by God, you're not making it very easy!"

Getting up from the bed, he began removing his coat

and tie and commenced pacing back and forth, rubbing his neck, to partially unclench his tight nerves. He was holding himself under rigid control.

Brooke's throat was so tight she felt she couldn't utter another word, but she knew Ashley would not rest until he had the whole truth. So plunging in head first, she said with bitterness in her voice, "Toni Lattimer came to see me today."

She watched closely to see his reaction. He stopped his pacing and stared at her with disbelief mirrored on his face.

"What!" he shouted.

"I *said* Toni Lattimer came to see me and took it upon herself to enlighten me as to why you married me."

Ashley's eyes narrowed. "And you believed her?" he asked with a deadly quietness in his voice.

"I . . ."

"You believed her all right," he stated harshly, "or else we wouldn't be having this discussion now, would we?"

"I—I guess not," she said, heaving a sigh.

"What exactly did she tell you, if you don't mind my asking?" he questioned sarcastically.

Stifling a sob, Brooke haltingly told him the gist of the conversation that had taken place between her and Toni. The whole time she was talking his expression kept getting more and more grim.

When she finished, his face mirrored frustration as well as despair.

Ashley turned away. "Where do we go from here?" he questioned, his voice weary.

"I've already told you what I want," she whispered.

"Well, you damn well can't have it!"

"Are you denying what Toni told me?" She held her

breath as she waited for his answer. If only he would deny it, everything would be all right. Just thinking about leaving him was tearing her to pieces.

"I'm not admitting or denying anything at this point. What would be the use anyway?" he said shrugging. "You have already condemned me without a hearing—you believed her without even giving me a chance to tell my side."

"I'm giving you a chance now."

"Well, I'm sorry, my dear, but it's a little too late. However, I do want to make one thing clear. There will be *no* divorce or separation now or ever. You are my wife and will remain so in every sense of the word. Is that clear?"

"I hate you, Ashley Graham, and you'll never lay another hand on me again, I promise!" cried Brooke.

"I could prove to you how very wrong you are my dear, but what I want in my arms right now is a warm-blooded woman, not some spoiled overwrought child!"

With those words, he stalked out of their room. She heard the car leave and was still awake when it returned at six o'clock the next morning. Brooke had never known such utter despair and sorrow as she felt that moment, knowing she had driven her husband into another woman's arms.

Chapter Ten

$\mathcal{D}$uring the next few weeks Brooke saw very little of Ashley. When they were forced to be in each other's company, the air was charged with tension.

It was totally opposite from the warm companionship they had recently shared; Brooke was finding it almost unbearable. The only time he was even close to being the Ashley she had known was at night when they were in bed. There he worshipped her body as ever before. He could not seem to leave her alone. If he were not reaching for her to make love off and on during the night, he was nuzzling up to her. Then, the next morning, he was polite but unapproachable. Brooke hated herself for letting him use her body like that but when he touched her, she was lost.

She had tried on several occasions to bring up again the subject of their quarrel to try and partially bridge the gap between them, but he refused to talk about it. Brooke had ceased to believe that he would ever forgive her for not giving him a chance to tell his side. His hostility was about to get the best of her. Her heart was breaking under the strain.

Her sister-in-law knew that something was bothering her and kept insisting that Brooke confide in her. But she was loath to do so. Anne was so obviously pregnant now, and Brooke felt it would not be the best thing for her health to be burdened down with someone else's marital problems. So she held all the pain and disillusionment inside of her, although she was not fooling Anne, or anyone else for that matter. Brooke was beginning to lose the weight that she had gained after coming to Hawaii and the circles under her eyes were returning.

If it were not for Anne and Jonathan, she did not know what she would do. Most of the time during the day was spent at their house and at the tennis club. She helped Anne get ready for the baby even though she had a few months to go.

Brooke felt best when she was pounding the ball against the hard surface of a court. She had improved so much that the country club was eager to include her in the next professional tennis match. To date, she had not given them an answer.

Today, as usual, she made plans to practice and then spend the remainder of the day with Anne.

She and Ashley had finished their breakfast, the conversation between them was impersonal and stilted. As he grabbed his briefcase and walked out the door, Ashley had informed her he would be gone to the mainland for about a week.

She had barely been able to hold the tears back until he was gone. For the past thirty minutes, she had been crying for what had been and what was never to be again.

It had been impossible for her to look Ashley in the eye this morning and be civil to him. It had been worse than usual because of her wantonness of last night. She had responded to Ashley as she had on their honeymoon, totally and without reservation. He had deliberately set out to make her respond to him in such a way. It was as if he were punishing the both of them by using their bodies. She was sore all over from being in his demanding arms. Just thinking about it now made her blush in shame.

With some effort, she pulled herself together enough to get dressed. She knew Anne was expecting her and would be calling to check on her if she did not show up soon. She hastily put on a pair of shorts, a matching shirt and her tennis socks and shoes. Grabbing her glasses and purse, she was ready to go.

All the time she played tennis, she cried. With no makeup to hide the stain of her tears, Anne was more than a little concerned about Brooke's appearance when she arrived later that morning. When Brooke sat down at the table to drink her coffee, the concerned look on Anne's face made her want to cry all over again. Absolutely everything made her cry these days. She knew that emotionally she had just about had it, something had to give soon or her heart would bear the brunt of it. She needed to go to the doctor since she had neglected her checkups since the wedding, even after promising Anne.

Seeing the tears glistening in her eyes, Anne asked, "Have you and Ashley been at it again?"

"No," gulped Brooke, "no more than usual. We're barely civil to each other, which isn't anything new as you well know."

"Brooke, I wish you would tell me what's going on. I know it's something you feel you shouldn't talk about with someone other than Ashley, but I think the time has come when you need to let it all out. You can't keep pain bottled up forever. It will soon explode and do irreparable damage."

"I know," whispered Brooke, "and I've just about reached that point."

"The more reason why you should talk about it."

"Oh, Anne, it seems as if I'm always burdening you with my troubles. I used you as a sounding board before Ashley and I married and here I am about to do it again."

"So what," shrugged Anne. "You'd do the same for me, wouldn't you?"

"Of course, you know I would but . . ."

"Well, my friend, I'm listening, so start talking."

Brooke began by telling her about her encounter with Toni Lattimer and repeated what she had said about why Ashley actually married her.

"Oh," interrupted Anne, "surely you didn't believe what she told you?"

Brooke moved her shoulders in a helpless gesture. "I did at the time, but now, I'm not so sure. However, the damage between Ashley and myself has already been done. He was simply livid with me because I found him guilty without giving him a chance to explain. Then when I did ask him if what she said was the truth, all hell broke loose."

"I can well imagine," said Anne, more to herself than to Brooke. "Well, go on," sighed Anne, "let's have the rest of it."

Brooke had actually saved the worst part for last. She hated talking about her health. However, she knew she had no choice. Anne was impatiently waiting with that determined look on her face for her to continue.

Brooke took a deep breath. "When I rammed into

that concrete embankment, I not only ended my tennis career, but I received various internal injuries as well. Due to the severity of the damage, the doctor advised me that if I married, I should *not* try to have any children. The worst part is that Ashley doesn't know."

The last statement fell into the deadly silence of the room.

"Oh, Brooke," cried Anne, when she finally found her voice, "I'm so sorry!"

"So now you see, Anne, how deceit has torn us apart. I can never give Ashley the child he wants to please his grandfather and he can never give me his total love and devotion. Now if that's not a mess, I don't know what is!"

"It's a mess all right, but not a total loss—yet. I know Ashley cares deeply for you," Anne continued gently. "He's a hard one to understand, but with time I know he'll mellow. Where there's a will there's a way, and I know you love him enough to find the way. You must concentrate on saving your marriage."

"You're right of course," confessed Brooke. "I have no choice—I need him to survive, but until I can be assured of Ashley's love, if ever, I can't afford to give up my chance to play professionally again. There again is another problem—Ashley is against my playing tennis one hundred percent. He's concerned about my health. Can you imagine how he's going to react to this bombshell?"

Trying to relieve the tension and depression somewhat, Anne said as cheerfully as possible, "Right now, I want you to get in your little car and go home, grab a dress or two, and whatever else you may need and come right back here."

"Oh, I can't do that," began Brooke. "I . . ."

"Oh, yes you can! With Ashley gone there's no

reason for you to stay home alone, especially feeling the way you do now. You don't need to be by yourself! Anyway, tomorrow night we're having a small dinner party and it will do you good to get dressed up and be around other people. And I need your help to get ready for it."

"I'm sorry, but I just can't," cried Brooke. "There's no way I want to be involved in any type of party. Surely you can understand that!"

Anne shook her head. "No, I don't understand that! It's only a few of our closest friends. You already know most of them. It will do you good. So please don't argue, okay?"

"Okay," said Brooke. "You win for now, but we'll see . . ."

Anne smiled. "Exactly how long is Ashley going to be away this time?" she questioned as Brooke was getting ready to go back home to get her things.

Shrugging, Brooke replied, "About a week, at least that's what he said! Our communication is practically nonexistent," except in bed, she finished bitterly to herself. But that was a problem that she could not bring herself to discuss, even with Anne.

Staying with Anne and Jonathan turned out to be very good therapy indeed. Even though Jonathan sensed that something was wrong, he made no mention of it. He just made her feel welcome and loved. The only time he came close to admitting his concern for her was when he inquired if she had been to see her doctor lately.

Brooke knew that as soon as she returned home she needed to make an appointment. But if the truth be known, she knew he would be angry when he saw how emotionally down she was and would insist on telling Ashley. She would have to prevent that at all costs.

When Ashley found out, it would be from her and no one else.

Anne was true to her word and put Brooke to work getting ready for the dinner party. Even though she was listless, Brooke put what energy she could muster into arranging flowers and helping Anne prepare the food. Although Anne had daily help if she wanted it, she preferred to do her own preparation for her parties.

The night of the party, Brooke felt that she simply could not get herself together to go downstairs. She knew Anne was counting on her and would be hurt if she didn't at least make an appearance.

Sighing, she got up from the dressing table and walked across the room to the closet to put on one of the two dresses she grabbed on the run yesterday.

As she was stepping into a knit sundress, she was overwhelmed by how lonely she was without Ashley. She would sorely miss his warm hard body next to hers and probably would not sleep at all as a result. Although he traveled a lot during the week from island to island, checking on his various investments, he was always home at night—at times very late, but home nevertheless.

This trip to the mainland upset Brooke greatly because she was afraid he might have taken Toni with him. There was no doubt in her mind that she was still trying to get Ashley back and was just waiting and biding her time.

She told Anne that tomorrow she needed to return home. She had left a note for Lano, telling him where she was but she wanted to be home just in case Ashley tried to call her. Also, the maid was due to clean the apartment and she wanted to be there when she arrived.

Forcing herself to finish dressing, Brooke turned and

took one last look in the mirror. None of her inner turmoil was showing. She wore more makeup than usual to cover the dark circles under her eyes and hide the pallor of her skin. The white sundress did wonders for the light tan that was now so much a part of her. Her hair was getting long and was much lighter due to the sun. She had it pulled back away from her face with colored combs.

Upon arriving downstairs, she was met by her brother and introduced to the couples present whom she did not know. She tried hard to be pleasant and get through the evening. Brooke knew that Anne meant well, but she was sorry she had let her ramrod her into attending this dinner party. She was miserable.

When Jonathan escorted her to the last group, standing in a circle, she found herself staring into the face of Cody Roberts, her ex-fiancé. She was so astonished that she practically shouted, "Cody! What in the world are you doing here?"

"Hello, Brooke, how are you?" responded Cody in his mild mannered voice, completely ignoring her rather tactless question.

"I'm fine, but, but, how did you . . ."

"Please excuse us for a moment," laughed Cody. "I think Brooke needs a drink to recover from shock." Casually guiding her arm, he led her away from the main stream of the party, into a relatively quiet corner. "Now for the drink I promised you. Still a Tom Collins?"

"Yes, that will be fine," murmured Brooke. What was Cody doing in Hawaii? Did he know she was married? Surely he had not come all this way just to see her. These questions and more kept buzzing through her head as she waited for his return.

Watching him make his way back toward her with

drinks in hand, she noticed he had not changed at all. He was the same solid, stoic Cody. He couldn't compare to Ashley. Of course, it had been a few months since she had last seen him, but so much had happened to change her life that somehow she expected Cody to be different too.

"Have you recovered now?" he inquired, smiling as he handed her a drink.

"I'm okay. It was just that you were the last person I expected to see at my brother and sister-in-law's."

"You could say you're glad to see me," he said quietly.

"Of course I'm glad to see you," assured Brooke. But not in the way you mean, she said to herself.

"When did you get married?"

"Oh, about two months ago."

"Rather sudden, wasn't it?"

"Not really."

"Oh, Brooke, my darling, you are so easy to read," laughed Cody. "There's no reason for you to get such a stiff upper lip. I came to visit some friends of mine who recently moved here. It certainly crossed my mind that I might see you, but I didn't set out deliberately to plan this meeting."

Brooke felt herself relax. Smiling she said, "I'm sorry, I didn't mean to appear so touchy. I'm really glad to see you." She found she meant it, too.

"Good," grinned Cody warmly. "Will you not turn cold on me again if I ask you a question?"

"What is it?" she asked hesitantly.

"Are you happily married? From what I've observed, I would presume not."

Averting her eyes, Brooke snapped, "Well, you presumed too much. I'd really rather not talk about it

220

though, if you don't mind. My husband happens to be out of town for a few days, that's all." She knew he was expecting her to say more but she was going to disappoint him. She certainly did not intend to share any of her marital problems with him!

Seeing that he could not persuade her to say anything else, he changed the subject and began telling her about some of their mutual friends in Houston.

After that, the evening passed rather pleasantly. She enjoyed Cody's undemanding company and revelled in the news concerning their friends. They discussed her roommate, whom it turned out Cody was dating quite often.

Brooke felt a twinge of guilt that she had not written to Cindy since coming to Oahu. She did not even know Brooke was married.

Before Cody and his friends left, he persuaded Brooke to have lunch with him the next day and show him some of the sights. She felt only a slight quiver of guilt as she accepted the invitation, but she was lonely and being with Cody gave her something to do other than brood about her errant husband.

Brooke knew that Jonathan and Anne did not exactly agree with her seeing Cody. They felt Ashley would not approve. But for once she didn't care what they thought.

So the morning after the party she went back home and around one o'clock Cody picked her up. From then on she spent a lot of time with her ex-fiancé. He was so unlike Ashley that she could relax and be completely herself in his presence. He was turning into a real friend.

It was during Cody's visit that Brooke played in the professional tennis tournament at the Waialae Country

Club. She had definitely decided not to participate but after a cancelation by one of the invited professionals she let Cody talk her into it.

Brooke had told him about her hours of working out, the exercises she had done to get her body back in shape and the practice games in which she participated. All she needed was a little encouragement. She wanted to prove to herself that she could again compete in a strenuous match as well as prove the doctors wrong once and for all.

She refused to let Ashley's disapproval daunt her.

Just thinking about the match set her pulse racing all over again. The day was perfect. People were everywhere. Excitement was in the air. Brooke and her partner, a young woman named Laurie Johnson, were competing against each other for the women's singles championship.

Brooke took her place on the baseline. The warm-up began and balls went backward and forward across the net. Brooke felt the strength surge through her limbs and she eagerly awaited the umpire's signal for play to commence.

Soon the signal came and each player once again took her position. Laurie Johnson was due to serve first and Brooke waited at the baseline, her racket clutched in anticipation.

Laurie's serve was low and fast, zipping across the net to land several yards short of Brooke's feet. With quick agility, Brooke lunged for it, returning it with accurate precision that drew a pleased murmur from the crowd. The point was taken by Brooke and her opponent served again. The serve went for several rallies with both women making brilliant moves but in the end, Brooke took the point.

There was no need to wonder if Brooke were in top

form. She was proving it not only to herself but to the crowd as well. The longer she played the better she felt. All the physical therapy, workouts, exercises and practice games were paying off.

Brooke won the first set without losing a game. She paused only long enough to mop her brow and rinse her mouth with water and returned to the court, ready to play.

She took the next three games without losing a point, breaking Laurie's serve twice. Laurie, however, rallied to win the next game, but Brooke won the next one, and with it, the set.

During the third and final set, Brooke was at her best. Her panther-like grace excited the crowd. She smashed the ball time after time across the court, her serve unanswerable. She lobbed the ball when a baseline shot was expected. She used her drop shot to perfection causing her opponent many forced errors.

She was all over the court, serving and volleying like a fanatic. The crowd loved her; they hollered and cheered and chanted her name.

Brooke took the final set in six straight games. She and Laurie walked off the court to a standing ovation. But the trophy belonged to Brooke. Grasping it close to her chest, it finally dawned upon her that she had done it! She had accomplished the impossible.

Where, however, was the satisfaction she was positive would follow? She still had that empty feeling inside her. It was because of Ashley. She realized attaining his love was the most important goal in her life.

Brooke knew she was going to miss Cody's gay companionship, which she had enjoyed these last few days. After spending this last evening with him, she was awfully tired as she let herself in the door. Lano had already gone to bed, so she had the house to herself. Cody was leaving in the morning and in a way she was glad. Ashley was due to come home in a couple of days. She just couldn't seem to get over being tired and listless. Brooke chided herself once again for not making her doctor's appointment. Maybe she would take care of that the following day.

Finally getting the key into the lock, she opened the door. Seeing the light under the den door, she hesitantly cracked it and peered inside to find Ashley sitting casually in his chair with a drink in his hand.

Brooke was not fooled by the way he was watching her so nonchalantly. He looked as deadly as a tightly coiled rattlesnake ready to spring at any moment. Her gaze fell before the penetration of his. She moved with reluctance further into the room.

"Hello, Ashley," she said as she laid her purse on the table with care. "Did you have a good trip?"

"It was all right," he responded tightly.

"Good, I'm glad." Forcing herself to look at him again, she saw the furious expression on his face. "I'm—I'm sorry I wasn't here when you got back. I went out with an old friend."

"So I was informed," he said as he took another gulp of his drink.

Brooke colored. This was going to be worse than she imagined.

"Did you go over to Jonathan's?" Brooke knew it was an inane question, but she asked it nevertheless. She was stalling for time.

"No, I called," he replied tersely.

"Yes. Well, I'm sure by now you've had something to eat."

"To hell with food," Ashley's anger exploded.

Brooke took a step backward. "Please, Ashley . . ."

"Don't please me!" Ashley slammed his glass down on the table. "Where have you been?"

Brooke swallowed. "Anne must have told you."

"I don't give a damn about what Anne said. I want to hear it from you."

"All right," shrugged Brooke. "I've been out to dinner with Cody Roberts." She defiantly looked him straight in the eye as she said it.

Ashley swore and Brooke winced at the language he used. "I can't believe you have the nerve to stand there and tell me you've been out with another man."

"Good heavens, Ashley! You're making something out of nothing!"

"I don't happen to see it that way. You're my wife! And I won't have you going out with another man, especially Roberts! Speaking of Roberts, I was informed that because of his encouragement, you played in the club's tennis tournament. I was totally against you doing that and you were well aware of my feelings!"

She had never seen Ashley this angry before and she was at a loss as to how to cope with him in this state.

Brooke clenched her fists. "Why are you acting like this? You've barely been civil to me. Why shouldn't I do something that brings me a little happiness and enjoyment? Answer me that!"

Turning his tormented eyes upon her, he said, "I'm concerned about your health! Can't you see that! You played in a strenuous tournament without even a doctor's examination, much less his approval. Do you realize what the consequences could have been? *And* because I won't have people talking about us! As I said before, you're my wife and you'll behave accordingly!"

"And you? Do those same rules apply to you?" Brooke asked quietly.

With his mouth drawn in a harsh line, he said, "Just *what* do you mean by that?"

"How am I to know that you didn't take Miss Lattimer with you on your trip to the mainland?"

"You don't! But if I did, are you saying that entitles you to do likewise?"

"Oh, Ashley, for God's sake, we're getting absolutely nowhere with this conversation. I did nothing wrong! I only played in the tournament to prove that I could play again and as for Cody—well, we're friends and nothing more. Anyway he's leaving tomorrow."

"Don't let him come near you again or I won't be responsible for my actions! I blame him for the fatigued look you're wearing."

Brooke took a deep breath. "I've had enough. I'm going to bed."

Ashley crossed the room and grabbed her arm and pulled her up against the rock hardness of his body.

"You're not going anywhere until you give me your word that you won't set another foot on a tennis court."

"Let go of me!" she pleaded.

"No!" growled Ashley.

Brooke began struggling in earnest to try and break the firm grip he had upon her arms. But she only made him more determined not to let her go.

"You brute!" she cried. "Are you drunk?"

"Ha! So you think I'm drunk, is that it? Well, let me assure you, I'm not. At least not in the way you mean," he added.

"Oh, you're not making any sense! All I want to do is go to bed!"

"All right. Let's go. We'll fight it out in bed if that's

the way you want it. But *I'll* win, and *you* will do as I say."

"No, Ashley," said Brooke shaking. "I do not intend to share a bed with you tonight! Go take your vile temper out on whomever you please. Just leave me alone!"

"That I can't do, my dear," he rasped as he swept her into his arms and headed for their bedroom.

Brooke began her struggle anew, but she knew she was fighting a losing battle. He was much stronger than she, and Brooke decided to save what energy she had left for later. Let him think she had given in to his demands.

Dumping her unceremoniously on the bed, Ashley began removing his coat and tie.

"You don't honestly think I'm going to let you make love to me after all those things we've said to each other?"

There was silence. Ashley's eyes flickered intensely over her.

Sitting up, Brooke made a dive for the other side of the bed, but Ashley was too quick for her. He grabbed her and pulled her roughly against his chest. "Quit fighting, you little wildcat. I aim to tame you and you know it!"

"Ashley, no!"

Brooke began pushing her hands hard against his chest. She tried to keep his mouth from claiming hers. Her heart was beating like a frightened rabbit and she felt herself weakening toward him. He had proved once again that he excited her, no matter how she tried to deny it.

Although he had stripped away her protective armor, she still had her pride and that was what she was desperately clinging to now.

"Please, Ashley, we've got to talk."

The grim expression on his face told her that he was in no mood to talk.

"Talking is not what either of us needs right now," he said thickly. Before she could say another word, his mouth was against hers, savagely seeking a response. She tried to remain passive, but a jerk on the back of her hair caused her to cry out in pain. When she did, he assaulted her mouth once again. This time he got the response he was seeking.

Ashley was the first one to pull away. He began removing his shirt which was already unbuttoned to the waist. She lay watching him shed the rest of his clothing, taking in his dark, hairy chest, flat stomach and narrow hips. It was all she could do to keep from crying out for him. But that would never do, because then she would be completely at his mercy. Even though her senses were clamoring for him, she was not ready to yield to him the fruits of her body.

"Please, Ashley," she pleaded. "I'm not ready for this."

Instead of listening to her, his fingers began undoing the buttons that held her silk blouse together. After he had discarded it, the same adept fingers began unfastening the hooks of her lacy bra. Upon removing it, he feasted his eyes upon the round softness already swollen with desire. She gasped at his touch on her bare skin and despite her earlier statement that she did not want him to make love to her, she found her arms slowly moving up his shoulders to his neck and drawing his mouth down to hers.

The kiss was gentle but filled with longing and hunger. The tip of his tongue began tantalizing her mouth. He then began nibbling, cajoling and teasing with his mouth, never staying in the same place for long.

Brooke began moaning and tried to stay his roving mouth and hands. He was setting her on fire and he knew it. "Do I make you hungry?" he whispered against her mouth.

"Yes, Ashley!" she choked.

"Do you want me?"

"You devil!" she sobbed as his lips continued to torment hers.

From her mouth Ashley took his plundering to her smooth tanned shoulders and to the creamy whiteness of her breast.

"Oh, please, please," she breathed, tears erupting from her eyes.

"Oh, Brooke!" he groaned.

"Please don't," she wept.

Suddenly tired of playing, Ashley reached over and turned off the lamp, plunging the room into a soft moonlit darkness and began caressing her in earnest now. He was trembling as his hands roamed freely over the slimness of her body and his lips were everywhere at once.

It was flesh against flesh as he moved his body over hers. There was desperation in his lovemaking and she met him with the same driving need and together they climbed the heights.

He reached for her again during the early morning hours and this time she drove him to the brink of insanity with her mouth and tongue, before he took her again with a deep driving urgency.

Later in the morning when Brooke awakened, she was alone.

Chapter Eleven

*M*aking herself get out of bed was one of the hardest things Brooke ever did. To make matters worse she was sick to her stomach and dizzy as well. Forcing herself to take deep breaths, she made it to the bathroom before she lost the contents of her stomach.

It was nearly an hour later before she was able to get up again. After taking a shower and putting on some clothes, she felt a little better, although the fatigue was still with her.

She went immediately to the kitchen in search of food. After munching on a few crackers and drinking a Coke, she felt more like her old self.

After last night, it came as no surprise to her that she felt ill. She couldn't bear to let her mind dwell on it. The situation between her and Ashley, as it was, could not continue. She simply couldn't take any more. She hated herself when she responded to him, but she always had and would continue to do so as long as she stayed with him. That was the root of the whole problem. She wanted more, much more than body contact from Ashley.

After she had been up for a while, she began to have that uneasy feeling in her stomach once again. She wondered if she could get in to see the doctor today. Maybe someone had canceled. Keeping her fingers crossed she picked up the phone and dialed the number. She really needed to go to the doctor anyway for a good checkup. She had gone too long without one.

She was in luck. There had indeed been a cancelation. Dr. Norman's receptionist told her to come right away. After grabbing her purse and sunglasses, she was on her way.

Pregnant? She was pregnant! As Brooke walked out of the doctor's office a few hours later, she was still in a state of shock, stunned was perhaps a better word for her feelings. But it was true. Dr. Norman had confirmed it.

He kept her in his office almost three hours examining her from head to toe while he ran various tests. He came back into the examination room with a grim look on his face. When Brooke saw his expression, she was frightened. Seeing the uncertainty mirrored in her eyes, his mood lightened. He patted her hand and said, his voice calm, "You're pregnant, my dear, you're pregnant."

She looked up at him as if he had lost his mind, her eyes as big as saucers. "But, but—are you . . . ?"

"Yes, I'm sure." He smiled softly.

A lump rose in her throat. She tried to swallow it, but couldn't. Then the tears came, only to be followed shortly by heartfelt laughter.

When Brooke finally settled down, she confessed

231

about playing tennis, concerned that she may have harmed her baby. He assured her, however, that the baby was fine. But he was furious because she hadn't seen a doctor before taking it upon herself to play again.

"You're tired and listless because you're anemic as well as pregnant. Between the two, you don't have a chance to feel good."

She did not tell him about her problems with Ashley and how upset that had made her. That was why she was so shocked when she found out she was going to have a baby. Brooke knew her normal body functions were off schedule, but she had blamed it on her depression and unhappiness associated with Ashley.

A baby! A life that she and Ashley had created together. Maybe, just maybe, there would be a chance for them after all. Now she would be giving him one of those things he had married her for—a child. Brooke knew Eli would be delighted and she hoped they could tell him together. Even if Ashley did not love her, hopefully their baby would create an unbreakable bond, and the reasons for their marriage would not be as important anymore.

Right now, Brooke believed she could survive if she had Ashley's loyalty and commitment, even if she could never have his undying love. The baby was sure to make a difference and she couldn't wait to tell Ashley.

Immediately after leaving the doctor's office, Brooke went straight to a restaurant around the corner from the office. Dr. Norman was adamant that she get something to eat before going home. He told her part of her problem was her poor eating habits. But she was excited and found it hard to eat now. However, she had managed to eat a grilled cheese sandwich and a small bowl of fruit. All she wanted to do was rush home and be ready for Ashley when he got home from work and tell him the good news.

Although she had plenty of time, she was nevertheless in a hurry as she made her way to her car. She wanted to wash her hair and put on her new silk lounging outfit and prepare a candlelight dinner for two. She couldn't wait to see his face when she told him!

It was while she was waiting to cross the street that she saw them.

Brooke's heart plunged to her toes as she watched her husband carefully help Toni Lattimer into the taxi and get in after her. People were jolting her as she stood heartbroken on the curb. At the moment, she was too ill to move.

"Lady, are you all right?" asked a young Polynesian man.

Coming out of her stupor enough to answer him, she stammered, "I—I'm fine. I was feeling a little sick to my stomach, but I'm okay now, thank you."

"Well, if you're sure . . ."

"I'm sure. My car is parked right around the corner, so I don't have far to go."

"All right. Good luck to you." He smiled and slightly bowed as she strode away.

Brooke laughed bitterly to herself. Even a stranger could see that her whole world had fallen to pieces. Her dreams were shattered. That's exactly all they were— dreams. But it didn't matter, nothing mattered anymore—nothing at all.

Somehow she managed to make it home. The only thing on her mind as she walked in the door was just how long it would take her to pack her things and be gone. She was leaving Ashley.

She began throwing her clothes and personal items in

her suitcase as fast and furiously as she could. Tears were running down her face and into her mouth faster than she could wipe them away, but she kept on until their bedroom and bath was devoid of anything that belonged to her.

After leaving here, her first stop would be Jonathan and Anne's. Although her brother would be at work, she would be able to say goodbye to Anne and thank her for all they had done for her. From there, she planned on catching the first available plane to the mainland. Hopefully Ashley would choose tonight to either work late or not come home at all.

Brooke did not even bother to hide the tears as she paid the driver and hastily climbed the steps to the house. If she did not have Anne to turn to, she didn't know what she would do.

She rang the doorbell and by the time Anne answered it, Brooke was shaking all over. A nervous reaction had set in.

Taking one look at her sister-in-law's face, Anne quickly put her arms around Brooke and led her into the den, sitting her down on the couch. Anne sat down beside her. "My God, Brooke, what in the world has happened?" she asked urgently.

Brooke tried to swallow the lump in her throat so she could speak. "I'm—I'm leaving, leaving . . ." She gulped. "I mean I've—I've left Ashley," she cried in anguish.

"Now, now, Brooke, calm down. Everything's going to be all right, you just wait and see," crooned Anne, trying to soothe her with gentle talk.

Brooke sobbed for a moment longer against Anne's shoulder. She shuddered as she raised herself. She was silent and pale as death itself.

Anne was worried.

When Brooke calmed down enough, Anne questioned her gently. "Can you tell me what happened?"

Brooke took several deep breaths, forcing herself to speak calmly. "I'm pregnant, Anne," she said in a dull voice. She paused. "But Ashley doesn't want me or the baby." Her voice quivered.

Anne looked stunned. "Pregnant?" She puckered her eyebrows. "But—I thought you couldn't get . . ."

"I did too!" Brooke cut in shrilly, "But I am pregnant. I just came from the doctor."

Anne frowned and spread her hands. "I don't understand. Have you seen Ashley?"

Tears welled up in Brooke's eyes again. "Yes, I've seen Ashley," she said bitterly.

Anne looked puzzled. "Let's have the whole story," she said, her tone flat.

It wasn't easy reliving it all over again, but she managed to relate to Anne in detail exactly what had happened.

When she had finished, Anne smashed her fist on the coffee table. "Why, that bas—" She caught herself and stopped. "I'd like to . . ."

"Please," cut in Brooke, "I don't want to talk about *him* anymore." She paused and licked her dry lips. "All I want to do is catch the next flight to Houston." Ignoring Anne's gasp, she continued. "I'm going back there and try to pick up the pieces of my life once more."

Anne rose abruptly to her feet. "Oh, Brooke, no! Please . . . You can't possibly go to Houston by yourself. Where would you live? Who would take care of you? If you don't care about yourself, think of the baby." Anne was very upset.

"Oh, Anne," wailed Brooke, "I need to get as far away from Ashley as possible."

Anne's eyes narrowed. "Are you sure about that? Are you sure leaving Ashley is the wisest thing to do, especially since you haven't even heard his side?"

Brooke shook her head. Her lips thin, she said, "My mind's made up. I'm going, with or without your help." Her voice had risen.

"Shh, calm down," shouted Anne. "Of course, I'm going to help you. You know that, silly." She paused. "Why don't I go call Jonathan . . ."

"No!" Brooke cut in rudely. "Don't do that. I'm afraid he'll tell Ashley."

"All right," said Anne, shaking her head. Then her face brightened. "I do have another idea, though!" She licked her lips. "See what you think about this. Why don't you go to Kauai and stay with Eli for a while instead of going to Houston? Now what would be wrong with that? At least you'll be well taken care of there."

Brooke looked at her in astonishment. "Surely you jest? Or even better, have you taken leave of your senses?"

"Now, hold on a minute," said Anne. "Just think about it a minute before you get yourself ruffled. What I've suggested makes good sense."

Brooke's eyes widened. "But why on earth would you suggest going there? I still don't understand . . ."

Anne regarded her steadily. "Kauai would be the last place Ashley would ever think to look for you. Right? Of course, I'm right," she continued, answering her own question. "So what do you say? Are you game?"

Hope shone from Brooke's eyes, although her voice was hesitant. "Do you really think it would work?"

"Well, I don't see why not," she said, her tone confident. She grabbed Brooke's hand and pulled her up from the couch. "Let's go call Eli."

Anne was right. Eli *was* delighted that she was coming for a visit. Brooke talked to him only for a moment, but when she hung up, his gruff voice still rang in her ears, "You come on girl, I'll be waiting." He didn't act as if he thought it strange in the least for her to be coming without Ashley.

The more Brooke thought about the idea of going to Kauai, the better she liked it. Especially after talking to Eli. The doctor had told her she needed to rest and to do absolutely nothing strenuous for at least a few weeks. She would stay on Kauai until she could make future plans for her and her baby.

It was no problem getting a flight to the island, even on such short notice. So it was with bitter disappointment and utter frustration that Brooke found herself on the way to stay with her husband's family and to an uncertain future.

As she tried to relax aboard the plane, the pain hit her once again full force. She fought back the tears. She still couldn't believe that it was all over between her and Ashley, but it was. She must learn to accept that. Knowing she had part of him growing inside of her was the only thing that kept her sane.

With her out of the way, maybe Ashley would find happiness with Toni.

Later she might even share the baby with him, but not for a long time. Her emotions were much too raw to even contemplate it now. She loved Ashley enough to give him up even though it was tearing her to pieces.

The money she had in savings would tide her over until she could make other plans. Maybe one of these days she would be able to return to the tennis circuit. But right now she was thankful she had enough money to be self-sufficient—she didn't intend to take one penny from Ashley.

The one thing she was concerned about was Anne telling Ashley where she was. Not that it really mattered because he wouldn't come looking for her unless pride forced him to do so. Anne had promised she wouldn't tell Ashley where she had gone until she had already left for Houston sometime in the not too distant future. Just how trustworthy her brother and sister-in-law would be under these circumstances remained to be seen.

Brooke strolled slowly along the beach. It was lovely this time of late afternoon and she was enjoying being by herself immensely. The waves breaking along the shoreline somehow helped soothe her troubled thoughts.

Although Eli and Aunt Madge were doing everything in their power to make her comfortable and her stay as enjoyable as possible, she nevertheless needed breathing room and time to think. That was why she coveted these walks along the beach.

Ashley's family blamed him for the breakup of their marriage, although Brooke said nothing that would put the blame upon his shoulders. But they were not blind and could see how troubled and unhappy she was.

Brooke had been on Kauai a few weeks now and although she didn't feel much better mentally, she was in good physical health. The hollowness of her face had filled out and the dark circles were no longer as noticeable as they had been when she had arrived.

For a while she tried to hide her morning sickness from Aunt Madge, but she was not too sure she had succeeded. It didn't matter anyway because the thickening of her waistline and the fullness of her breasts gave her secret away.

Feeling her stomach now as she continued her leisurely pace, she thought again of how she wanted this baby above all else—except Ashley himself.

During the time she had been here, Ashley's aunt had talked to her a great deal about Ashley and tried to make her understand him a little better. She didn't really know the man she married and even though their time together was virtually over, she nevertheless yearned to know more about him.

"My dear, you mustn't judge him too harshly," Madge had said one evening after she had arrived here. She went on to tell Brooke that his parents had died when he was young and at a vulnerable age. As a result, he was never allowed to be a little boy. Although his grandfather adored him and still did, he expected more out of a small boy than Ashley was capable of giving. There was love but not the right kind. She told Brooke that she tried to do what she could, but Eli had definite ideas about how he wanted his only grandson to be reared and he would take no interference from anyone. He never learned how to love or to be loved as others know it. The old man had mellowed somewhat over the last few years, but it was too late where Ashley was concerned.

She told Brooke how she had prayed for someone like Brooke to come into his life and cultivate the good in him and make him know love.

Thinking about those words now as she had so many times after they were said always brought a lump to Brooke's throat. The tears came easily. It was almost more than she could bear at times knowing she had failed not only herself, Eli and Aunt Madge, but most of all Ashley.

During the past weeks, she spent a great deal of time with Eli. She had come to dearly love the old gentleman. In his own way, he loved his only grandson and wanted the best for him.

Although they never discussed Ashley, Brooke sensed his feelings. He treated her like a daughter. They played cards and visited as long and as much as his health would permit.

If he were aware of her pregnancy, he never mentioned it. He was aware of her deep hurt and refused to add to it.

Hunching her shoulders, Brooke cast these thoughts aside. She glanced at her watch and noticed she had been walking quite a while. Although it wasn't late, Eli and Madge would worry if she were gone too long.

As she made her way back toward the house, she had a feeling that she was not alone.

Pausing, she looked up and what she saw made her eyes darken with anguish.

If she had fared well physically, the same was not true for Ashley. He looked awful. He was thin to the point of gauntness and he looked haggard. What he really portrayed was a man who had been through hell, but she could not let herself think it had anything to do with her.

"Brooke." There was a waver in his voice along with uncertainty.

"Yes." Brooke answered breathlessly.

"I've been waiting to talk to you."

Brooke wasn't sure she was up to this. Seeing him again after all these weeks was too much. She would like to tell him to go away, but she knew he would not until he had his say.

Running her tongue over her upper lip, she finally said, "All right, say what you must. I'm listening."

"You're not going to make it easy, are you?"

"No."

"Okay," sighed Ashley as he rubbed the back of his neck showing his utter weariness. "Shall we sit here on this rock—that is, if you'll be comfortable enough."

"I'll be fine," she whispered.

The spot he chose was certainly private and relatively well hidden. There was lush greenery surrounding them and the sweet smell of flowers filled the air. It was a place to make love—not war.

Brooke turned to face her husband and asked, "How long have you known I've been here?"

"Only four days," Ashley ground out harshly.

"What! Are you serious?"

"I assure you I'm serious." Bitterness was reeking from his voice.

"I just assumed," she stammered, "that Anne or Jonathan would have told you a long time ago."

"Oh, they did."

"Well, then why on earth did you say only four days. I don't understand . . ."

"I called my grandfather two days after finding out where you were and he said that you were no longer here—that you had flown to Houston to stay with some friends for a while."

"No! No!" cried Brooke shaking her head. "I don't believe you. He wouldn't do a thing like that!"

"Well, I assure you he would and he did! Damn him!"

"But, why?"

"I'll tell you why. Because he enjoys playing God. He wanted to teach me a lesson or so he said. Well, he damn near killed me. You have no idea the torment

241

I've been through not knowing where you were or whom you were with. I was just about at my wit's end when I called Eli one more time from the airport in Houston to see if by any chance he had heard from you."

"You went to Houston!" cried Brooke.

"Hell, yes, I went to Houston. I was determined to find you and bring you back. Anyway, when I called, he finally admitted that you were here and had been all along! I swear I would have strangled the old man if I could have gotten to him."

"Oh, Ashley, how awful!"

"From Houston, I flew straight here. However, I did call your brother and sister-in-law immediately. They have been out of their minds with worry also. Eli has really played havoc with our lives."

"I was wondering why I didn't hear a word from Anne and Jonathan. Now I know."

"You have no idea of what you've put me through with the help of my own grandfather."

"But I thought you didn't want me anymore . . ." Brooke's mouth was so dry she couldn't utter another word.

"Where the hell did you get an idea like that?"

"I—I saw you with Toni the afternoon I left," confessed Brooke.

"Surely you didn't think—!"

Seeing the hurt look on her face, he groaned and said, "Oh, honey, what you saw that day was the tail end of my last conversation with Toni. I had just told her to get out of my life and stay out. And I also told her never to go near you again. I put her into a taxi and haven't seen her since."

Brooke's face lost all color. All those wasted weeks!

"Do you care about me at all, Brooke?" asked

Ashley quietly. "If not, I don't have a reason for living."

Brooke stared at him with her heart in her eyes. "Care about you! Of course I care about you! I love you, more than you'll ever know, my darling!"

The words were barely out of her mouth when Ashley pulled her fiercely into his arms. He crushed his lips to hers in a kiss that left them both devastated with its intensity. But one kiss did not quench their thirst for one another. They drank from each other's lips until they were both completely drained.

Somehow they had drifted from the rock to the sand and lay with their bodies entwined as the beauty of the early evening surrounded them.

"Oh, Brooke," he said thickly, "promise me you won't ever leave me again."

Laughing with pure delight, Brooke said, "I'm afraid you're stuck with me from now on!"

"That's music to my ears!" His arms tightened around her and they lay basking in their renewed pledge to one another.

Shortly, Ashley broke into the quietness and said, "Brooke, there's one more thing we have to discuss. I talked to Anne and to your doctor in Houston at great length about you."

Brooke felt herself stiffen in his arms. She would never forgive Anne if she told Ashley about the baby. No, Anne would never do that, she reassured herself.

"Honey, now please don't be upset. It's only fair that I know about your health problems. I want you to listen to this and listen well. I love you and you alone. I married you because I loved you and for no other reason." The silence that followed those words allowed Ashley to continue.

"It's partly true what Toni told you that day she came

to our apartment. I, as well as the other board members in our company, have been trying to get Eli to retire because of his health. He is far too old and ill to be working and having the kind of pressures our job involves. And it was true that he did not want me to marry Toni." He paused, the lines deepening around his mouth. "But as far as pushing me into marrying and having a child before he would turn over the company to me, that was a lot of hogwash, spoken by a jealous and vindictive woman."

His words disarmed her. "Oh, Ashley," she cried, "I should have listened to Anne. She tried to convince me not to leave until I heard your side of the story, but I . . ."

"Hush, honey," demanded Ashley, softly placing a finger against her lips. "I'm not blaming you. But I've been to hell and back these last few weeks."

"So have I," she returned huskily, looking up at him with her heart in her eyes.

She heard the sharp intake of his breath before he leaned down and touched her lips lightly. It was not enough. He molded her closer to the contours of his body and drank again the sweet nectar from her mouth like a man with an unquenchable thirst.

When he let her go, they were both shaken.

"Oh, God, the smell and taste of you drives me insane," he muttered indistinctly.

"Me too," she echoed, smiling sweetly.

He kissed her again soundly. He grinned. "That's for looking at me like that."

"Ashley?" she questioned tentatively, not wanting to break the magic spell. "Can we go see Eli and tell him we're back together. I know he didn't mean . . ." She licked her suddenly dry lips. "He was only protecting me. You see, we've grown quite fond of each other . . ."

He frowned and rubbed the back of his neck. "Now?" he questioned, perturbed. "But what about us?" He hesitated. "We still have so much to talk about—so much to straighten out."

"I know," she said lightly, "but Eli would want to know that everything is all right between us now." She flashed him a beautiful smile. "After all, we have so much, we can afford to forgive him. Please—"

"All right, you win," he said, expelling a sigh. "But don't expect me to turn the other cheek, at least not right now. For heaven's sake, let's make it short. I want you all to myself." He grinned.

As they walked toward the house, hand in hand, Brooke's thoughts were deep. Later, when they were alone, she would share the secret that was nestled close within her body. She couldn't wait to see the expression on his face when she told him.

Eli was sitting alone in the den, peering out the patio door. His eyes sparkled when he saw Brooke, but an immediate shadow appeared when he saw Ashley with her.

When they entered the room, Ashley remained silent, his features brooding. Brooke sighed to herself. It was certainly not going to be as easy as she had thought to get these two back together.

Eli, however, took the bull by the horns and said, looking at Brooke, "You all right, girl?" His voice was more gruff than usual.

"Of course she is," retorted Ashley. "Surely you don't think I'd harm my own wife."

Eli flushed, clenching his jaw.

"Ashley, please . . ." begged Brooke softly.

"Dammit, I— Oh, all right," he said, changing his mind after looking at Brooke's pleading expression. He then took her hand and raised the palm to his lips, his eyes never leaving her face. It was such an intimate gesture that it left Brooke feeling weak all over.

Pulling her eyes away, she turned toward Eli and said, "We just wanted you to know that we have everything straight between us and that I don't hold a grudge against you." She hesitated for a second and then rushed on, "And neither does Ashley. We—"

"Now wait a minute!" cut in Ashley. "I didn't say—"

"Son," interrupted Eli, his voice full of emotion. "I thought I was doing the right thing by Brooke here. I've come to love her, and dammit I didn't want to see her hurt anymore." He turned his face away.

Brooke blinked back the tears as she went to the old man and sat down beside him on the couch. She put her arm around his bony shoulders and patted him. She turned and fastened her eyes on Ashley pleading with him to make amends.

For a moment, he remained still as a statue, his gaze locking with hers.

"Oh, what the hell," he muttered, more to himself than to anyone else and walked toward his grandfather.

The old man insisted on getting up with Brooke's help. By the time Ashley reached the old man, he was standing on two shaky legs.

Eli searched Ashley's face before saying, "Son, I'm sorry. I . . ." His voice broke.

Ashley looked concerned as he grabbed his grandfather and gave him a quick, but intense hug. "I'll forgive you this time, you old geezer," he said, lightening his tone. "But don't you ever do anything like this again."

Eli never replied, because Brooke jumped between the two of them and began hugging and kissing them and crying all at the same time. Her eyes shone as she looked up at Ashley and silently whispered her thanks.

Shortly thereafter, Madge joined them and they all enjoyed a drink to celebrate Ashley's return. Soon, however, she took Eli upstairs to bed, tired but radiantly happy.

Alone at last! Ashley suggested they go for another walk along the beach where they would be assured of complete privacy. Brooke nodded her agreement.

They strolled along the water's edge, hands entwined, listening to and feeling the waves lap against their bare feet. Not a word passed between them. They were both savoring these rare moments of utter contentment, afraid to break the spell with words.

Finally Ashley stopped her at the same private place where they had talked earlier and pulled her down beside him on the sandy beach.

The silence was prolonged as Ashley outlined her face with his finger, the moon being his only light. He moved his head back to look at her. "I want you to forget about having a child." His words, though softly spoken, fell into the quiet night like cannons on the Fourth of July. He paused, trying to read her expression, "We don't need one to make our life complete."

Brooke flinched inwardly. "But I'm . . ."

Ashley leaned forward and planted a firm kiss on her parted lips.

"Please don't interrupt. Let me finish." His voice softened. "I love you and I will *not* risk your health in any way." He shrugged. "Eli will be disappointed, but so what. He'll soon get over it. And," he grinned in the dark, "I'll even let you play tennis—but only in moderation, mind you," he finished on a teasing note.

Brooke felt sick to her stomach. Do you mean, she accused him in her mind, that you *don't* want a child? *After all this?*

Pulling away from him Brooke said in misery, "I'm sorry Ashley, but I can't go with you after all. I'm going to stay here for awhile and maybe return to Houston later."

Rising swiftly, Ashley spun her around angrily and said, his voice edged with steel, "Just exactly what do you mean by that statement?"

"Oh, Ashley, don't ask me please," cried Brooke. "Go away and leave me alone." She was crying out loud now.

Groaning, Ashley folded her into his arms and rocked her. "Don't cry, tell me what this is all about. There's nothing we can't work out together."

"I'm going to have a baby!" sobbed Brooke.

"Oh, my God!" he whispered, his eyes glowing.

Upon hearing the disbelief in his voice, she pulled away and searched his face. What was he thinking? She could picture his mind working, trying to take it all in. Would he accept it?

"It just happened, Ashley, I didn't even know. And then when I . . ."

"Hush now, Brooke," demanded Ashley. "You are going to make yourself sick. We'll talk as soon as you're quiet."

Folding her closely once again within his arms, he led her back to the rock and sat down with her.

"Will you ever forgive me for doing this to you?" he begged. "I'm so sorry."

She raised her tear-stained face to his and said softly, "Oh, my love, I'm not. I'm delighted." She smiled through the tears. "I can't think of anything more wonderful than having your baby growing inside of me."

In an unsteady voice he replied, "You don't know what it does to me to hear you talk that way. But according to Dr. Todd, it's too much of a risk."

"I know, but Dr. Norman in Honolulu said my heart was actually stronger and that if I took good care of myself, the chances of survival for both myself and the baby were excellent."

Hearing the word "survive" made Ashley's blood run cold. "It was my fault, I should have used precaution when we were making love. But when I have you in my arms, I can't even think straight. It's just like you've cast a spell on me. I'm completely at your mercy."

"I know the feeling," responded Brooke. "I knew the doctor advised me against getting pregnant, but I guess because I'd had so many problems, that I *couldn't* get that way, so I just didn't worry about it. I also want you to know that I have everything I could possibly want and more. I don't care if I ever pick up another tennis racket as long as I live. You are my love, my life and my career."

Ashley's only response was to lean down and kiss her sweetly for a long moment before whispering, "It's hard for me to believe that we're making a baby. Your stomach is still so flat." His hands began softly caressing where their baby was growing.

"Oh, no, it's not and you know it, Ashley Graham! Just look how fat I'm getting." Her hands went to her waist.

Ashley's eyes grew gentle. "You look beautiful to me," he said thickly. "You look *beautiful*."

Later as they strolled toward home, arms entwined, Brooke's thoughts were at peace. Their marriage was reborn. They had created a living bond that could never be broken.

All their tomorrows were finally within their grasp.

If you enjoyed this book...

...you will enjoy a Special Edition Book Club membership even more.

It will bring you each new title, as soon as it is published every month, delivered right to your door.

15-Day Free Trial Offer

We will send you 6 new Silhouette Special Editions to keep for 15 days absolutely free! If you decide not to keep them, send them back to us, you pay nothing. But if you enjoy them as much as we think you will, keep them and pay the invoice enclosed with your trial shipment. You will then automatically become a member of the Special Edition Book Club and receive 6 more romances every month. There is no minimum number of books to buy and you can cancel at any time.

Coming Next Month

Bitter Victory by Patti Beckman

She had left him years ago, but when Slade
appeared in her office, Veronica still felt the
burning desire and hatred that had driven her to
leave her husband. Could their love
mend their differences?

Eye Of The Hurricane by Sarah Keene

There were two sides to Miranda: the practical
miss, and the daring, wild dreamer. And in Jake
she found a searing passion that would weld the
two together.

Dangerous Magic by Stephanie James

Elissa fought her way up the corporate ladder and
into Wade's arms. Her sultry innocence intrigued
him, and his desire for her was overwhelming.

Silhouette Special Edition

Coming Next Month

Mayan Moon by Eleni Carr

Beneath the Mexican moon, beside the Sacred Well of Souls, Antonio Ferrara, a man of fierce Mayan pride, took Rhea on a journey that encompassed the ages.

So Many Tomorrows by Nancy John

Having been mistaken in her first marriage, Shelley wasn't thinking of love—until Jason found her and taught her the meaning of life, and of a love that would last forever.

A Woman's Place by Lucy Hamilton

Anna's residency under Dr. Lew Coleman was difficult—especially when she saw the answer to all her hidden desires and dreams in his compelling gaze.

Look for More Special Editions from
Janet Dailey and Brooke Hastings,
and a New Novel from
Linda Shaw in Future Months.

Silhouette Special Edition

MORE ROMANCE FOR
A SPECIAL WAY TO RELAX

March Special Editions
Available Now

Silver Mist by Sondra Stanford

To free her mind from a disastrous affair, Laurel
concentrated on the business she was organizing. Then a
charming local rancher entered her world
—and her heart.

Keys to Daniel's House by Carole Halston

All of Sydney's energies went into her family and her
career in real estate, until Daniel lured her away and
made his house their home.

All Our Tomorrows by Mary Lynn Baxter

Brooke lost a successful past in a tragic accident, but in
the tropical splendor of Hawaii, Ashley Graham
challenged her to love again.

Texas Rose by Kathryn Thiels

Returning to her old Texas stomping grounds to
interview a ranch owner, reporter Alexis Kellogg was
stunned to learn that he was actually a man
she once loved.

Love Is Surrender by Carolyn Thornton

Amid the lush splendor of New Orleans, a blue-eyed,
sensitive man taught Jennifer about passion,
jealousy—and love.

Never Give Your Heart by Tracy Sinclair

Gillian was thrilled to land a new account, but all too
soon her client, Roman Barclay, aroused more than
professional interest.

Dear reader:

Please take a few moments to fill out this questionnaire. It will help us give you more of the Special Editions you'd like best.

Mail to: **Karen Solem**
Silhouette Books
1230 Ave. of the Americas, New York, N.Y. 10020

1) How did you obtain **ALL OUR TOMORROWS**

( ) **Bookstore** 10-1 ( ) **Newsstand** -6
( ) **Supermarket** -2 ( ) **Airport** -7
( ) **Variety/discount store** -3 ( ) **Book Club** -8
( ) **Department store** -4 ( ) **From a friend** -9
( ) **Drug store** -5 ( ) **Other:** _____ _____
(write in) -0

2) How many Silhouette Special Editions have you read including this one? (circle one number) 11- **1 2 3 4 5 6 7 8 9 10 11 12**

3) Overall how would you rate this book?
( ) **Excellent** 12-1 ( ) **Very good** -2
( ) **Good** -3 ( ) **Fair** -4 ( ) **Poor** -5

4) Which elements did you like best about this book?
( ) **Heroine** 13-1 ( ) **Hero** -2 ( ) **Setting** -3 ( ) **Story line** -4
( ) **Love scenes** -5 ( ) **Ending** -6 ( ) **Other Characters** -7

5) Do you prefer love scenes that are
( ) **Less explicit than** ( ) **More explicit than**
in this book 14-1 **in this book** -2
( ) **About as explicit as in this book** -3

6) What influenced you most in deciding to buy this book?
( ) **Cover** 15-1 ( ) **Title** -2 ( ) **Back cover copy** -3
( ) **Recommendations** -4 ( ) **You buy all Silhouette Books** -5

7) How likely would you be to purchase other Silhouette Special Editions in the future?
( ) **Extremely likely** 16-1 ( ) **Not very likely** -3
( ) **Somewhat likely** -2 ( ) **Not at all likely** -4

8) Have you been reading . . .
( ) **Only Silhouette Romances** 17-1
( ) **Mostly Silhouette Romances** -2
( ) **Mostly one other romance** _____ -3
(write one in)
( ) **No one series of romance in particular** -4

9) Please check the box next to your age group.
( ) **Under 18** 18-1 ( ) **25-34** -3 ( ) **50-54** -5
( ) **18-24** -2 ( ) **35-49** -4 ( ) **55+** -6

10) Would you be interested in receiving a romance newsletter? If so please fill in your name and address.

Name _____

Address _____

City _____ State _____ Zip _____

19 ___ 20 ___ 21 ___ 22 ___ 23 ___